Praise for *T*

'A haunting, deadpan tale.'   *Washington Post*

'Echoing work by Marge Piercy and Margaret Atwood, *The Unit* is as thought-provoking as it is compulsively readable.'
NPR

'What a striking, remarkable book – one of the best I've read in a long time.'
Frank Huyler, author of *Right of Thirst*
and *The Laws of Invisible Things*

'Orwellian horrors in a Xanadu on Xanax – creepily profound and most provocative.'   *Kirkus*

'Like Margaret Atwood's *The Handmaid's Tale*, this novel imagines a chilling dystopia: single, childless, mid-life women are considered dispensable.'   *More* magazine

'Holmqvist handles her dystopia with muted, subtle care...a feminist, philosophical page-turner.'   *Time Out Chicago*

'Haunting.'   *The New Yorker*

'A chilling, stunning debut novel... For Orwell and Huxley fans.'   *Booklist*

'An exploration of female desire, human need, and the purpose of life.'   *Publishers Weekly*

'Holmqvist's is a book of quiet cruelty, and perhaps the most harrowing twist of all is that the world outside the walls of the Unit – one with married couples, one with children – seems even worse. In that way, *The Unit*'s strength is uncovering beauty in bleakness.'   *GQ*

'A remarkably thought-provoking novel.'   *Reading Matters*

'This is one of the best books I've read over the past two years...thought-provoking and emotionally moving.'
Orlando Sentinel

'A stunning debut that deserves to become an instant classic.'
Elizabeth Baines, author of *Balancing on the Edge of the World* and *Too Many Magpies*

'Holmqvist paces her revelations superbly and the reader is gripped by the atmosphere of slowly mounting claustrophobia.'
New Internationalist

'Savagely dystopian...remarkably deft.'
Barnes and Noble Review

About the Author

Ninni Holmqvist lives in Skåne, Sweden. She published her debut short story collection *Kostym* (*Suit*) in 1995 and has published two further collections of short stories since then. She also works as a translator. *The Unit* is her first novel.

About the Translator

Marlaine Delargy has translated novels by Åsa Larson and Johan Theorin, with whom she won the CWA International Dagger 2010 for *The Darkest Room*. She serves on the board of the *Swedish Book Review*. She lives in Shropshire.

the
UNIT

ninni holmqvist

Translated by Marlaine Delargy

A Oneworld Paperback Original

First published in Great Britain and the Commonwealth by
Oneworld Publications 2010
Originally published in Swedish as *Enhet* by Norstedts, Sweden 2006

Published by arrangement with Other Press LLC
This edition published 2018

ISBN 978-1-78074-721-7
eISBN 978-1-85168-773-2

The translation of this work was supported by a grant
from the Swedish Arts Council

Text design by Simon M. Sullivan
Printed and bound in Great Britain by Clays Ltd, St Ives plc

Oneworld Publications
10 Bloomsbury Street
London WC1B 3SR

Stay up to date with the latest books,
special offers, and exclusive content from
Oneworld with our newsletter

Sign up on our website
oneworld-publications.com

MIX
Paper from
responsible sources
FSC® C018072

PART 1

1

It was more comfortable than I could have imagined. A room of my own with a bathroom, or rather an apartment of my own, because there were two rooms: a bedroom and a living room with a kitchenette. It was light and spacious, furnished in a modern style and tastefully decorated in muted colors. True, the tiniest nook or cranny was monitored by cameras, and I would soon realize there were hidden microphones there too. But the cameras weren't hidden. There was one in each corner of the ceiling —small but perfectly visible—and in every corner and every hallway that wasn't visible from the ceiling; inside the closets, for example, and behind doors and protruding cabinets. Even under the bed and under the sink in the kitchenette. Anywhere a person might crawl in or curl up, there was a camera. Sometimes as you moved through a room they followed you with their one-eyed stare. A faint humming noise gave away the fact that at that particular moment someone on the surveillance team was paying close attention to what you were doing. Even the bathroom was monitored. There were no fewer than three cameras within that small space, two on the ceiling and one underneath the washbasin. This meticulous surveillance applied not only to the private apartments, but also to the communal areas. And of course nothing less was to be expected. It was not the intention that those who lived here should be able to take their own lives or harm themselves in some other way. Not once you were here. You should have sorted that out beforehand, if you were thinking along those lines.

I was, for a while. I thought about hanging myself or jumping in front of a speeding train or doing a U-turn on the highway and driving toward the oncoming traffic at full speed. Or simply driving off the road. But I didn't have the courage. Instead I just obediently allowed myself to be picked up at the agreed time outside my house.

The first snowdrops had just appeared in my flowerbeds, which had been blazing with yellow winter aconite for several weeks now. It was a Saturday morning. I had lit the fire earlier. A transparent, quivering plume of smoke was still rising from the chimney as I stood waiting by the side of the road outside the gate. There wasn't a breath of wind, and the air was cold and clear.

The SUV was a metallic wine red, so shiny that it cast reflections of the sun as it slowly moved down the hill and through the village, then stopped in front of me. All the windows except the windshield and the front side windows were tinted black; apart from that the car was completely anonymous, with no logo or sticker to reveal where it had come from or where it was going. The driver, a woman in a black quilted jacket, climbed out and greeted me with a nod and a friendly smile. She hoisted my large suitcase into the trunk and waved me into the back seat. I fastened my seat belt and placed my shoulder bag on my knee, my arms around it. The driver put the car in first gear, released the handbrake, and we moved off. There were only the two of us in the car. We didn't say anything to each other.

After a drive of about two hours, behind those windows that were so dark I would have found it difficult to follow our route even if I'd tried, or to work out in which direction I was being taken, we suddenly plunged downward and the sound of the engine and the tires changed and became muted and echoing at the same time, as if we were traveling through a tunnel. First it became darker, then lighter on the other side of the windows, then the car stopped and the engine was switched off. The door by the back seat where I was sitting was opened from the outside. I saw a man's face and a woman's face. The woman's face was smiling, her mouth open, and she said:

"Hi there, Dorrit! You've arrived."

I got out of the car and saw that I was in a parking lot, an underground one from the look of things. The man and the woman were both dressed in green shirts the color of linden flowers, with the logo of the unit in white on the breast pocket—I recognized it from the information packet that had been sent to me at home a few months earlier. The man and woman introduced themselves as Dick and Henrietta. Henrietta added:

"We're your section orderlies."

She went around the car, opened the trunk, lifted out my suitcase and set off toward a row of elevators at one end of the parking lot where some fifty cars were parked, most of them ordinary family cars, SUVs or minibuses, but I also saw a couple of ambulances. Dick picked up my shoulder bag from the concrete floor where I'd put it while I shook hands. I would have preferred to carry it myself, as it contained my most private possessions, but he insisted and I didn't want to make a scene, so I shrugged my shoulders and let him take it. He gestured toward the elevators. I followed Henrietta empty-handed with him directly behind me.

The elevator went up only one floor. When we got out, Dick said:

"We're on level K1 now. That's the upper basement floor."

We walked along a wide corridor with a red ceiling, floor, and walls until we reached another row of elevators. We got into one of them, went up several floors and came out into something that resembled an ordinary stairwell with two doors that looked like ordinary apartment doors, one at each end. Dick, who had less to carry of the two functionaries, went ahead and pushed open one of the doors labeled SECTION H3 and held it open for me. I walked into an open common room of the kind usually found in hospital wards or student corridors, a lounge really. On a sofa in the corner sat a woman with red frizzy hair, just starting to turn gray, reading a magazine. In front of her on the table was a steaming cup of tea. Judging by the aroma, it was peppermint. The woman looked up, smiling.

"This is Majken," said Henrietta. "And this is Dorrit."

I managed to croak something that was supposed to be hello, and noticed that my mouth was completely dry.

"I live two doors down from you," said Majken. "If there's anything you're not sure about, or if you just want to talk—or not even that; if you want to be quiet in someone's company, or anything at all—then I'm either here or in my room for the next few hours. It says Majken Ohlsson on my door."

"Okay," I managed to get out.

She looked at me, her gaze steady. Her eyes were flecked with green.

"Don't hesitate," she added. "You mustn't feel you're disturbing me. We always have time for each other here."

"Okay," I said again. Then I thought I ought to say something else, so I said: "Thanks."

A hallway led off the lounge, with five doors along one side. On the second door was my name. Dick pushed down the door handle, opened the door, and we walked straight into the living room.

Henrietta put my suitcase down on the floor. Dick placed the shoulder bag on top of it, then turned to me and asked pleasantly:

"Would you like us to stay for a while?"

"No," I replied, a fraction less pleasantly.

"In that case we'll leave you in peace," he said. "Just don't forget the orientation meeting at two o'clock."

He looked at me searchingly, as if to check that I could really manage all on my own until two o'clock. I couldn't help snorting. Then they left, closing the door behind them.

So there I stood.

It was warm in the room; it must have been about seventy degrees. I wasn't used to such a high temperature indoors, especially not at this time of year. I shrugged off my peacoat, untied my winter boots, took off my cardigan and finally my socks. For the time being I just left everything lying in a heap on the floor. I stood next to the heap, barefoot, contemplating a simple beechwood dining room set, a deep sofa and two armchairs upholstered in eggshell white; at the far side of the room in an alcove was a desk. To my left, the kitchenette, to my right, the bathroom door, and next to that the bedroom, with the door standing open. To my surprise I saw that there was a double bed in there. I'd never had a double bed in my entire life. I laughed, and that was when I heard the faint hum of one of the cameras for the first time, as it turned its little dark eye toward me and— or so I imagined—zoomed in on my face. I automatically looked away.

2

Yes, I did actually have a house. When I say that I was picked up outside my house, I don't just mean my home, my residence, but my actual house. Despite my very low and irregular income, I had managed to get a bank loan some eight years earlier, just before I turned forty-two, to buy a little place I'd been to look at several times, and one of my life's dreams had been fulfilled: a house of my own and a garden of my own on the open, rolling plain between the Romele Ridge and the south coast.

But I hadn't been able to afford to maintain the house. The bargeboards and the window frames were rotten, the paint was flaking, the roof leaked in at least two places, and new drainage was needed all the way around the house. My income just about covered the interest on the loan, paying it off in the smallest possible installments; wood and electricity and maintenance costs, plus insurance, taxes, gas, and food for myself and my dog. And I don't think it could have made much difference to the state coffers when the confiscation authority sold the house at auction—that is if they managed to sell it at all in its present condition.

But despite the fact that I'd let the house get so run down, and despite the fact that it was old-fashioned and impractical, and cold and drafty in the winter and damp and stuffy in the summer, at least it was my very own home, my sanctuary, a place over which I and no one else had control, where my dog could run free and I could work in peace most of the time: no noisy neighbors on the other side of the wall, no footsteps clattering up and down an echoing stairwell, no squabbling kids in the shared courtyard, no communal outdoor spaces where families with children or friends could come along and sit down just as I was relaxing in the sun, noisily snacking or partying around me as if I didn't exist. I felt at home here, both indoors and out-doors; this was my domain, and if anyone—a neighbor or a friend who happened to be passing by—noticed that I was sitting in the garden, and stepped in through the gate for a chat or a cup of coffee, then at least it was me they wanted to talk to or drink coffee with. And if I didn't have the time or the inclination for a chat, then I had the right to tell them that, and they would have to go away.

It very rarely happened that I would ask someone to go. I didn't have very many friends, and not so many neighbors either, and if visitors turned up unannounced at an inconvenient moment, I usually let them stay for a little while anyway. If you live alone in the country you can't afford to push away your neighbors, or fall out with them. In fact, the way I see it, you can't afford to fall out with anyone at all if you live alone and no one needs you. Therefore I was friendly and welcoming from the very start each time someone turned up in my garden or at my door, even those times when I was absorbed in my work and they really were disturbing me.

At that time, when I'd just moved in, I still regarded the future with optimism. I still believed and hoped that it wasn't too late to have a child. Or at least to start earning money from my profession and become financially secure, or find a partner, someone who would love me and want to live with me. Almost to the very end I had hopes, futile and desperate hopes, of Nils.

Nils was several years younger than me, tall and strong and with tremendous sexual vitality. We had the same secret desire. The same sexual fantasies. The same hopelessly politically incorrect attitude. We were like a hand in a glove. He was actually living with another woman already; they had a child together, a boy. He never said he loved me, but for him, as for me, the word "love" was a big thing to say. But he said he "almost loved me"— he said it many times—and for me that was wonderful to hear. To be almost loved is as close as you can get to being loved without actually being loved.

Perhaps it was because of this "almost loving" that as late as six weeks before my fiftieth birthday, in a final attempt at least to gain a dispensation with regard to the date, I turned to him and asked him to save me—yes, in my desperation I actually used that expression—by separating from his partner and becoming mine instead, and, regardless of whether it was true or not, supplying a written declaration to the authorities stating that he loved me. When I asked him this outright he became terribly upset. In fact, he cried. He sat there naked on the edge of my bed, and that was the first and last time I saw him cry. He sat there with his eyes glistening, sobbing, and he pulled a corner of the duvet over his penis, apparently unconsciously, and said:

"Dorrit, I think more of you than I've ever thought of any other woman, and it isn't just sexual feelings, you know that. I admire you and respect you, I almost love you, and I would be more than happy to live with you and share my life with you. But for one thing, I want my son to grow up with both parents living in the same house. And for another, I can't actually say I love you, because I can't lie. I . . . I'm just not made that way. I can't say it to you, and I can't say it to the authorities; I can't put my name to something that isn't true. That would be perjury. I would be committing a crime. You have to understand this, Dorrit. I . . ."

He paused, took a deep breath, swallowed a few times, sniveled, rubbed his finger under his nose, and went on, virtually breathless, almost whispering:

"I'm so sorry, I'm so sorry. I . . . you know what you've meant . . . what you mean to me. I'll miss you so much, I . . ."

And he wept and wept. He put his arms around me, clung to me, howling like a child. I didn't cry. Not then.

I didn't cry until I said good-bye to Jock, my dog; we'd been so close for so many years. He's a Danish-Swedish farm dog, white with black and brown patches, brown eyes, and ears that are as soft as velvet, one black and one white. I gave him to a family I knew and trusted, not far from where I lived. Lisa and Sten and their three children. They've got a smallholding with horses and chickens, and they were very fond of Jock. The children loved him. I knew he liked them too, and that he'd have a good life there. But even so. He was mine, after all. And I was his. Between him and me you really could—without committing perjury —talk about love. The feeling was mutual, I'm convinced of that. But dogs don't count; a dog's dependence and devotion are not enough. And it was when I had left Jock at Sten and Lisa's and I was driving away that I wept.

Loving and leaving don't go together. They are two irreconcilable concepts, and when they are forced together by outside circumstances they require an explanation. But I was unable to give Jock that explanation. Because how do you explain something like that—or anything at all—to a dog? Nils could at least explain to me why he couldn't be with me properly and make me a needed person, and I could understand that. But how will Jock, if he's still alive, ever be able to understand why I drove away without him that day? How will he ever be able to understand why I never came back?

3

The suitcase wasn't particularly heavy. All I had to do was get a good grip and swing it up onto the table. I opened it and started unpacking. It was mostly clothes, nothing out of the ordinary: sweaters, shirts and pants. A black jacket for festive and formal occasions. Clothes for exercising. Sneakers, walking shoes, sandals.

But at the last minute and after much deliberation, I had stuffed my little black dress into my shoulder bag, along with my blue skirt, my fitted white blouse, a push-up bra, a few pairs of stockings and my high heels. I had no idea if I would get the chance to wear them here. I didn't think so, but then they didn't take up much room. Besides which they were mine, after all, and they had been expensive and not all that easy to get hold of. And

I knew myself well enough to know that if I suddenly got the urge to feel feminine, I would be very unhappy if I didn't have the means to satisfy that urge.

I stood with my back to the surveillance camera on the ceiling, fumbling with the dress, skirt and blouse I'd just taken out of my bag, then opened the closet door to hang them up—and that was when I saw there was a camera in there too. It was pointing straight at me, and it made me feel as if I'd been caught red-handed. I could feel myself blushing. Then I got angry, gave the camera the finger, put my clothes resolutely on hangers and shut the door on them.

I had also packed a couple of books, and I put them on a side table in the living room for the time being; I placed my laptop on the desk in the alcove. I put my favorite pen, a notepad and an envelope containing some photographs in the drawer of the bedside table.

The envelope contained a photo of Jock, one of Nils, one of my house and one of my family from when I was a child. It was a Polaroid, taken on the sofa in my parents' house. Mom and Dad in the center, Mom with the baby, Ole, on her knee. Next to her Ida and me, and next to Dad the two eldest, Jens and Siv, sitting close together. We're all smiling. Ida and I are actually laughing. I was eight when the picture was taken by Mom's best friend; I remember I really liked her a lot. She loved kids but had none of her own, and she'd insisted on taking a photo of us all with her new Polaroid camera that day. It was actually the only photo of the whole family gathered together, so I was glad she'd got her way. Unfortunately, I can't remember her name.

My family was all over the place now, scattered to the winds like a dandelion clock. Both my parents had died a long time ago. If they had still been alive, I could probably have received a dispensation for a few years to look after them. Jens, Ida and Ole had families of their own, living and working in different parts of Europe. My older sister Siv didn't exist anymore, at least I didn't think so. She had no children and was seven years older than me, so the probability that she might still be alive wasn't particularly great, that's if she had become dispensable—I didn't even know that much for certain.

I finished unpacking, pushed my suitcase, peacoat and winter boots into the top part of the closet, then began—indifferently at first, then restlessly, finally almost manically—wandering to and fro through the two rooms and into the bathroom; I turned on the faucets, flushed the toilet, opened drawers and cabinets, checked out the appliances in the kitchen, made sure the refrigerator and freezer were on and that the ice maker, ceramic cooktop, convection oven, microwave and kettle were all working. Went over to the alcove and sat down on the chair in front of the desk. It was a nice chair, made of molded wood, but it wasn't particularly comfortable. It didn't give support to the lower back, but higher up, just below the shoulder blades, and there were no arms. I knew from experience that if I sat and wrote for just a few hours a day on a chair of this quality, I would have an aching back and shoulders within a week. But I was sure I would get a better chair if I asked for one. From now on it was important that I was kept in good condition and good health in every way. That was the whole point, after all.

I got up from the chair and went over to the sofa to try that out. It was wonderful, both to sit on and to lie on. I settled down and picked up the remote from the coffee table, pointed it at the TV, pressed a button at random and the picture quickly appeared. It was a German channel broadcasting a talk show. I flipped here and there, established that there appeared to be lots and lots of channels, and that at least the world came here, even if I couldn't reach the outside from now on, not by mail, e-mail, text messages or telephone calls. From now on the telephone existed for me only in the form of a fixed internal line, and as for the Internet, I was allowed to surf only under supervision, which meant an orderly or another member of staff sitting beside me, and I was not allowed to join chat forums, contribute to blogs, create or respond to advertisements, or vote in opinion polls.

After flipping at top speed through fifty or so channels, I switched off the television, got up from the sofa, stretched, then looked around the room. What should I do now? A glance at the clock on the DVD player under the TV told me there was still quite a while before the meeting at two o'clock. This was not good. I'd begun to get the creeps. Whether it was from anxiety or anger, I didn't know and I didn't want to know. If there had been a window I would have gone and stood by it to look out. That usually had a calming effect on me, standing by a window and looking out. But—I only realized it now—there were no windows, not anywhere. I had probably registered it subconsciously as soon as I was shown into the apartment, but it was only now that it struck me. No windows. And yet it was daylight in here. How could that be? Nor did the light appear to be coming from any kind of lamp. It didn't seem to be falling in a particular direction; it was more that the room seemed to be filled by it. I looked around the living room in confusion. The only light that was on was the bulb above the sink in the kitchenette. In a vain attempt to solve the mystery, I went over and switched it off, but it didn't make much difference. I gave up.

It wasn't until a couple of days later that I found out about the daylight. It was when I got on top of a chair to put a shelf above the alcove where the desk was. I happened to glance up at one of the rectangular air vents mounted in the walls, high up, close to the ceiling, a couple in each room. They turned out not to be air vents at all, because when I was standing on the chair looking diagonally through the upwardly angled slats—

roughly like Venetian blinds when you adjust them to let in the light, but not direct sunlight—I was dazzled by the harsh white glare of the diodes inside.

Because I couldn't go and stand by a window to calm myself down, and because the creepy feeling in my body was threatening to get out of hand and take over, I wondered about going to the lounge or maybe knocking on Majken's door. But when I thought about it, I didn't feel ready. I was also very tired, so I went into the bedroom and lay down on one side of the double bed. Lay there, looking up at the ceiling and trying not to think. Took deep breaths and concentrated on exhaling slowly. After a while I must have fallen asleep, because when a loudspeaker somewhere in the room suddenly crackled, I opened my eyes with a start. The crackling gave way to a friendly exhortation from a male voice:

"This is a message for today's new arrivals. We would like to remind you that the obligatory welcome and orientation meeting will be taking place in conference room D4 in ten minutes. You will find conference room D4 on staircase D on the fourth floor. The easiest way is to take the optional elevator down to level K1, follow the blue corridor then take elevator D up to the fourth floor. Welcome, everyone! End of message."

4

There were eight of us. Only two were men, which wasn't that strange as the age limit for them is sixty. It's perfectly natural; after all, they produce viable sperm much later in life than we produce eggs. Even so, I had thought for a long time that the difference in age limits for men and women was unfair. That is until Nils informed me that there were lots of men—I think he even knew a few—who had been conned out of parenthood by women who just wanted free sperm.

"It's really only fair that men get more time, so stop moaning!"

I was very upset when he said that, not least because I felt found out. One of the reasons I had sex with Nils was that I secretly hoped the condom he so carefully slid over his penis before we had intercourse might split. I also made sure we got together immediately before or during ovulation. But it was also his harsh words, and the hardness in his voice when he said them, that upset me, and from then on I never spoke to Nils about my anxiety as I approached my fiftieth birthday.

There was still a minute or so before the orientation began. We went around shaking hands and introducing ourselves. Everybody looked pale and serious. Resolute. I was feeling slightly unwell and just a little bit groggy and only half awake after my unintended nap. An orderly who had been by the door welcoming us and ticking us off on a list was now standing by a table up on the podium at the front of the room, arranging some papers, a bottle of water, a bottle opener and a glass. She gave an introverted impression, as if she were shy. But if you happened to meet her eye, she smiled warmly. Her legs were disproportionately short, and she must have been seven or eight months pregnant. When she had finished arranging everything on the table, she climbed down and moved with short, waddling steps to the other end of the room. The way she walked reminded me of a penguin, which made me feel a little better, and the next time she smiled at me, I smiled back.

There was something familiar about one of the other new arrivals, a tall slender woman with high cheekbones and slanting eyes who seemed to be looking at everything around her with narrow-eyed skepticism. I recognized the girl in her through all the layers of age, but at first I couldn't place her. When she introduced herself as Elsa Antonsson, I remembered.

"Elsa! It's Dorrit—Dorrit Weger."

"I can see that now," she said, smiling tentatively. "Elementary and middle school. We were in the same class.

"Time passes . . ." she added slowly, in a voice that was only just holding. She was noticeably moved.

"Yes," I said. "Time passes."

□ □ □

We sat down in a semicircle facing the podium. The director of the unit was now standing behind the table, neatly and impeccably dressed in a dark maroon suit and a gray shirt. She looked at us, allowing her gaze to rest on each person in turn. Made sure she met everyone's eyes. This made her appear extremely sincere. She smiled, unbuttoned her jacket, cleared her throat and took a deep breath, and as she breathed out she began to speak:

"My name is Petra Runhede, and I am the director here at the Second Reserve Bank Unit for biological material. First of all I want to welcome you here. I would also like to take the opportunity to congratulate you on your fiftieth or sixtieth birthdays. Congratulations! This evening we will be throwing a big party for you all. A combined welcome and birthday celebration. Everyone in the unit, residents as well as staff, is of course invited. If everyone attends there will be something in the region of three hundred people. There will be a dinner, entertainment, and dancing. Don't miss it! Our welcome parties are usually a lot of fun! We hold one each month, as you might be able to work out. Because those of you who are here, the eight of you, have certain things in common, including the fact that you were born in the same month. You are all February children."

Petra paused and took a sip of water.

"You all know why you're here," she went on, "so I won't bore you by going through all the whys and wherefores."

She had tilted her head slightly to one side and was smiling now, confident but still immensely engaging.

"Or to put it more accurately: you know *the main reason* why you are here. But there is also something more positive for you in all of this."

She paused again, for slightly longer this time, looking at us with a serious expression.

"I have no doubt," she said slowly, once again allowing her gaze to move from one to another, stopping briefly on each of us, "you have found that people were often unsure of you, felt nervous in your company, sometimes seemed afraid, or behaved in a condescending or scornful way. Isn't that the case? Do you recognize that kind of situation?"

Nobody replied. There was complete silence in the room, apart from a faint hum from the air-conditioning. I was staring like an idiot at Petra, and presumably the other seven were doing the same. After a while she continued:

"Is there anyone who doesn't recognize that situation?"

We burst out laughing, grinning at each other in embarrassment, responding to her with a mumble of denial.

"Okay," she said, "this is what I mean. For the majority of you it isn't until you come to the reserve bank unit that you will experience the feeling of belonging, of being part of something with other people, which those of us who are needed often take for granted. And the icing on the cake, as explained in the information packet you've been given, is that you need never worry about your finances again. You have food on the table, a roof over your head, free access to medical care, dental care, physical therapy and so on, and it won't cost you a thing. You may move around freely within the unit and make use of all its facilities. There is a large winter garden here, almost a park in fact, for recreation and the enjoyment of nature. There is a library, a cinema, a theater, an art gallery, a café and a restaurant. There is a huge sports complex. And you can pursue more or less any hobby or professional activity you wish: art, crafts, electronics, mechanics, botany, architecture, acting, film, animation, you name it—there are workshops and studios for most activities. But above all"—and now she leaned forward, supporting herself on her fingertips on the edge of the table as if to give her words additional emphasis. "But *above all*," she repeated, "you have *each other*! And now it's coffee time."

□ □ □

I would venture to say that this welcome speech made us all feel better about things. It would be an exaggeration to say that there was a cheerful atmosphere during the coffee break, but the deathly pallor had left most people's faces, and as we drank coffee and ate homemade cinnamon buns in a cafélike room next door, the conversation was lively. We were starting to become interested in one another, asking questions about jobs and activities. Roy and Johanna were long-term unemployed; before that Johanna had delivered the mail and Roy had been some kind of consultant—I didn't understand what kind. Annie had been a hotel receptionist, Fredrik a mechanic in a truck factory, Boel was a violinist and Sofia had done lots of different things, including delivering newspapers and junk mail, proofreading, cleaning in a hotel and packing goods for a mail-order company. Elsa, finally, had worked in the same shoe store ever since she finished high school.

After coffee, the meeting continued with practical information about everything from the procedures surrounding research experiments and donations to finding our way around the unit. Staff from the residential department, the health center, the surgical department, the restaurant, the art gallery, the sports center, and the podiatry and massage clinics came along, one after another, introduced themselves and told us what they did.

When we were finished my head was spinning from all the information we'd been given during the afternoon, and I had to go and lie down again for a while so I'd be able to cope with the welcome party that evening.

5

I remember the debate and the referendum. I also remember that it wasn't really much of a debate to begin with, because the idea came originally from a newly formed party called the Capital Democrats, or something like that, and very few people took their proposal seriously.

I wasn't particularly interested in politics, and I was far too young to be able to identify with concepts like middle age. Every time the topic came up, in the media or with other people, I heaved a bored sigh and turned the page or switched channels or changed the topic of conversation. Social issues of this kind just had nothing to do with me, in my opinion, and when I got pregnant by accident during the first phase of the debate, I had an abortion. I was young, after all, I was in high school, I wanted to travel, go to college, do some casual work here and there, paint, write, dance and enjoy myself. It was just as impossible to imagine myself as a mother as it was to imagine myself as middle-aged. But if I had known that at the very moment when I allowed myself to be anesthetized and scraped out I was throwing away the only chance of becoming a parent I would ever have, then things would probably not have been quite so clear cut. If I had been able to work out how things were going to be in the future, if I'd had the slightest idea, I would have given birth to my child. At least I would like to believe that's what I would have done.

The question came up again in different guises and different packaging, and somehow it had slipped into the manifestos of some of the bigger and more established parties, and when the referendum finally took place, opinion had shifted. At that stage I was already more or less a grown woman with my sights set on a career as a writer. As I got by with various odd jobs I was determinedly working on what was to be my debut book. Around that time I started to toy with the idea that I would probably like to have a child before too long. But as I was living just below the poverty line and without a partner or other adult who could share the responsibility and the expense with me, I never pursued the idea. And when the new law came into force, I was well over thirty. I was a complete person with my character fully established, and unfortunately stamped more by the spirit of the times I had grown up in than that of the present situation.

When I was a child and a teenager, the ethos of the day advocated that a person should acquire some life experience and some experience of working life; you should learn about what made people tick, look around the world and try out different things before settling on a way of life you enjoyed. Enjoyment was important. Self-realization was important. Earning lots of money and buying lots of things was regarded as less important, in fact it was hardly of any importance at all. As long as you earned enough to get by. Getting by, coping, standing on your own two feet—financially, socially, mentally and emotionally—was important, and that was sufficient. Children and a family were something that could come later, or even something you could choose to do without. The ideal was first and foremost to find yourself, to develop your character, become a whole person who loved and respected yourself and who was not dependent on others. This was particularly important for women. It was extremely important not to become dependent on a man who would provide for us while we were with the children, looking after the house. At that time such a division of labor was actually still possible, and something my mother often warned my sisters and me about. From time to time she would gather the three of us together and give us a feminist talk. It started when Ida was just about three years old, and I was five. Siv was twelve, and the only one who had any idea what my mother was talking about for the first few years.

"Don't you go having kids before you can stand on your own two feet," Mom would say. "Don't go letting some man support you, not financially, not intellectually, not emotionally. Don't you get caught in that trap!"

Getting caught in a trap became my greatest fear. To begin with, it was a very concrete fear. I looked carefully for traps around me, and didn't like to go into narrow passageways or enclosed spaces, for example elevators or airplanes—what if there was a man in there threatening to support me! I didn't know what this supporting business actually was, but I was sure it would hurt a lot and that it might kill you. In stores, museums, cinemas, theaters and other large public indoor spaces I always wanted to stay near one of the doors, and the first thing I looked for when I went into an unfamiliar building was the emergency exits, the fire escapes, the escape routes.

When I got older and understood more clearly what my mother meant by children and men and supporting and traps, my fear of crowds and narrow spaces diminished somewhat. It no longer had such a concrete expression. But I was still—and would remain—afraid of getting caught. In every situation where there was a choice, I opted for the alternative that would give me the most freedom, even if that usually meant I was also opting for the alternative that was the least financially rewarding. For example, I have never had a permanent job with regular hours, a monthly salary, a pension and paid holidays. My jobs were always on an hourly or freelance basis so that, at least in theory, I could choose from day to day whether I wanted to work or not. Whenever I was forced to sign a contract—of whatever kind: a rental agreement, a book contract, a purchase agreement—I did so with great unease. I would sometimes get palpitations and break out in a cold sweat as I stood there with the pen in my hand, about to sign and therefore lock myself into something, irrevocably.

In my mind it was strictly taboo to be, or even to dream of being, emotionally or financially dependent on anyone, or to harbor even the tiniest secret desire to live in a symbiotic relationship with another person. And yet—or perhaps for that very reason—I have always felt a strong attraction to that kind of life. An attraction and a secret longing to be dependent and taken care of. That's right: to be taken care of, to be taken in hand—financially and emotionally and sexually, and preferably by a man.

I sometimes managed to live out this longing, which found its expression through daydreams and fantasies, in my sexual relationships. This would take the form of a kind of role-playing, where my partner and I would pretend we were an old-fashioned married couple: married man who is the provider comes home to housewife who has dinner on the table. And after dinner: active male subject services passive female sex object.

But, as I said, I only managed to live out these fantasies to a certain extent, because just as I have never had a permanent job, I have also never had a long-term relationship, only casual liaisons.

These days there is no trap of the kind that my mother talked about and warned my sisters and me about. First of all there was the law stating that parents must divide their parental leave from work equally between them during the child's first eighteen months. Then day care became compulsory for eight hours a day for all children aged between eighteen months and six years. The housewife and her male provider have not only been out of fashion for a long time, they have been eradicated. And children are no longer a drag, a hindrance, for anyone. There is no longer the risk of ending up as a dependent, or falling behind on the salary scale, or losing skills in the workplace. Not because of the children, at any rate. There is no longer any excuse not to have children. Nor is there any longer an excuse not to work when you have children.

6

The welcome party started off with a five-course Italian meal: Parma ham with melon, minestrone, pasta with pesto and chicken fillets, aged cheese with pears and grapes, and for dessert, *panna cotta*. Freshly baked white bread was served with the appetizer and main course. Only the wine was missing. During dinner I sat next to Majken, who told me she was an artist; Alice, a short, plump woman who had been a stagehand at the theater in Malmö, and Johannes, a fellow author I had often come across in literary circles, but had never really spoken to. I had always thought he seemed difficult and deliberately kept his distance. Now, however, he turned out to be quite the opposite—easy company and socially adept. He seemed to be in good form, despite the fact that he had been in the unit for more than three years.

But then so far he had only donated sperm to the sperm bank and one kidney to a father of five who was a primary school teacher. He had also taken part in various experiments.

"At the moment I'm involved in a completely safe psychological investigation to do with cooperation and trust and that kind of thing," he said.

Then he told us about the time he took part in an experiment with a new kind of medication for depression and chronic exhaustion, and ended up so lively and talkative that they had to bring in extra staff working around the clock just to socialize and chat with him—or rather listen to him, since he was babbling nonstop—and to keep an eye on him so that he didn't overexert himself or disturb his neighbors too much. He had been seized by an uncontrollable urge to make things and to renovate, and took the opportunity to convert his kitchenette and part of the living room into a proper little kitchen.

"I didn't get much written at that time—I was way too restless and desperate for company—but I had a really good time," he ended his story.

Majken had been in the unit for four years, Alice for four months. Majken had, among other things, donated eggs for stem-cell research, one kidney, and the auditory bone from her right ear. As she was now deaf in that ear, she always wanted people to be on her left, she explained.

"And in a few weeks," she went on, "I'm going in to donate my pancreas to a student nurse with four kids. So I guess this will be my last welcome party."

She was moving her spoon around in her dessert, a distracted movement, it seemed to me—as if she didn't mind, as if it didn't bother her, as if it were completely okay. All of a sudden I felt completely powerless. Majken stirred and stirred with her spoon and I followed her hand and the spoon with my eyes, and with every rotation it felt as if the air in the big room were becoming thinner and more difficult to breathe. My body grew heavy, my

arms ached, there was a thudding and rushing noise in my ears,
I couldn't see properly. I broke out in a cold sweat, and through
a black, flickering mist I saw Majken's hand stop its movement,
let go of the spoon and grip my hand as it lay there in front of
me next to my dish, limp and damp and cold. As if from far, far
away, beyond the rushing in my ears, I heard her voice:

"Darling, you get used to it. Don't you, Alice?"

I couldn't see Alice. My field of vision had shrunk. I could
only see Majken's hand resting on mine. Alice said something,
she was talking, reassuring me, but I couldn't hear what she was
saying because her voice was surging and fading, growing in turn
stronger and weaker as if she were speaking in a strong wind,
and only odd words were getting through. I opened my mouth,
tried to say that I couldn't hear her properly, but there wasn't
enough air. I couldn't get my breath. I couldn't focus. The dark
flickering mist grew more dense and became a dark veil, a curtain. I could hardly see at all, and it felt as if the chair and the
floor were about to give way beneath me, as if I were being sucked
down into a hole. But then Alice was there too, stroking my arm
with her hand, and now I could hear her. She was saying:

"It's okay, darling, it's okay . . ."

And Johannes, who was sitting beside me, put one arm around
my shoulders. He placed his other hand on my forehead. As if I
were a little child who might have a temperature. But it worked,
it felt as if he were propping me up, keeping me there, stopping
me from being sucked down into that hole or falling headfirst
into the *panna cotta*. It felt as if they cared about me, all three
of them, and I have always been calmed by the feeling that someone cares about me. Johannes said:

"There now . . . Take a deep breath. There. And breathe out
slowly. Good. And again, Dorrit, nice and calm. That's it, there
now . . ."

We sat like that for quite a while: Majken holding my hand,
Alice stroking my forearm and Johannes stroking my back slowly,

and they all carried on murmuring "There now, it's okay" until my senses and my breathing returned to normal. When Johannes finally took his hand away from my forehead, he did it by allowing it to slide down over my cheek, like a gentle caress.

There was entertainment. There was dancing. A rock band played. I danced with Johannes, Majken and Alice. And with Elsa and lots of other people. But I danced the most with Johannes. He had rhythm and feeling, and he knew proper ballroom dancing, with the right steps and everything. He could lead like a real old chauvinist, like an old-fashioned gentleman. At first I found it a bit difficult to keep up. Partly because I had never done this kind of dancing before, I'd only seen it in old films, partly because I felt a little bit exposed somehow, it almost felt dangerous, not being in charge of your own steps. But after a while I decided to ignore that feeling and just let myself be led and managed. And then it felt just wonderful, right up my alley.

It grew late. Elsa and I were standing at the bar, each with a pear drink. They served only nonalcoholic beverages, and if you didn't want a soda there was only orange juice and a pear drink to choose from.

"Would you like to meet up tomorrow morning and have breakfast together?" I asked.

"Would you like to have breakfast tomorrow and then spend the next four days together?" Elsa asked.

As new arrivals we had four consecutive free days, Sunday to Wednesday. It was so we could make ourselves at home in the unit before the compulsory health check; after that we would be allocated to appropriate humane experiments or begin to donate. We were being given a gentle start. And when Elsa mentioned spending the next four days together I felt—to my surprise—an enormous sense of relief, and it made me realize that I was afraid of those four free days. It made me realize that for the first time in my adult life, I was afraid of being alone. So I accepted her invitation. No, I didn't want to be alone. I didn't want to be alone in a building without windows, where there wasn't a living thing to fix your gaze on, not a thing to stop me from thinking about the fact that I would never again experience the feeling that flooded through me that morning in March each year when I opened my door and saw the first crocus of the year in bloom on my lawn. Or the first scilla or the first hepatica or the first scented violet. Or when I saw the cranes, trumpeting as they flew over in wide skeins on their way north to Lake Hornborga. And I didn't want to think about Nils and our times together, his hands on my body, his kisses, his penis, his words telling me how much I meant to him. Above all I didn't want to think about Jock, about the fact that we would never again run together in the forest or by the sea. Or take our walk along the tractor route to Ellström's farm to buy fresh eggs and vegetables for me and a pig's heart for him. I needed to erect a barrier of new experiences, a buffer zone between there and here, between then and now, before I had the courage to be alone with my thoughts again.

On the other hand, I wasn't so afraid of the night. I wasn't afraid to sleep without company. Since I wasn't used to sleeping with other people in the same room, or even in the same house, I actually preferred it that way. And to be on the safe side I'd made sure I got myself some sleeping pills. Of course they were the kind that can't send you off to sleep forever; they were the suicide-proof kind with a built-in antabuse effect: if you take more than two, you throw up.

When Elsa put her empty glass down on the bar and said she was tired and off to bed, I asked her if she wanted a sleeping pill.

She laughed.

"Thanks, but I've been to the doctor too and got myself some!"

We decided that whoever woke up first the next morning would ring the other, and after breakfast we would set off to explore the unit and make the most of everything being free. Then we hugged each other, said good night, and she left.

The last dance was a ballad. The singer stood in the middle of the stage, alone in the spotlight, the orchestra hidden in the darkness behind him. He sang: "This is for my girl, this is for my woman, for my world. Baby, baby, this is all for you . . ."

Johannes came over to me as I stood there with my lukewarm pear drink, swaying to the beat and humming along with the refrain. He bowed briefly and asked, very politely:

"May I have the pleasure?"

It was charming, I was charmed by his old-fashioned manner and his words, and without a second's hesitation I put my glass on the bar, nodded graciously and held out my hand to him. He took it and placed his other arm quite formally around my waist. And we sailed out onto the dance floor. He led so confidently, in such a relaxed way and with such perfect timing that I didn't even feel as if I couldn't really dance like this. I almost fell into a trance, following him as easily as if I were a part of him, as if we were the same body.

"Thank you for the dance, Dorrit," he said when the music ended. "And thank you for this evening."

He took my hand, raised it to his lips, and just brushed it with them. I had read about this in novels, I had seen it in films and plays. I had dreamed about it. But this was the first time in my life that someone had actually kissed my hand.

7

I was just leaving the party when I heard hurrying footsteps behind me and turned around. It was Majken.

"I presume we're heading in the same direction," she said. "I can show you a nice detour. If you're not too tired, of course."

"No, I'm not particularly tired," I said. Actually I was grateful to have some company for a while longer.

We took elevator B from K1 to the fifth floor. The doors slid open and we stepped out into a very wide and apparently endlessly long corridor, more like an indoor street or—I realized after taking a few steps—a running track. It had the same kind of surface as outdoor tracks usually have: with a little bit of give, and the ability to absorb sounds. On the other side of the track, opposite the row of elevators, was a glass wall the height of a three- or four-story building, looking out over something that in the half-darkness looked like a real primeval forest.

"That's the winter garden," said Majken. "One of the wilder areas."

Above us, high above, a glass dome covered both the winter garden and the broad track we were on. And up above the night sky curved over the dome, the infinite reality of space.

"This," said Majken, gesturing toward the floor, "is the Atrium Walkway. It goes all the way around the winter garden, and measures 130 yards from corner to corner. A total of 520 yards. So if you jog around it ten times, you've done a good three miles."

We followed the Atrium Walkway for fifty yards or so, until the forest on the other side of the glass wall gave way to a kind of galleria, with small glasshouses and orangeries, small shops that were closed, and workshops for drying flowers, arranging flowers, coloring plants, and so on, and a broad staircase curving upward to something that looked like a café.

"That's the Terrace," said Majken. "They serve breakfast and lunch every day. The rest of the time it's an ordinary self-service café—you can make your own coffee or fruit drinks, make a sandwich and take any cakes you like, or anything you fancy from what's there."

"It looks really lovely," I said.

"What?" she said, and I realized we'd somehow managed to swap places as we came around the corner into the galleria, so I was now on her right side, where she didn't hear so well.

She stopped and turned her left ear toward me.

"It looks lovely," I repeated.

She nodded. "It is. You can see almost the whole winter garden from up there. I always have lunch there on weekdays."

At the far end of the galleria, where the high glass wall once again turned into a background of dense greenery, was a door.

Majken opened it and let me go ahead of her into a warm air lock, where she opened another door, and we stepped out into a nocturnal garden.

There was a fresh, slightly sweet smell of flowers and plants. The moon, which was almost full, was shining in through the glass ceiling from its winter night. But inside here, under here, it was already spring, almost early summer, and flowers in hundreds of colors and shades seemed to glow in the white moonlight.

There was a different climate in the winter garden from our northern European one. A network of paths meandered among palms, wild hibiscus, climbing vines, trailing bougainvillea, olive trees, stone pines, plane trees, citrus trees and cedars, leading over small paved patio areas with fountains and benches where you could sit and read or philosophize, continuing around a huge lawn—where you could lie and read or philosophize—and then back into a wilder, darker area, and finally to the area Majken really wanted to show me: an almost exact, if somewhat reduced, copy of Monet's garden at Giverny. The only thing that was really missing was the pink house where he lived with his family, and of course this replica wasn't as mature as the French original. The garden, which had been laid out by a group of gardening enthusiasts who were interested in art, was like an Impressionist painting: an explosion of colors, a perfect, conscious composition, dotted, its contours slightly blurred—at least that's how it appeared to me at this time of the night—but unequivocally clear in terms of the combinations and contrasts of the plants and the colors.

As we strolled in silence along the gravel paths through the flower garden and across the little wooden bridges in the water garden, the scents of flowers and herbs gave way to one another—violet, lavender, thyme, rosemary, sage, rose, apple blossom, peony—and all these scents and sights had a pleasantly anesthetizing effect on me.

When we reached the big pool, where the reflections of the moon glimmered between irregular rafts of water lilies just beginning to flower in shades of yellow, blue, green and pink, we stopped and sat down on a wooden bench, painted green and damp with dew.

"I often come here," said Majken after a while. "It's as if this were real."

I understood what she meant. It felt exactly as if we were outside, outdoors, in a normal garden down on the ground, not on the top of a windowless fortress, with earth that had been brought in, artificially constructed ponds and streams, beneath toughened glass that couldn't be smashed and no doubt had some kind of alarm system built in.

"Those Impressionists," she said, "they certainly knew about color. And about light and shade. Different kinds of shade: thinner shadows that let the light through, and heavier, denser ones. And it's as if Monet made this garden to show the world how he saw colors. How he saw their power, their potential and their purpose. I think he wanted to show that the world is color. That life itself is color. That if we can just see the colors, really see them, life will be beautiful. And meaningful. Because beauty has a value of its own, that's how I see it anyway."

She looked at me, smiled. The moonlight made her lips appear dark red, like pomegranate, her eyes almost emerald green, her skin like ivory, her hair like gold and ash. I tried to smile back, but I couldn't do it, there was a lump in my throat dragging the corners of my mouth down, and if she had said "life" one more time I wouldn't have been able to hold back the feelings that were lying there whimpering and throbbing beneath the pleasantly numbing veil all these different impressions had wrapped around me. Fury, grief, fear, hatred—everything would have burst through the veil and surged up and come roaring out through all the orifices in my face: my eyes, my nose, my mouth. And I didn't want that to happen—not because I was afraid of showing my feelings to Majken or to other people, not because I was particularly bothered about keeping up a facade of strength and self-control, but just because I didn't want anything to disturb this period of stillness. I wanted to keep the stillness, intact, for as long as possible.

But she didn't say anything else for quite a while. We just sat there. And eventually we got up from the bench and set off again. Then we heard a faint mechanical humming somewhere in the bushes behind us—so sudden and so unlike the other faint sounds of rustling leaves and lapping waves that I jumped and turned around.

"It's nothing to worry about," said Majken. "It's just someone on the surveillance team wondering what we're doing out here in the middle of the night."

"Aren't we allowed out here at night?" I said.

"Oh yes, sure. It's just a little unusual for anyone to actually come here then."

The stillness had been disturbed, as if someone had drilled right through it and smashed it to pieces. All of a sudden I felt cold, frozen.

8

The breakfast buffet in the Terrace restaurant was groaning with fruit and vegetables, freshly baked white and brown bread, cheeses, pâtés, salami, ham, eggs, oatmeal, yogurt, cereals, jellies and marmalade, and on a table nearby was coffee and hot water on hotplates, and milk and juice in thermoses to keep them cool.

Elsa just took a cup of coffee and a bowl of yogurt with granola and sliced fruit, while I piled up my tray with as much as it would hold: coffee, freshly squeezed orange juice, cinnamon toast, yogurt with raspberry jelly and cornflakes, a boiled egg, three sandwiches—one with Emmental cheese, one with honey-smoked ham and one with ginger marmalade. I didn't expect to be able to eat it all, but it smelled so good, looked so attractive, and as it didn't cost anything I saw no reason to stop myself or hold back.

We moved through fifteen or so other diners to a table where we could look straight down onto a circular patio with marble benches and a fountain, surrounded by low palm trees and hibiscus bushes with bright red flowers. The winter garden extended around and beyond the patio. The morning sun was shining in at an angle from above. I could see birds, butterflies, bumblebees. Far away I could just glimpse a weeping willow, a wisteria, a big copper beech and Monet's lily pond. Elsa gazed at all the greenery, and in a tone of voice that I interpreted as tired, but later would realize was more likely to be apathetic, or possibly ironic, she said:

"Isn't that lovely."

"Yes," I said.

I was feeling pretty good, almost confident after the walk and the time spent with Majken the night before, and I had slept surprisingly well without needing to take a sleeping pill, and even if I hadn't managed many hours of sleep before Elsa rang just after eight, I felt rested. I took a cautious sip of my coffee, which was steaming hot, black, and smelled fantastic. Closed my eyes, swallowed.

"Oh, that's good!" I exclaimed spontaneously, and went on:

"This is such a treat, isn't it? Being able to go out for breakfast."

"Out?" said Elsa, raising an eyebrow and looking around and up toward the dome, which in daylight turned out to consist of several large sheets of glass, set in lead—at least I presumed it was lead—and put together in a symmetrical, starlike pattern. There was something British or colonial about it, like the roof of an orangery in the gardens of a palace. The sky on the other side was clear blue. Individual clouds sailed majestically by, and the word "galleon" came to mind.

"I don't mean 'out' as in 'outside,'" I explained, "but more as in the opposite of being at home. Going out, sort of."

Elsa mumbled something inaudible. Not a morning person, I thought. She's got out of bed on the wrong side.

"I've never been out for breakfast before," I went on, taking a bite of my cheese sandwich. Chewed. Swallowed.

"Have you?" I asked Elsa, who—I now noticed—wasn't eating or drinking, just poking her spoon listlessly around in her yogurt with granola and sliced strawberries and mango.

"No," she replied in a flat voice. "Not as far as I can remember."

It was now I realized she wasn't tired, or at least that wasn't the main problem. This wasn't about being in a bad mood because it was morning, she just felt bad all over. I was ashamed. I put my sandwich down and said:

"Elsa, I'm sorry!"

"For what? Because you can manage to be positive? There's nothing wrong with that."

"No, because I'm so caught up with myself I didn't realize that you . . ."

I broke off—I had absolutely no idea what words to use, so instead of finishing the sentence I reached across the table with my right hand and clasped Elsa's left hand, which was lying limply beside her bowl. Her right hand was still clutching the spoon in the yogurt, but it wasn't moving now. She closed her eyes. She screwed them tight shut. She bent her face over the bowl so that I couldn't see it, only her bangs, like a brown-and-silver-striped curtain. The hand I was holding was cold, and was shaking slightly.

"It's okay . . ." I said, tentatively at first, trying to sound as calm, as secure as Majken, Alice and Johannes had the previous evening. "There now, Elsa, it's okay. There now."

She was weeping now, silently but with drawn out, suppressed whimpers and quivering, hacking breaths as I squeezed her hand

and repeated "It's okay," because I didn't know what else to say or do.

The other people up on the Terrace this Sunday morning—the others who were having breakfast at tables around us, reading the morning papers or chatting quietly with one another, or simply eating in silence without reading, and the two breakfast hostesses who could have been either employees or residents, bringing in one pot of coffee after another, topping up the dishes on the buffet, wiping down tables, carrying out dirty dishes and providing clean plates and cutlery—started noticing Elsa. One or two put down their newspapers and took off their reading glasses, others put down their coffee cup, placed their spoon in their bowl of oatmeal, or pushed their tray away from themselves, slightly across the table. Conversations fell silent, one by one. One hostess stopped in the middle of the room carrying a dish of sliced papaya. Everybody was staring at us, and everyone looked serious. But no one seemed troubled, no one seemed upset. They were just paying careful attention. They were waiting, I realized just a little while later. They were waiting to see how things unfolded. And when Elsa was finally unable to control the sobs she had suppressed until now, when her cries became louder and more piercing and persistent, first one of the diners got up, then another, and a few more, and the hostess hurried over to the buffet table and put down the dish so that her hands were free. The next moment a crowd of people surrounded Elsa in a semicircle, some sitting on chairs they had dragged along with them, others standing. Those who could reach were touching her. With steady hands they held her shoulders, or stroked her arms, her back or the nape of her neck. As if they were holding her together.

9

The small shops and workshops in the galleria were open now. People were standing or sitting inside, working on different activities related to plants, herbs and spices. The whole galleria was flooded with sunshine, revealing that the air in here was filled with very fine particles, forming a gossamer-fine, yellowish mist. There was an aroma of spices and flowers.

It was warm in the winter garden, perhaps as high as eighty degrees, at least in the sun. Elsa and I strolled along in silence. Birds sang. Flies and bees buzzed. A squirrel leaped among the branches of a stone pine, stopping from time to time to grab small orange cones with his teeth; he would hold them between his front paws and eat quickly, then shoot off, leaping with ease and assurance to the next branch. We carried on through the olive grove, passed an area planted with rosebushes, and entered the citrus grove, where the trees were covered in white blossoms that filled the air with a sweet, fruity perfume, and came out again on the other side where the vegetation was dense and tangled. After an avenue of tall bushes and low-growing trees we reached the huge lawn, where people were lying and reading, or simply relaxing in the sun. We walked around the edge of the lawn and on past springs and small fountains and underneath trellises covered in vines, roses, sweet peas, honeysuckle, clematis and bougainvillea, through narrow overgrown passageways and thickets, and eventually reached Monet's garden. There, in front of a large bed of forget-me-nots and pink and red tulips, Elsa stopped dead. We were on the exact spot where the pink house would have stood if it had been the original garden. On the far side of the forget-me-not bed and two yew trees lay the flower garden, with its rows of flowerbeds and gravel paths in between. Elsa looked around in confusion, then exclaimed:

"But . . . I've been here! I don't mean here, but . . . I was here with my . . . With a good friend. She treated me to the trip. We had that book with us, you know, that children's book . . . We'd read it at home together when we . . . And that's why we came here. There."

Her cheeks were red. She was thrilled, but also agitated, it was obvious that something inside her had been stirred.

"*Linnea in Monet's Garden*," I said quietly. "I think that's what it's called."

She didn't reply, but started walking again, and I followed her, the gravel crunching beneath our feet as we moved between the multicolored flowerbeds. The same scent of flowers and herbs from the night before drifted toward me, but drier now, not quite so distinct. We went through the underground passage to the water garden, into the shadows beneath the trees, and followed the path by the pond. We reached one of the green benches, and Elsa sat down. I sat beside her. She was sitting up very straight, not leaning against the back of the bench, and she stared straight ahead, down into the lily pond. She didn't speak. Nor did I. I wondered if I should ask how she was feeling, or if she wanted to tell me about the woman she went to Giverny with, but something held me back. And after a while she sighed, then leaned back and crossed her arms and legs. Then she shrugged her shoulders, sneezed, and looked normal again. No red roses in her cheeks, just that watchful expression, her eyes slightly narrowed.

"It's strange," she said. "But this feels completely real. Totally genuine."

"Yes," I said. "I know."

"Genuine, and at the same time . . . romantic," she said, and her voice once again had something of that toneless quality, which might be either apathy or irony. "Perhaps they want it to be romantic for us. Warm and romantic. Eternal summer."

She didn't yet know—nor did I—how right she was when she talked about eternal summer. In the winter garden it was in fact spring and summer all year round. Mimosa, bougainvillea, rhododendrons, roses, peonies, tulips and forget-me-nots flowered week after week, month after month. Everything was either just coming out or in full bloom, but never yellowing, withering or dead. Nothing died in the winter garden. And yet everything was real; there were no silk flowers or plastic bushes or trees from some stage set. These were real plants, real living flowers with stamens and pistils, and real live bumblebees buzzing around them. Flowers and leaves that could be picked and arranged in a vase, or used to make tea or dye clothes. If you picked them and put them in a vase with some water, they gradually faded like any other flower, but in the beds or on the trees, where you'd picked them from, delicate new plants or buds soon emerged. And the lawns were real grass; they needed cutting and fertilizing and watering, just like any other lawn. The bushes and trees also had to be trimmed and pruned at regular intervals so that the paths and patios wouldn't get overgrown. Everything was green all the time. The color of the leaves never changed from green to yellow to red to brown, they never dried up and they never fell. On the citrus trees the oranges, lemons, mandarins and grapefruit never ripened. However, their small white scented petals did fall after the brief flowering period, filling the air between the trees and forming a snowy carpet on the ground. But the buds from which the petals had fallen never developed into fruit. Instead they came into blossom once again after a while. But Elsa was not yet aware of any of this as she went on:

"Perhaps they want us to experience summer and romance. One last time."

"Or for the first time," I said.

"Maybe," said Elsa. Then she asked:

"Do you think you'll miss the Scandinavian winter? Snow and wind and cold?"

I thought it over.

"Autumn and late winter," I replied. "Late winter moving into spring, the way it is out there right now," and in my mind's eye I could see my garden as it had looked the previous morning: the winter aconite and the snowdrops that had just appeared. And I could see the outside of my house with its flaking white paint and its roof covered in patches of moss, with the chimney puffing out the transparent, quivering smoke from the stove. And I saw myself coming out of the door in my warm jacket, hat, scarf, and gloves along with Jock, setting off for a long walk in the wind in the low, early spring sun. I shook myself to get the images out of my head, but it didn't work. So I stood up quickly and said:

"Can we go a bit further, I just feel I . . . I need to get moving."

It must have been obvious that there was something I needed to shake off, because Elsa nodded and got up straightaway; she took my arm and we went through the nearest warm air lock into the Atrium Walkway, where two joggers came steaming toward us, their feet almost soundless on the surface of the track.

"Hi Dorrit!" panted one of them, wiping the sweat from his eyes with his sleeve. "Thanks for yesterday."

It was Johannes. He stopped. His companion stopped too, and jogged in place.

"This is Dorrit, who's such a good dancer," explained Johannes, turning to his companion. I felt ridiculously flattered. I don't think I blushed, but I might have.

Johannes introduced his friend to us and I introduced Elsa, and we all shook hands, then they jogged away and Elsa and I took elevator A to the next floor, where we walked out directly into the library.

It wasn't large. It was just like an ordinary rural branch library: one big room divided up by shelves. But as we walked around I could see that it was well organized and impressively up-to-date; I noticed a number of titles that had just been published. The CD and DVD section wasn't large either, but it too was varied and current.

The librarian, a skinny man in saggy brown corduroy pants, came over to us as we stood checking out the selection of films. He stopped directly behind us, his hands in the back pockets of his pants. It was a little while before he spoke, and when he did it was with a sullen whining quality that we would soon realize was somehow inherent in his voice. Whatever he said, it sounded negative. He said:

"You can of course order music CDs and films on loan from the real library out in the community."

"So you mean this isn't a real library?" I said, amused.

He didn't reply. Instead he took his right hand out of his back pocket and held it out slowly, first to me and then to Elsa, shook us by the hand and introduced himself as Kjell.

"I used to work for the library service in Lund," he said. "I actually saw you there once, recording one of your books as an audio book. Anyway, I've been looking after all this for two years now," he said, making a sweeping gesture around the room. "Full time—at least. There's a certain amount of overtime, if I can put it that way."

"I see," I said.

"Well, it's because there are so many intellectuals here. People who read books."

"I see," I said again.

"People who read books," he went on, "tend to be dispensable. Extremely."

"Right," I said.

"Yes," he said.

I looked for Elsa, who had moved discreetly away and was now leafing through a gardening book a few shelves away.

Kjell slipped his hand back into his pocket, and for a moment it looked as if he were going back to the issue desk, but he stopped.

"Yes, that's the way things are," he said. "Books, on the other hand, can't be ordered from the main library. Either I have to buy them," he said, sighing, "or you can download them as an e-book. You can sign out a reader each from here, if you haven't already got one."

We did that. And we sorted out our library cards as well. Then we sat down in the armchairs in the corner and flipped through the daily newspapers and magazines. A man was fast asleep in one of the other armchairs. The newspaper he had been reading was lying on the floor in front of him. He was breathing audibly—not exactly snoring, but it sounded as if there was something wrong with his airway. He was making a grating, whistling noise.

Perhaps he has a cold, we whispered to each other, and neither Elsa nor I wanted to catch anything, so we got up and left.

During those early days at the unit I would come across several people who just fell asleep anywhere, and who breathed in the same way, almost snoring. It would soon be explained to me that this was a side effect of one of a series of tranquilizing drugs being tested here. The people involved in this particular experiment found their ability to absorb oxygen was seriously impaired, and at the same time the yawn reflex was canceled out. A consequence of these two side effects was that they found it very easy to fall asleep. A few were also affected by minor but permanent brain damage, presumably as a result of the lack of oxygen, and in the worst cases had difficulty walking, talking, and knowing where they were or what day it was.

In other words, the man sleeping in the corner probably didn't have a cold, and there was no need for us to worry about our health.

We didn't borrow anything from the library that first day, but left empty-handed apart from our readers. As we were passing the issue desk on the way out, we nodded to Kjell.

"Thanks for popping in," he said gloomily. "Come again any time."

We emerged into a large indoor square, surrounded by a department store, lots of smaller shops, a cinema, a theater, an art gallery and a restaurant with tables outside. In the middle of the square, which was paved with mottled gray polished slabs of the kind you often find in churchyards, in the form of gravestones, was a rectangle of thick glass, with several stone benches surrounding a bronze sculpture representing a fishing boat. Through the glass we could see shifting, constantly moving shades of blue and turquoise. We realized the swimming pool must be directly beneath us.

Among the small shops around the square were two boutiques, one offering new clothes and one secondhand, a music store with guitars, wind instruments, electric organs and drum kits in the window, a craft shop with goods made by artists in the unit, a hardware store and a shop with hobby items as well as office and art supplies. The words "shop" and "store" are perhaps misleading, and I must stress that no money changed hands. Or to put it more clearly, it wasn't really a question of shopping at all. You just went in and picked up what you needed, apart from certain items that had to be signed out. Sometimes you also had to order things that were temporarily out of stock, or fill out a request for some specific product or a specific brand to be stocked in the future.

The cinema had two screens. At the moment they were showing *The Double-Headed Crane*, a psychological drama about a family in crisis that had received very good reviews, and an action comedy, *The Maniac 3*.

The art gallery was closed while a new exhibition was being mounted, and it would open the following Saturday. It was Majken who was exhibiting. She had told us during dinner at the party: "My first solo exhibition!"

The theater was also closed. But a poster informed us that Chekhov's *The Seagull* would shortly be having its premiere, and later in the spring they would be putting on Shakespeare's *The Merchant of Venice*.

"What a shame," I said. "Now that we can actually afford to go to the theater, they're only doing the same old classics."

"It doesn't really matter, though, does it?" said Elsa. "A play is a play. The whole thing about going to the theater is actually going to the theater, isn't it?"

I laughed; there was certainly some truth to what she said.

"Okay, let's go for a swim!" she said, grabbing my arm and dragging me with a certain amount of gentle force in the direction of the elevators at the opposite end of the square.

10

I have always loved exercise, and in the unit's sports complex
there was everything I could have wished for, and more: a small
sports ground with a running track—as if the Atrium Walkway
weren't enough—and equipment for all kinds of athletics, a big
hall for various ball and racquet sports, a bowling alley, a classic
gymnasium with wall bars all the way around, and a storeroom
next door with a vaulting horse, a vaulting box, baseball bats,
hockey sticks, and nets containing balls of various sizes. And on
two floors there were smaller rooms for aerobics, Friskis & Svettis
gym training, spinning, dance, yoga, fencing and so on, as well
as a weight room. And the swimming pool was right in the center of everything.

My mouth was almost watering as Elsa and I wandered around. We saw people practicing the high jump, long jump and discus, playing badminton, tennis, hockey and volleyball. And as we cautiously pushed open the door of each of the smaller rooms in turn and peeped in, we saw two women playing squash, a group in cotton outfits learning judo, another group doing something that sounded and looked like African dance, a man on his own practicing tai chi, plus a group exercising around a Friskis & Svettis instructor to some music with a powerful beat. When she saw us in the doorway she waved to us to come and join in, but we smiled and waved our refusal, pointing at our clothes and shoes by way of explanation. Elsa was wearing loafers and I was in sandals. The instructor nodded and we closed the door and went into the gym next door.

It was small but well equipped, the air fresh without feeling chilly, the music pulsating energetically but with the volume relatively low. Five or six people were exercising at the moment. None of them took any notice of us; they carried on lifting, walking on the treadmill, pulling and pushing as they puffed, grimaced and concentrated as hard as they could on one muscle group at a time, one repetition at a time.

"I don't get it," muttered Elsa as we made our way between rows of well-oiled, perfectly functioning machines.

"Don't get what?" I said.

"All this luxury! How much is all this costing the taxpayer?"

"That's true," I agreed, although I was actually more excited than upset. "We seem to be expensive to run."

"Exactly. And for what purpose?"

I didn't reply. Not because I had nothing to say, but because at that moment I caught sight of something that took my attention away from the topic of luxury. On the leg-curl machine was a man in a T-shirt and shorts, exhaling audibly each time he pulled the weight down toward himself with the back of his legs, keeping an even rhythm. On his face, arms and legs he had some kind of outbreak: blue-black and reddish brown spots and blotches, the smallest the size of the nail on your little finger, the biggest about as large as a medium-size birch leaf. Some of the larger blotches had burst and were suppurating. They looked revolting. It looked like a disease, and it made me think of Kaposi's sarcoma, which I had seen an AIDS patient suffering from when I was young and working in health services and home care. It certainly looked like Kaposi's, and the lumps were swelling and shrinking according to the movement of the man's muscles. As we passed him I glanced curiously and as discreetly as I could at the weights on the machine, and saw that he was lifting four hundred pounds with the back of his thighs. Not bad for a man between sixty and sixty-five. Whatever he was suffering from, at least it wasn't AIDS.

Elsa, who didn't seem to have noticed either the man's skin or the strength of his legs, sighed and carried on her argument.

"We're like free-range pigs or hens. The only difference is that the pigs and hens are—hopefully—happily ignorant of anything but the present."

Suddenly a long-forgotten memory surfaced; I laughed and said:

"You know what, Elsa—you haven't changed at all."

"What do you mean?"

"Do you remember our class trip to the zoo in fourth grade?"

"Er . . . vaguely. Why?"

"The sight of all the animals wandering back and forth behind bars made you absolutely furious. Particularly the beasts of prey and the elephants. And the big birds that didn't have room to fly properly. You were probably the only one of us who realized that their restless wandering wasn't natural behavior. Do you remember? Do you remember what you did?"

"Let them out? No, I don't remember at all."

"Every time you caught sight of one of the keepers or anyone else employed by the zoo," I said, "you crept up behind them,

and when you got there, right behind them, you yelled out: 'Ge-
stapo!' Do you remember?"

She giggled and said:

"Now you come to mention it, yes I do. But do you remember
when you and that Lotta . . ."—and we were off, chatting about
childhood memories as we carried on out of the gym and into
the echoing foyer of the swimming pool, with its smell of chlorine. This sort of talk was calming, soothing. It was as if we were
wrapped in a kind of cotton wool, insulating us from everything
around us.

We hadn't brought swimsuits, but Elsa had heard that there was
a small selection of used but clean ones that could be borrowed,
so we went over to the nearest attendant, dressed in white, and
made inquiries. He showed us to a closet containing trunks,
bikinis, and one-pieces neatly sorted according to size. Next to
it was another closet containing hand towels and bathing towels.

"Just help yourselves," said the attendant. "When you've finished, put them in the laundry bags in the changing room. Towels and swimming gear in separate bags. Simple and practical,
isn't it?"

He smiled. We thanked him, took what we needed and went
to the ladies' changing room, where we each found a locker, got
undressed and tramped along to the showers barefoot and top-
less, each with our bathing towel wound around our hips.

There weren't many people in there, which was fortunate,
because the few naked bodies we did see made the insulating
cotton wool of our old childhood memories loosen and fall away.
In front of us were six naked women. Three of them had the
same kind of outbreak on their bodies and faces as the man on
the leg-curl machine. They all had one or more scars from surgery, most on their bellies. Two of the women had distorted,
swollen joints, their movements slow and jerky, as if their whole

body ached. Another was clearly finding it difficult to breathe. She was also moving very slowly, and was always within reach of something that she could use for support—a wall, a faucet, a friend—when she had to stop and gasp, gasp, gasp for air, before tottering unsteadily on.

Elsa and I had stopped dead on the tiled floor, just inside the doorway of this wet, steaming room, with our borrowed swimsuits in our hands and the bathing towels wrapped around our hips and thighs. We just stood there. The women turned toward us where they were, under the showers or beside the rows of faucets where a couple of them were rinsing out their swimsuits. They all gave us a friendly smile and said hi—except the one who was having difficulty breathing; she just nodded wearily as she stood there with one hand pressed against the tiles on the wall.

Elsa was the first to start moving again. Resolutely she pulled off the bathing towel, stepped forward and hung it on a hook, then carried on into one of the showers and turned on the water. Mechanically I followed her example, and when we had put on our swimsuits we went out into the pool area. There were two big pools, a deep one 75 feet long, with a trampoline and diving boards, and a shallow one 150 feet long. There were also two Jacuzzis. No children's pool.

Without a word Elsa marched straight over to the diving boards and began to climb. There were four different levels, each with a board extending out over the pool. I assumed she was going to walk out onto one of the two lower ones, get ready, then jump feetfirst into the water, but she didn't. She kept on climbing, past the third level, all the way up to the top—from where I was standing it looked as if she were only a few feet from the ceiling.

With relaxed, confident steps she walked out onto the board, which bounced slightly under her weight; she positioned herself right at the end, with her toes just over the edge. Extended her arms out in front of her, stood completely still, staring straight ahead until the movement of the board stopped altogether. Up above her I could just make out the blurred shape of the soles of a pair of shoes through the thick glass ceiling, as someone walked across the square on the floor above. At the same time I became aware of a dragging feeling of dizziness in the soles of my own feet as I waited there watching Elsa by the side of the pool down below. I've always had a tendency to feel dizzy easily.

Then she began to bend her knees, once, twice, so that the board began to bounce, and the third time she pulled back her arms and seemed to collect her body, somehow. And when she straightened her knees and pushed off, her arms shot up in a straight line above her head, and the whole of her body formed a single straight line from the tips of her toes to the tips of her fingers. She was like a spear as she took off from the board— or perhaps it was the board that fired her into the air, like a spring. She flew upward at an angle, toward the ceiling. And when she had gone a short distance up in the air she bent her upper body forward, downward, toward her legs, then straightened her body once more by extending her legs backward and upward, once again forming that same straight spear, but this time hurtling downward. The next moment she cut through the surface of the water with a sound that was most reminiscent of a whiplash, then she was underwater without the slightest splash. At least that's the way I remember it, the way I see it in my mind now as I try to describe it: as if she went through the surface of the water with a whistling, cracking noise, without even a drop of water splashing up around her. The only trace I remember her leaving behind was a series of gently undulating rings spreading across the surface of the pool from her point of entry.

She swam underwater, the contours of her body rippling beneath the rings on the surface; she came up at the far end, climbed up the metal ladder, pushed her wet hair back from her face and shook the water out of her ears.

"Oh, I can't tell you how good that feels!" she said when I had made my way around the pool to join her.

I was amazed, admiring, and asked stupidly:

"Where did you learn to do that?"

"Oh," she said, laughing, "I used to dive when I was young. I'd already started a little bit in middle school, in fifth grade if I remember correctly. Then after a few years I started competing."

"You must have been good," I said. "I mean, you *are* good."

"Thanks. Yes, I was pretty good, actually. Won a few prizes, that sort of thing. It was fun. I mean, diving was fun. But I wasn't competitive enough to carry on at the top level. I only did it because it felt so liberating, so beautiful somehow. It was the experience of beauty and the slight sense of danger I wanted, not a load of trophies and medals and fuss."

I gazed at her, lost for words.

"I know what you're thinking," she said. "You're thinking that if I'd gone in for competing at the top, I might not have ended up here."

"Something like that, yes," I admitted. "For example, if you'd won an Olympic medal . . ."

"I know," she said. "Then I would have become a great, positive role model for many young women, and would have been protected for the rest of my life. But I have to tell you, Dorrit, that I don't regret getting out of that particular rat race for one single second. It's not my thing, I've never understood the point of winning just for the sake of winning. What's the point in putting all your energy into being better than other people at just one thing, which is in fact completely irrelevant? Why do it? Do you understand it?"

"No," I replied truthfully. "I don't, actually."

"No," she said, "I can see you don't. If you did, you probably wouldn't have ended up here either. Shall we have a swim now?

We'd better go for the other pool so we don't risk somebody like me landing on our heads."

We swam twenty lengths, back and forth. After the first three or four warm-up lengths I speeded up. I was swimming breaststroke, I've never managed to learn anything else, but I had strong arms and legs and could swim pretty fast when I was in the mood, which I was at the moment. It felt as if I were literally splitting the water in half as I pushed it aside with huge, rapid strokes and kicked it away with my legs.

When I had swum my laps and came up I was as heavy as a whale; I heaved myself out onto the side of the pool with a particularly unattractive splash and waited for Elsa, who had taken things a little more slowly and still had a couple of lengths to go. I was out of breath, my heart pounding rapidly, steadily, rhythmically. I really did feel alive.

PART 2

1

I didn't think about Nils. I didn't think about my house. I didn't think about Jock, but it didn't help. Not thinking about Jock didn't help, because the way I missed him was different. It was in my body. It was in my heart. And it was painful.

For anyone who has never experienced or set any store by being close to an animal, it is perhaps difficult to understand that you can miss a dog so that it literally hurts. But the relationship with an animal is so much more physical than a relationship with another person. You don't get to know a dog by asking how he's feeling or what he's thinking, but by observing him and getting to know his body language. And all the important things you want to say to him you have to show through actions, attitude, gestures and sounds.

People, on the other hand, can always be reached through talking. A bridge of words grows easily between people, a bridge of information, explanations and assurances. For example, one person can say to another: "It's my birthday on August twenty-sixth," which is a piece of information, or: "I'm late because I couldn't get the car started," which is an explanation, or: "I will love you until death do us part," which is an assurance. But words between people also act as a kind of shock absorber; those in close relationships often choose to talk about something other than the matter that is weighing them down, worrying them or annoying them. Just like when Elsa and I were sharing our childhood memories. Or when an established couple immerse themselves in a discussion about the fact that the children need new shoes, or start enthusiastically planning a house extension, instead of talking about why they're always mad at each other these days.

Between Jock and me there was no bridge, no shock absorber. The contact between us was what it was, with no shortcuts, diversions or beltways. We couldn't talk to each other about our relationship, couldn't sort out misunderstandings or explain how much we meant to each other. We lived completely separately, because of the conditions imposed by our respective species. But we also lived side by side, body to body, without promises, lies or small talk. And irrespective of whether I thought about him or not, during my early days in the unit I could feel his coarse coat beneath the palm of my hand, the rapid beating of his heart under the coarseness, his cold nose, his warm tongue against my cheek, the smell of his breath and his fur. I could hear and see him: his brief bark when he caught sight of me and came bounding toward me, his legs wide apart, but his head held elegantly high; his excited snuffles and constantly wagging tail; his panting breath as he ran alongside me, his paws rhythmically rasping against the ground. And in bed at night I could feel his weight on my leg, and when I woke up in the morning I would sit up straightaway, and for a fraction of a second I would imagine I could see his expectant expression meeting my eyes from the foot of the bed. Each one of these sensory perceptions, these phantom emotions surrounding Jock's presence was immediately followed by the realization that it bore no relation whatsoever to reality. This realization was always equally brutal, like being struck hard by a fist or stabbed with a knife, and then it turned to a constant, nagging ache.

The only thing that could alleviate this kind of pain was physical activity. As long as I was on the go, the body was producing endorphins, and as long as the body was producing endorphins, life was bearable. Elsa seemed to be thinking along the same lines, because without ever discussing it or even commenting on the reasons, we were more or less constantly on the move during those first free days. We went for long, brisk walks around the Atrium Walkway and in the winter garden, swam, went to Friskis & Svettis, did strength-building exercises, joined in with various dance groups—salsa, hip-hop, jazz, step, belly dancing—and tried to keep up as best we could. In the evenings we had dinner at the restaurant on the indoor square on level 4, chatting about old school friends or talking for a while with whoever happened to be dining in the restaurant. This was something completely new for me, this idea of whiling away the time just chatting and socializing with other people. I had never looked at time or at people that way before. I had always valued my time and I had always regarded people as individuals, I had never reduced them to "just anybody" who might keep me company. Never before had I valued company for its own sake. I had never valued small talk. Now I noticed that small talk had a soothing effect; it was like a cold compress placed on a twisted ankle, counteracting swelling and bruising. And when the night came and Elsa and I left each other to go to our own apartments, I was so exhausted from all the physical activity, all the chatting, all this intense time killing, that I literally collapsed into bed and slipped into a black, dreamless sleep. Eight hours later I woke feeling rested, and with each new morning my perceptions of Jock were slightly less overwhelming.

2

"What if they find something wrong with me?" I said.

"Like what?" said Majken.

"Well, I don't know," I said. "But what if I'm not good enough, if it turns out that I'm . . ."—I was searching for the right word— ". . . that I'm unusable. What will happen to me then? What will they do with me?"

We were standing in the elevator. It was morning. It was Thursday. We were on our way down. She was going to her studio on level 2 to finish things off before her exhibition, which was due to open on Saturday. I was heading for lab 2 on level 1 for the obligatory health check for new arrivals. The elevator stopped on level 2 and the doors slid open, but instead of stepping out Majken put her arms around me and stroked my back.

She was warm. She was calming. She didn't speak, she simply stood there holding me and stroking my back, while the elevator doors closed and it set off downward. We started to laugh, and she had to come down to level 1. I got out, turned to her and raised a hand to say good-bye. She waved back, the door closed, and the elevator took her back up again with a humming noise.

I was in a corridor not unlike a hospital's, with white doors and pale yellow walls, decorated with the kind of reproduction paintings you often find in hospital corridors. I passed a Van Gogh, a Carl Larsson, a Miró and a Keith Haring before I reached the door with LAB 2 on it.

I was early, but Fredrik, Boel and Johanna were already sitting in the waiting room. They were sitting in a row along one of the walls. They were silent, simply nodding to me as I came in. I sat down next to Fredrik.

On the wall opposite us hung two large appliqué pictures. One of them represented an autumn landscape, with dark brown, golden brown and pale yellow fields, a sky in tones of white and yellowish gray, and flocks of black and white birds, both on the ground and in the air. The flocks of birds formed a pattern, an image; after a while I could see that it was a face. Siv, my older sister, had often worked in the same way. I got up and went over to see if the picture was signed, but it wasn't. I carefully lifted one of the bottom corners and peeped at the back, but there was no name there either. When I went back to my chair and sat down, Johanna, Boel and Fredrik were all gazing curiously at me.

"I just thought it reminded me of . . . of an artist I used to know," I explained.

Johanna made a small movement with her head to show that she understood. Boel nodded. Fredrik said:

"There are a lot of things here you thought you'd forgotten."

"Yes," I said. "But this wasn't someone I'd forgotten."

"A good friend?"

"A relative." I tried to smile, then turned away.

Fredrik didn't ask any more questions, but placed his hand briefly over mine for a moment.

We could hear lively voices from the hallway. The door opened and Elsa came in, along with Roy and Sofia. Her cheeks were red and her hair looked damp. She sat down next to me, smelling faintly of chlorine.

"Have you been swimming?"

"Diving."

"Nice?"

"Fantastic!"

Then I looked around and counted. There were seven of us.

"Who's missing?" I asked, but at that moment the door flew open and Annie burst in, out of breath, her hair standing on end, and with toothpaste at one corner of her mouth.

She looked around for a free chair, but didn't have time to sit down before a door opened, leading into a room with a breakfast buffet laid out. A nurse with crow-black dreadlocks appeared.

"Good morning," she said. "I'm Nurse Lis. Please come in!"

While eating our breakfast we each had to fill out a questionnaire about our health, ticking boxes in response to questions about whether there had been instances of diabetes, rheumatism, breast cancer or other chronic and/or hereditary diseases in the family, whether we ourselves were suffering from any chronic condition or had had any serious illness or injury, undergone any kind of surgery, had an abortion or a miscarriage, had or had had any kind of sexually transmitted disease, were on medication for any kind of somatic or psychiatric problem, were still menstruating and if so, whether our periods were regular or irregular, whether we were suffering from hot flashes, sleep disturbance or mood swings, whether we felt tired, stressed, anxious, depressed or completely healthy.

Once the questionnaires had been collected and breakfast was over, the examination itself began. We were weighed and measured. They took our pulse, blood pressure, blood samples, DNA, and gave us an ECG, a chest X-ray and a mammogram. They checked our sight, hearing and reflexes. We had a full gynecological examination, with a pap smear and tests for HIV, chlamydia, syphilis and gonorrhea. This went on all morning, on a rolling program where we moved one by one from room to room and station to station. It was like a kind of circuit training, where the pommel horse, vaulting box, ropes, weights, beam and mats had been replaced by various nurses and doctors with different items of equipment—syringes, sample bottles, blood pressure cuffs and stethoscopes, X-ray scanners, gynecological stirrups and so on.

I started with a mammogram, where Nurse Karl took care of me, gently pressing first one breast, then the other, in the big X-ray machine. Then I moved on to the gynecological room and Dr. Amanda Jonstorp. When I was finished there I went next door, where Nurse Lis and Nurse Hassan weighed and measured me, took my pulse and checked my blood pressure, then on to Nurse Yasmin who measured my reaction rate and hemoglobin and took some other samples, found out my blood group and took saliva from my mouth with a swab to get a DNA sample. And then on to the chest X-ray, ECG, eye and hearing tests and so on, until all eight of us had gone all the way around.

For lunch we were given a salad with boiled fillet of salmon. No bread, no potatoes or pasta—so that we wouldn't get tired and dopey, but would get some nutrition, because after just an hour's rest it was time for our fitness and strength tests.

On exercise bikes arranged in a semicircle, and with various cables and wires and sensors attached to carefully selected places on our bodies, we pedaled along, encouraged by music with a strong beat and an instructor yelling heartily in a shrill voice:

"Okaaay, let's do this! One and two and three and fooouur! Come on now, everybody, one and two and three and fooouur!"

Meanwhile the machines and monitors to which we were connected via the cables, wires and sensors were measuring our pulse, lung capacity, calorie consumption and fat burning in relation to the number of pedal rotations per minute. The bikes were on the interval setting, alternating between easy and difficult. About halfway through this fitness test, which lasted half an hour, it became harder and harder, and then harder still, until it felt like cycling up a steep hill in a stiff breeze. Our legs wanted to pedal slowly, in slow motion—or preferably to get off. But the instructor kept driving us on, more and more:

"Come on, come on! Get those pedals moving, one and two, one and two, let's get some speed up!"

She seemed almost deranged, and I decided that it probably wasn't a good idea to give up, so I carried on as best I could, releasing the lactic acid in my thigh muscles, panting and groaning and grimacing with pain as the sweat poured off me. After a while it felt as if my heart were getting heavier, being pulled down and down, and the air grew thinner and thinner. It was like being at a height of three thousand feet.

However, it did gradually get easier, first as if we were cycling on level ground, then on a slight downward slope, and after a short cool-down the music came to an end. Nurse Yasmin and Nurse Karl came in and removed our sensors, and we were finally allowed to get off the bikes to stretch and have a drink and eat some fruit, which was displayed in a big basket.

After our break it was time for each of us to go on a strength-building machine, Advance Home Gym model, to measure the strength in our legs, arms, shoulders, back and stomach. This was much more pleasant than all that frantic cycling. The instructor didn't shout at us, but just walked around explaining calmly and clearly how to set the machines for the different muscle groups, and we worked at our own pace.

All these measurements and the results from our samples and tests, from both the morning and the afternoon, were then fed into databases and toward the end of the day when the strength assessment was over, we each got our own printout with our individual measurements and values listed and compared with the average scores for dispensable individuals of the same age and sex. There was also a comparative table showing the average values of individuals who were needed. It was interesting—and surprising—to see that these were significantly worse than those of the dispensable in terms of fitness, physical strength and BMI, while at the same time, paradoxically, they had considerably better blood counts and lower blood pressure than the dispensable.

I was judged somatically healthy, even though my iron levels were a fraction low, but not below normal; I was just above average for the dispensable when it came to strength, and well above when it came to fitness.

But during a short conversation with Nurse Lis—we all had a brief chat with one of the nurses at the end of the day—I was assigned to a psychologist. And as if that weren't bad enough, I was already booked for a session with him the following day after lunch. This was because on the questionnaire I had ticked to say that I felt quite anxious and depressed. We had to choose one of these alternatives: I feel: 1) not at all anxious, 2) anxious sometimes, 3) slightly anxious, 4) quite anxious, 5) extremely anxious, 6) unbearably anxious, and the same for the extent to which we felt depressed, stressed and tired.

"If you've ticked number four, five or six for at least two of the statements, an interview with a psychologist is automatically arranged," explained Nurse Lis.

"But," I said, "isn't everybody here more or less anxious and depressed? I mean, wouldn't you say that was normal?"

Nurse Lis tilted her head to one side, her dreadlocks dangling. She smiled with her mouth open. She had dimples and small white teeth. She looked like a child when she smiled.

"You're right, Dorrit," she said. "Most people here get depressed now and again. And that's why we've got a dozen or so psychologists attached to the unit. We want you all to feel as good as possible. In body and soul. They go together, as you know. Isn't that right?"

"Yes," I said.

I got ready to get up and leave. The sweat had dried on my clothes, and I felt smelly and cold and wanted to have a hot shower and put on something clean. But Nurse Lis had something more to say, so I stayed put.

"We have a suggestion for you," she said. "A group of researchers are working on an experiment here; they need more people with physical stamina, and we think you'd be suitable."

"Right," I said. "And that would involve . . . ?"

"In purely practical terms," replied Nurse Lis, "it would involve devoting yourself to physical exercise every afternoon for a comparatively long period of time—we're talking about roughly two months. Pretty intensive exercise, from what I understand, because the point is that you become virtually exhausted, and then the level of various minerals and hormones in the body is measured. In other words, it's not that different from what you've been doing here today. The researchers want to investigate which nutrients and hormones are lacking and which the body produces itself or releases during intensive exercise. And how this lack or production works out over a period of time, and in relation to the subject's weight, sex and basic fitness. What do we gain and what do we lose from regular intensive physical activity, to put it simply."

I was surprised. This offer sounded too good to be true.

"And where's the catch?" I said.

Lis laughed, delighted, as if I'd asked the very question she wanted to answer most of all.

"There is no catch," she said. "It's difficult to get hold of volunteers for these studies out in the community, even for something as safe and comparatively pleasant as this. People are just too busy. It's partly because it does take up quite a bit of time: four hours a day, five days a week for a couple of months. And partly because you're going to get tired, and presumably will need to sleep and eat more than usual. And what person who is needed has time for that? Young people might volunteer if there was some kind of compensation, and top sportsmen of course, but they're not the groups the researchers are interested in for this study; they want middle-aged people who are comparatively fit."

She paused briefly. Then she asked:

"Well then, Dorrit. What do you think?"

I realized of course that this project would keep me off the operating table for a couple of months. It also sounded like a dream—exercising, eating and sleeping a lot. So my answer didn't need too much consideration. But I didn't want to sound too grateful or enthusiastic, so I drew it out a little bit.

"Well . . . ," I said. "I suppose I could give it a go."

"Fantastic!" said Lis. "In that case, you start tomorrow afternoon at two o'clock. That will be immediately after you've seen Arnold."

"Arnold?"

"Your psychologist. Arnold Backhaus. The research group works in lab 8. If you come here after you've seen Arnold, I'll take you over there. I'm actually"—and she said this in the tone of voice you use when you're passing on something that you expect will be an enormous and wonderful surprise to the listener—"starting as an assistant on this particular experiment tomorrow!"

She smiled her dimpled smile. Her eyes sparkled. I couldn't make any sense of her at all.

When I passed the waiting room on my way out, I stopped and looked at the appliqué landscape with the flocks of birds forming a face. The face seemed familiar to me, but I couldn't work out who it resembled. On the other hand, I was almost completely certain that the picture had been created by Siv.

3

I took a shower. It was the first time I'd done that alone, and in my own bathroom. Up to now I'd showered at the pool or in the sports complex, surrounded by other naked women the whole time. Now, with no one to talk to, I became very aware of the surveillance cameras, and in my mind's eye I could see someone sitting in a control tower somewhere in front of a bank of monitors, closely observing the particular monitor that showed me showering in my bathroom. It was as if I were showering for someone else, doing some kind of number, putting on a live show. It wasn't exactly unpleasant, but it gave me a feeling of unreality, as if I were playing the role of a person showering rather than actually showering.

By this stage I had already managed to get used to going to the toilet without bothering about the surveillance; I simply took it for granted that whenever a resident did something as intimate as carrying out their bodily functions, any observer would look away discreetly and turn their attention to another monitor.

After drying myself and putting on clean clothes, I realized I was hungry and thirsty. My first impulse was to go to the restaurant and eat a meal that someone else had cooked, but halfway out the door I stopped myself.

If I've managed to take a shower alone, I thought, I might as well try to eat on my own as well. So I closed the door, walked resolutely through the living room to the kitchenette, took a packet of crackers out of the cabinet and butter, cheese and orange juice out of the refrigerator. Poured myself a big glass. Drank it standing by the sink. Then I spread butter on a cracker, sliced some Port Salut and placed it on top. Ate—still standing, but leaning against the counter facing the room. Chewed. The hard cracker crunching between my teeth. When I'd finished I made another one the same. Then I remembered that I had some tomatoes, so I got one out, cut it into four thick slices, and placed two of them on top of the cheese. Ate. Poured another glass of juice. Just as I raised the glass to my lips, I happened to catch sight of one of the small camera lenses up in the corner of the ceiling. It was pointing straight at me.

I took the glass away from my mouth, raised it in the air, said "Cheers!" and drank. Then I made another cracker sandwich with cheese and the remaining two slices of tomato, turned my back to the camera, and ate. I was full after that, and I didn't know what to do next, so I put the butter, cheese and juice back in the refrigerator and went out anyway.

I took the elevator up to the Atrium Walkway, went through

one of the airlocks into the winter garden. Ambled—I made a real effort to walk slowly, strolling rather than behaving like someone consciously chasing the body's endorphins—along the gravel paths through arbors and shrubbery and past little fountains and marble benches where people were sitting chatting or reading; they would look up and nod or say hi as I wandered past and on into other darker, bushy areas. I stopped by a hibiscus with enormous flowers, pointing their stamens at me in a challenging way. A bumblebee, buzzing heavily, found its way right inside one of the flowers, where it fell silent for a moment before tumbling out, buzzing once again, and flew away. I moved on, nodding, smiling or saying hi to the people I met. I knew some of them already. I recognized most of them. There were a few I hadn't seen before. One or two I was seeing for the last time. I passed the olive grove, then spent a long time walking slowly among the extravagant flowerbeds. The whole time I was inhaling different scents: cypress, rose, jasmine, lavender, eucalyptus. I walked through the citrus grove and finally reached the big lawn.

Beneath a cedar tree a small group of people were sitting on a blanket having a picnic. A little way off a man on his own was lying on his stomach, also on a blanket, reading a book. I lay down on my back on the slightly damp grass which smelled of earth. I lay there with one leg draped over the other, gazing up at the sky through the leaded glass dome. It was striped, the dome, with running water. It was raining up there, out there, raining on the glass. Through the stripes I could see gray, sodden banks of cloud scudding across the sky. It wasn't only raining, it was blowing too. Hard. It looked as if it was almost storm force. I would have guessed it was blowing at maybe thirty-five miles per hour. But in here, down here where I was, everything was still. There was no wind to speak of here, and no rain of course, just a faintly humming air-conditioning system, but you could hardly hear it at this time of day when the air was filled with different sounds: people moving about, people chatting, bees, birds. Watering took place at night, automatically and in accordance with a carefully planned schedule.

It was pleasantly warm, very easy to relax. I was lying there half asleep when I felt a movement in the grass just behind my head: light, running steps, and in some strange, dreamlike way I was in my garden back at home, while at the same time I was here in the unit's winter garden; I was lying on the grass resting and it was summer, and the steps behind my head moved away, then came back, came closer, and closer still, and I heard the faint panting, felt the nose nudge my hair, the warm breath against my scalp, and I smiled and turned, but there was no one there. No dog. No person. No bird. Not even a mouse or a beetle. Nothing. I felt a sharp stabbing pain in my chest. But I steeled myself and managed to quell the impulse to sit up. I didn't even press my hand against my chest, but forced myself to lie still and focus my attention on the weather and the wind up there on the other side.

It was still raining. The racing clouds were darker now, shading from gray into blue-black. I realized it was twilight. The air quickly grew cooler and damper—an artificial dew came down—and when I eventually sat up it had grown dark around me. The picnic group was packing their things away. They were shadowy figures, silhouettes, until the lampposts around the lawn flickered into life and spread a yellowish muted glow over them. Then I saw that Alice was among the group. I hadn't seen her since the party almost a week ago.

Just as I got up and shouted to her and she turned and peered in my direction, I suddenly thought, "What if she doesn't recognize me, what if she doesn't remember me!"

This had happened before, it had happened quite often, out in the community; I would say hi to people who didn't recognize me, despite the fact that they'd been sitting opposite me at a party or some other event just a few days ago. But as soon as

Alice caught sight of me her face brightened, and she waved and shouted "Hi Dorrit!" and came over.

"If I'd known you were here earlier," she said, "we could have invited you to share Ellen's delicious raspberry pie. But it's all gone, unfortunately."

"I've only just seen you," I said. "Besides, I needed to be on my own for a while. It was that big health check today."

"Oh right, how did it go?" said Alice.

I told her about the exercise experiment.

"Wow! Congratulations!" Alice raised her hand and we gave each other a high five. "Does it feel good?"

"It feels absolutely fine," I replied.

"Alice!" shouted one of her companions, who had gathered up the blankets and baskets and was ready to leave. "You won't forget your injections?"

"No, I'm coming now!" Alice called back, then she turned to me: "I'm involved in some test with male hormones. Don't ask me what it's all about, because it's so complicated that I've forgotten, but I presume I'll soon end up with a beard and a hairy chest."

Just as she said that I realized her voice was slightly deeper than it had been on Saturday at the party.

"See you around!" she said, starting to move away, but then she stopped herself. "But I'll see you at the opening of the exhibition the day after tomorrow, won't I?" she said. "Majken's exhibition. You are coming?"

"Of course," I said. "Good luck with the jabs."

She gave me the thumbs-up sign in reply, turned and walked away.

I also set off across the lawn, but in the opposite direction. The man with the book had fallen asleep. He was still lying on his stomach. I stopped, hesitated. Should I wake him up, or leave him alone? He'd get cold, lying there. But maybe he wanted to be left in peace? I set off again. But he was lying so very still. What if he was ill? It was probably best to check after all.

When I got right up to the man I could see it was Johannes. He was lying with his cheek resting on the right-hand page of the book. I knelt down beside him, and a glance at the left page told me it was a play he was reading; I caught sight of a line roughly halfway down the page: "People who stand at a stove all day get tired when night comes. And sleep is something to be respected . . ."

I could have taken that as a message, an indication that I shouldn't disturb him. But Johannes was lying so strangely still and—it seemed to me—not breathing, and for a moment I was afraid that . . . well, I feared the worst, as they say, and I spontaneously put my hand on his shoulder and shook him gently.

"Johannes?"

"Mm . . . what is it, Wilma?" he mumbled from somewhere inside a dream.

"It's not Wilma," I said. "It's Dorrit. Are you okay?"

"Dorrit . . . ?" He stirred, raised his head, opened his eyes, first one, then the other. "Oh, Dorrit, my dancing queen. Hi there."

He winked with one eye, either flirting or still half asleep—I couldn't decide which, but went for the latter. Then he rolled over onto his back and sat up. He was supple, I noticed: how supple his body was, not stiff at all after lying there sleeping on the damp grass. But his thin white hair was standing on end and his face looked worn—slightly more so than the previous evening, when Elsa and I had met him while we were having dinner in the restaurant.

"How's it going?" I asked.

"Oh, I'm just really tired. Hey, it's gotten dark. Time passes, Dorrit."

"Yes," I said. "It does."

He got to his feet, closed his book, shook and folded his blanket, then we walked together through the garden toward one of the exits. He told me about the psychological experiment he was participating in.

"It's just a series of tiring exercises in cooperation, loyalty and trust. I don't know what they think they're going to get out of conducting this kind of experiment here. I mean, none of us here understand the business of trust. Do you?"

I laughed. "No, to be honest I don't suppose I do. I've never understood why it's regarded as such a good thing, being able to rely on other people. To me it just sounds naive."

"Exactly," said Johannes. "And loyalty? What do you think about that? Isn't it just a kind of blindness, in actual fact?"

"Or another name for dependence," I said. "And being at a disadvantage. An expression for obsequious respect. Perhaps even fear."

Johannes sighed. "You should see us trying to solve a problem together. Or attempting to reach a common standpoint on some issue. You can't imagine how much babbling it takes! It makes my ears hurt. That's why I get so tired. Do you know what I mean?"

I knew.

"But I shouldn't complain," said Johannes. "At least there's no physical danger, no chemicals and no scalpels involved. But how are things with you, Dorrit? What's happening with you?"

And as we left the Atrium Walkway via one of the warm air locks, I told him about the exercise experiment and was congratulated once again, only this time with a hug instead of a high five, a hard, warm hug that smelled of a man, and I became . . . what did I become? Not sexually aroused, but not far from it, something along those lines at any rate. My head was buzzing, it was like being dizzy, and a quiver ran through my body—a hormone specialist would presumably say I was reacting to Johannes's pheromones—and I suddenly felt embarrassed. When he let go of me I didn't quite know where to look.

To cover my embarrassment I asked him if he was going to Majken's exhibition on Saturday.

"Are you going?" he asked me.

I told him I was.

"In that case I'll come," he replied, winking at me, and this time it couldn't be because he was half asleep, so I said as firmly as I could:

"Are you flirting with me, Johannes?"

He smiled. Tilted his head to one side and said:

"What do you think?"

Out in the community I could have reported a man behaving like this for sexism or mild harassment—in fact I would virtually have been forced to do so. For the first time I was glad—yes, glad—that I wasn't out in the community, because I have always felt secretly flattered when men flirt with me; it makes me feel happy and sort of soft all over my body—soft in the same way as when I put on my black dress, nylon stockings and high-heeled shoes.

But despite my pleasure, despite the fact that I was flattered, I attempted to maintain an indignant facade, and looked sternly at Johannes.

But he just laughed at me and I blushed and looked away and felt completely foolish. To my shame, however, I liked it—which made me feel even more foolish; I felt like one of those silly women in old films, capable of nothing but giggling and fainting and busying themselves in the house and being seduced. And suddenly I thought of the cameras and microphones which, even if no one happened to be watching us right now, registered everything. I was worried that my body language would have consequences for me.

As if Johannes had read my mind, he said:

"Nobody minds, Dorrit. Haven't you realized that yet? Not here." And in a teasing, almost mocking tone of voice he added:

"You can be yourself here, totally yourself."

I considered whether to pretend that I didn't understand what he meant, to say that he had misinterpreted me and was presuming things about me that were untrue. But instead I just mumbled: "Okay . . ."

And so we separated. He went toward elevator F. I watched him go. He turned, winked. I couldn't help smiling in response.

I was just on my way to elevator H to head home when I remembered that I had no idea how Elsa's conversation with the nurse had gone, so I went to look for her instead.

She wasn't in her room in section A1, so I knocked on other doors until I found someone who had seen her. She had gone off with a small bag in one hand and a bathing towel around her shoulders.

I found her in the sauna by the swimming pool along with Lena, a cheerful woman with white, short, unruly hair and eyes as bright as a squirrel's, and Vanja, whose appearance was the exact opposite of Lena's: a serious expression and iron gray hair caught up in a long braid.

"Hi Dorrit!" said Elsa when she spotted me in the doorway. "Come on in and sit down!"

I grabbed a towel, got undressed, took a shower, stepped into the dry heat and sat down on one of the top wooden benches.

We chatted for a while about this and that. Eventually Vanja left, then Lena, and Elsa and I were left on our own. I was sweating like mad, and kept wiping my forehead so that the sweat wouldn't run into my eyes; I enjoyed the feeling of little rivulets of sweat trickling down my spine and between my breasts.

"How did things go for you today, Elsa?" I asked. "The chat with the nurse, I mean."

"Oh, I think I got lucky," she said. "I'm joining an experiment that's already under way, where they want more so-called ordinary people, people who've been in employment and are used to colleagues and compromises and fixed working hours, that sort of thing. It's to do with testing people's ability to work together, and with mutual trust and loyalty. Working in a group to allocate and delegate tasks in order to solve a problem together. It sounds really interesting, actually."

"That must be the one Johannes is involved in," I said.

"Oh yes? How does he find it?"

"Too much time spent talking rubbish, according to him. But completely safe, of course. It's just that he gets very tired."

I told her about finding him lying on his stomach on the grass, fast asleep, and Elsa laughed.

"I've got nothing against getting tired," she said.

"Me neither," I said.

4

"Who's Wilma?" I asked.

Johannes turned quickly to face me; his expression was surprised, but there was something else, something strained, like anger or suspicion, and I immediately regretted asking.

We were standing in front of one of Majken's paintings, each of us with a sparkling fruit drink in our hand. The picture showed a skinny old woman in a hospital bed. She was lying on her side in the fetal position, her arms and legs locked in contractures— the picture was actually called *Contractures*. The woman was wearing green incontinence pants; apart from that she was naked. Above her, in the air, a shoal of white, long-tailed sperm was circulating.

"What do you know about Wilma?" asked Johannes.

"Nothing. When I woke you up on the lawn the other day, you said: 'What is it, Wilma?'"

"Oh!" His expression softened, his eyes became calm again, less watchful.

"Wilma is my niece," he said.

"Right," I said. I wanted to ask questions—How old is she? Did you see her often? Did you get on well? Did you look after her sometimes? The questions stuck in my throat. I wanted to know what it was like to be close to a child, to be part of its social network, to look after a little relative, to be woken up by a niece or nephew who wanted to play with you or wanted help with something.

I had hardly ever seen my own nieces and nephews, let alone looked after them. After our parents died—with less than a year between them, first my father, then my mother—the gaps between telephone calls, letters, e-mails and visits grew longer and longer. It became clear that our parents had been the link that held us together, and when they were gone there was no longer anything for us to gather around or stick together for. Ole, Ida and Jens had been living in Brussels, London and Helsinki respectively with their families for a long time, and were very busy with their careers, which had vague titles like management consultant and marketing operator. I had never been to visit any of them, and couldn't even imagine one of their children waking me up by gently shaking my shoulder and saying: "Dorrit? Auntie Dorrit?" The concept was just as unreal as the idea of a child shaking me and saying "Mom!"

At any rate, I just couldn't bring myself to ask Johannes any more questions about Wilma.

After a little while we moved on to the next picture. It showed another woman, significantly younger; she was dressed in a long white dress and a tulle veil, and was swimming underwater with a net, chasing another shoal of sperm, but this time they were trying to escape from her. The sperm with their wriggling tails were swimming away from the woman and her net. This one was titled *Fertile*.

The next painting was small, around twelve inches square, and showed a bluish fetus in its fetal sac, against a warm, blood-red background with blue veins. The fetus was shown in profile, but was twisted in an unnatural shape: the narrow, still transparent arms and legs were bent into the fetal position, while the upper body and head were turned to the front, facing the observer. The head was also bent slightly backward, and the slanting, very dark oval eyes were squinting unseeing, it seemed to me, in different directions. The nose was a still-undeveloped bump without nostrils in the middle of the pale blue face, with its thin, downy skin. And the mouth was the most striking part— unnaturally wide with full red lips, locked in a twisted, gaping expression, perhaps a tortured grimace, perhaps a scornful grin, it was hard to decide. It was also difficult to decide whether the fetus was dead or dying, or capable of life but severely deformed. I leaned forward to read the title: *To be or not to be— that is the question.*

I started to laugh—involuntarily. Johannes looked at me and started laughing too, a low, rumbling, and slightly hesitant laugh; perhaps he was laughing out of politeness because I was laughing, or so that he wouldn't seem stupid, or perhaps he was just as torn as I was; perhaps this was his way of laughing involuntarily.

Majken, who had been standing a little way off in the room talking to Alice and Vanja and some other visitors, was now on her way over to us with a half full glass in her hand.

"Do you find it funny?" asked Majken, gesturing toward the picture of the fetus.

"Yes," I said. "Or no. Or both. It's . . . unpleasant. And yet it's funny."

"Hm . . ." said Majken. "That's actually how I felt when I was painting it. The other way around, though. My first feeling was a kind of angry humor. But as I worked the fetus became more and more distorted and frightening. In the end I was actually slightly afraid of it. And I still am, I think."

I was watching her as she talked, her green eyes exuding a sense of calm and harmony. But at the outer corner of one eye a tiny nerve was vibrating, almost imperceptibly; it twitched and quivered beneath the skin. This quivering, together with just the tiniest hint of tension around her mouth, was the only thing that gave away the fact that this harmony was not complete, that there was something inside that was not calm, and I was seized by an almost irresistible urge to put my arms around her, to console and protect. To try to save her. But just as during our nighttime stroll in Monet's garden a week ago, I was afraid I would ruin the atmosphere if I gave in to my emotions and impulses.

The gallery was, as galleries usually are, light and airy—polished wooden floor, white walls, high ceiling—and in this particular gallery there was daylight despite the fact that it was evening. Since Majken was principally a visual artist, the exhibition consisted mainly of paintings, colorful and figurative. But at the far end of the bright hall was a wall painted black. There was a doorway in the wall with a heavy black curtain in front of it. Above the doorway was a sign in big blue neon letters: HERE.

As you approached the doorway and the curtain, you could hear, very faintly, a whispering voice from inside. It was enticing, this voice, there was something meditative and magnetic about it, and I was drawn all the way to the door; I moved the curtain aside slightly and looked into compact darkness. I walked in and let the curtain fall behind me. I stood still in the darkness, waiting for my eyes to grow accustomed to it, and after a little while I could just make out a faint, bluish light farther in.

I started to walk cautiously toward the light and the whispering, and immediately I could hear not one but two whispering voices. Or perhaps three, or even more, it was hard to make out, they were speaking out of the darkness, but from different directions. They were different distances away from me, coming and going, sometimes continuing on from one another, sometimes talking over one another. The voices were eager, but in a good way, not angry or pushy. It was impossible to make out what they were saying, but I had the impression that they were calling to me—well, not just to me, of course, but to me in my capacity as a visitor. The floor beneath my feet felt soft and silent, like a fitted carpet, and I couldn't hear my own footsteps. I couldn't see anything either, apart from the distant, bluish light far ahead; there was only black darkness around me, and I had the feeling that I was moving in a tunnel of some kind. After a while I also got the impression that there were several people around me. I couldn't see anyone, but sometimes I thought I could hear breathing that wasn't my own, or I felt a faint movement of the air as someone passed me, but I wasn't sure.

The voices, the whispering voices, grew in number as I moved farther in. They didn't get any louder, I was the one approaching them. I passed individual voices, leaving them behind me, but only to approach several more. Suddenly I was surrounded by these gentle, enticing, whispering voices. There were both women's and men's voices at first, but after a while I could hear the occasional child's voice, shriller and higher, among the rest.

The blue glow ahead of me grew brighter and expanded; I was getting closer and closer, and it was getting cooler now, not cold but cool, and the smell of damp earth crept toward me. It was as if I were going into a cave, and when I got even farther in I heard, in the distance, something dripping among all the whispering voices, then the echo of slow footsteps. The whole thing was very calming: the sounds, the darkness, the smell of earth and the coolness, and I could feel my heartbeat literally slowing down and finding a more measured rhythm. My arms, shoulders, and the back of my neck felt pleasantly relaxed. My steps also grew slower, lighter, almost as if I were moving in slow motion. I was completely calm; my brain was lying there with its full weight inside my skull—for the first time in my life I could feel the weight of my brain. It lay there, heavy and silent. It wasn't thinking, it wasn't having opinions, it wasn't arguing, it wasn't analyzing. It was only controlling my bodily functions and sensory organs, and I don't think my senses had ever been so sharp before. And in this very clear, highly receptive and yet incredibly relaxed state I stepped into an oval room with high, small glass paintings along the black walls, my footsteps echoing on a marble floor. There were obviously people in here; it was their footsteps I had heard, accompanied by the whispering voices and the sound of dripping.

The people were dark shadows, moving as if they were in a trance. The dripping sound was louder now, closer, the whispering voices as before, some close, some farther away, children's voices and adult voices, women and men, and the words were still impossible to make out. It was dark in here too, but the glass paintings, with abstract motifs in shades of blue and turquoise, were illuminated and in their faint glow I could see, apart from the figures moving slowly around the room, a large rounded stone, a natural rock, about the same height as the withers of a small pony or a large dog, in the center of the room. And from somewhere above a drop of water fell at regular intervals, perhaps every five or six seconds, straight down into a hollow in the top of the stone. The hollow was full of water and the water was overflowing, running down the curve of the stone into a round black vat in which the stone was standing.

I stood there watching the falling droplets and the running water, covering the stone like a clear veil, until I became conscious of the warmth of another body at my side, and looked up. It was Majken herself, and she nodded silently at me. I nodded back. The whites of her eyes were luminous in the bluish glow of the glass paintings; her hair had its nocturnal golden gray sheen and looked very soft and silky, like angora, and without thinking about what I was doing I raised my hand and stroked her hair gently and slowly with the tips of my fingers—it really was very soft—and let them glide down over the nape of her neck and along her spine. When I reached the base of her spine I stopped, and slowly withdrew my hand.

And now I felt someone doing the same thing to me—exactly that: *someone*, because it wasn't Majken, it was someone standing directly behind me, moving their fingertips lightly down from the top of my head over my hair, down the nape of my neck and my spine, stopping at the base of my spine and disappearing. Afterward I turned around, but too slowly, I didn't see who it was, I just heard the echo of measured footsteps moving away and dissolving into the darkness.

5

I was woken by a shot, sat up in bed with a start and gazed around, half awake. It was still almost dark, not quite morning yet. It was Monday. A couple of weeks had passed since the exhibition.

A shot? Was that possible? Perhaps it was a dream. Or someone, one of my closest neighbors, slamming a door. But why should anyone be slamming doors in the middle of the night? Could the noise have come from outside? When it came down to it, I didn't really know exactly where I was. I didn't know what was outside the walls of the unit. Was it a village or a city? Was it just a forest? Or an industrial neighborhood? Nor did I know whether any of the walls of my apartment faced outward, if any were outside walls. The noise I had heard—the shot, the crash, the bang—could have been a bomb, an explosion, a truck

carrying flammable goods crashing into another vehicle, spring-
ing a gas leak and blowing up. Perhaps there was a fire out there
like the fires of hell, with thick black smoke. Poisonous. Was I
in danger? Were *we* in danger? Probably not. In the end I decided it must have been a dream; I lay down and tried to get
back to sleep. But it was impossible; I was wide-awake. So I got
up, made some coffee and took a cup back to bed. Then I sat
there under the duvet as the day slowly dawned, the light that
was so very much like the real thing filtering in through the slats
in the walls, and drank my morning coffee.

It almost felt like home. That's the way my days used to begin.
Well, they actually used to begin with me pulling on a pair of
thermal pants and a padded jacket over my pajamas, ramming a
hat with ear flaps firmly on my head, and going for a sleepy walk
with Jock. But after that I would drink my coffee in bed as the
day dawned. With my notepad close by.

I turned on the light, pulled out the drawer in the bedside
table and lifted up the envelope containing the pictures of Nils,
Jock, my house and my family, and took out my pad and my
favorite pen. Then I put back the envelope, pushing away the
thought of the photographs—I hadn't looked at them since I
arrived, and doubted that I ever would—and closed the drawer.

Then I began to write, but not my novel. I started a short story
about a single woman around age forty-five who gives birth to a
deformed child, not unlike the fetus in Majken's painting, although the child in my story was not a fetus, but a fully developed child. Fully developed and born, but seriously deformed.
Large parts of the brain were missing, as if they had been erased;
it was only the centers for hunger and thirst and for certain other
bodily functions such as swallowing and emptying the bladder
and bowels that worked. It was uncertain whether the child would
survive for weeks, days, hours. And if, against all the odds, it
survived the first highly critical period, it would in all probability be completely helpless, unable to see, hear, smell, taste or

feel, without the ability to recognize or make a connection with other people. An exhausting burden that would need looking after twenty-four hours a day throughout its entire life; the mother would never be able to manage its care without an enormous amount of support from society. The question was: Is this mother to be regarded as a parent in the practical, concrete meaning of the word? Is she to be regarded as needed? The question was: Is a person needed if she gives birth to a child that will never be able to bond with her, and will never be able to make any kind of contribution?

At about half past eleven I had to stop so that I could get dressed and eat a proper lunch to be able to cope with my afternoon session in the physical exercise experiment. In five hours I had filled three and a half pages; not bad. I tore them off the pad and placed them upside down in a plastic folder on the desk next to the computer. My intention was to type them up and continue the story the next morning.

I went to the Terrace. They usually had tasty, substantial salads. I chose one with tuna, eggs, peas, rice, iceberg lettuce and tomatoes, got myself a large glass of freshly squeezed fruit juice, and sat down in my favorite spot where you could see all the way to the lily pond in Monet's garden.

At this time of day there was hardly anyone here; it wasn't until about half past twelve that it started to get noisy and crowded. I had thought I might see Majken, since she usually ate lunch early as well. But she wasn't here, nor did she turn up.

When I had eaten I went down into the winter garden, lay down on the lawn and looked up at the sky through the glass dome, then when it was time for me to take the elevator down to my exercise session I stopped off at level 2 to see if Majken was in her studio. I wanted to tell her that her picture of the deformed fetus had inspired me to start writing again. I thought she ought to know that, I felt it was important. Her studio was between the room where they edited films and a studio that was shared by two animators, Erik and Peder.

Majken's door was ajar. I knocked but got no answer, so I pushed it open, and a heavy aroma of linseed oil, turpentine and charcoal dust struck me.

"Majken?" I called, but still there was no reply. Half finished and completed sketches and paintings were stacked along the walls. On an easel in the center of the room stood a painting that had just been started, while tubes of paint, jars containing clean brushes, other jars with the lids screwed on (presumably containing oil or turpentine), two palettes, and multicolored pieces of rag were crowded together on a small table beside the easel. There was a side room with a little kitchen and a sink where you could clean brushes and palettes. I went in, but that was empty too. It felt a little bit as if I was snooping, as if I was invading Majken's private domain, which I was in fact, so after I had established that she wasn't there, I hurried out.

On the way to the elevators I passed the animators' studio, and knocked on their door.

"Yes?" I heard from inside.

I opened the door and stepped in. On a threadbare sofa crammed in between a drawing board and a computer desk, and surrounded by a mess of sketchpads, pens and pieces of chalk thrown down anywhere on the furniture and the floor, sat Erik along with Vanja. They were drinking coffee. Erik had his arm around Vanja's shoulders. There was no sign of Peder.

"Have you seen Majken?" I asked.

"Not for a while," replied Erik. "Maybe she's gone to give blood. Shall I give her a message if she turns up?"

I said there was no need, I was bound to bump into her in H3 tonight. Then I left them and carried on to the elevators, went down to my exercise session and didn't give Majken another thought until the day's work—four hours on a rowing machine—was over, and I went home to section H3, exhausted and with trembling upper arms, and saw that Majken's door was ajar, just as her studio door had been. The only difference was that through this door I could hear voices, two of them, neither belonging to Majken.

My legs started trembling now as well, and on these trembling legs, which were threatening to give way, I went over to the door and pushed it wide open.

Dick and Henrietta were in there. They were chatting away quite normally as they wandered around among Majken's things, Henrietta with a black garbage bag, Dick with a big metal box on wheels—it reminded me of the kind of gurneylike contraption they use in hospitals to transport patients who've died, although this box was shorter and deeper.

Dick was the first to notice me, as I stood in the doorway.

"Oh dear!" he said, looking at me but speaking to Henrietta. "Looks like we forgot to lock the door."

"Oh dear!" echoed Henrietta; she put down the bag, came over to me and took hold of my arms, tilted her head to one side and was presumably about to say something sympathetic, something comforting. But I didn't want to hear it, so I tore myself free, turned on my heel, rushed into my room, slammed the door—hard—and turned the key. (This was a symbolic gesture more than anything, since all staff members had their own master key that opened all the residents' rooms.)

After that I stood just inside the door of my apartment, not knowing where to go next. For the first time I was seriously bothered by the surveillance cameras. Eating, sleeping, reading, writing, watching TV, talking on the telephone, cleaning your teeth, picking your nose or poking about in your ears, taking a shower, having a pee or a shit, changing your tampon: it was fine to do all that with someone watching. But, I asked myself, why should the bastards see this?

This—this was when my legs finally gave way and I sank helplessly to the floor and just sat there, not moving, with my back against the door, and, without being able to stop myself or even keep the noise down, howled like a mortally wounded animal.

6

When my older sister Siv was about to turn fifty I called her to
ask if she wanted me to come over, but all I got was an auto-
mated message: "There is no subscriber at this number." When
I tried to e-mail instead, the message bounced back; no one with
that address existed. Then I got in touch with my other sister
and my brothers, but they said they hadn't heard from Siv for
several years and knew nothing. In the end, after having written
an ordinary letter to her and gotten it back with her name and
address crossed out and RETURN TO SENDER written across it, I got
in the car and drove to Malmö, to her apartment on Kornetts-
gatan. But there was a different name on the door, and when I
rang the bell, a young man answered. He said:

"No, there's no Siv Weger. My boyfriend and I have lived here for over two years."

He was lying! Or . . . ? I was confused. As far as I could remember, I had seen Siv at home here in this very apartment as recently as a year ago, on her forty-ninth birthday. We would try to meet up at least twice a year, on each other's birthdays, and sometimes over Christmas and New Year's as well. It could happen that a birthday get-together might occasionally be postponed or canceled because we didn't have time to travel to see each other, or because we couldn't afford it. Therefore I now came to the conclusion, if somewhat reluctantly, that my memory was playing tricks on me, and that I was mixing up the last couple of years—as so often happens when we hit middle age. The order in which things had happened, and the length of time between events in my relatively recent past, tended to be a little unclear in my mind these days. Time, the past, had lost its linear structure to some extent, my memory had started to prioritize as it had never done before, breaking up time and rearranging my experiences and reference points, putting them in an arbitrary and changeable order. I therefore decided it must have been over two years since I was last in Siv's apartment.

But of course I didn't just leave it at that; the fact remained that she had gone off somewhere without getting in touch with me, and that wasn't like her. I therefore reported her disappearance to the police, even though of course I suspected she had been taken to a unit. But I wasn't sure; it was true that she had no children, but she could easily have become successful in her profession all of a sudden, or managed to find a steady partner who loved her. Or both. We weren't in the habit of asking about each other's love lives, and Siv wasn't the kind to start talking about that sort of thing. So it could have happened without my hearing about it. She could, for example, have met someone from another part of the country and moved there with him or her, and simply forgotten to tell me. Or something terrible could have happened: she might have moved to another part of the country with her partner, intending to tell me, but hadn't had time because she had been involved in an accident or a violent crime with a fatal outcome. Perhaps she was buried in some forest or bog, or had been dumped in the sea, or perhaps her dismembered body was in someone's freezer. Or maybe she had decided to go mountain climbing and had fallen without anyone seeing and had landed somewhere where people hardly ever went. Anything could have happened. That was why I reported her disappearance.

However, the police investigation led nowhere. At least that's what they said whenever I phoned to ask how it was going. "We are doing everything in our power to find out what happened to your sister. But so far our leads have unfortunately been unsuccessful."

Sometimes when I had to visit Malmö I would bump into one of Siv's old friends, and I always took the opportunity to ask if they'd heard from her or if they knew anything. I might get an answer like this:

"No, it's ages since I had any contact with Siv. But you know what she's like; she's probably just given notice on the flat, sold everything and taken off on a long trip somewhere. You'll see, she'll be sitting in some ashram chanting a mantra, or sailing around Cape Horn on a raft or something like that. I'm sure she'll pop up like a jack-in-the-box any day now."

Or they'd say something along these lines:

"Oh, you know, contact between Sivan and me has always been pretty sporadic. I haven't a clue what she's up to these days."

Later, after a year or so, when I had accepted the fact that Siv was gone and wasn't coming back, I did think that one of her friends must have known what had actually happened to her, but hadn't said anything. I thought she might have told someone in confidence that she was going to be dispensable, and that this person had promised to say nothing if I or anyone else should ask. I really wanted to believe that this was what had happened. I really wanted to believe that Siv had a friend like that, someone so close to her that she could confide in them. I really wanted to believe that she hadn't only had "sporadic contacts."

7

"What's the meaning of life?" asked Arnold, my psychologist.

For the third time in the week after Majken's final donation I was sitting in the armchair in his office. The first time had been an emergency. Henrietta had followed me to my apartment, where I had locked myself in and sunk down with my back against the door. She had stood outside listening to me—as if it weren't enough that someone was sitting in a control tower (or wherever it was that they sat) both watching and listening. This person was evidently in contact with Henrietta via a mobile phone or some other kind of transmitter, because I could hear her talking quietly to someone.

She said "Yes" and "Yes, Dick's here" and "Ready, yes" and "Just say the word" and shortly afterward she had unlocked the door and opened it carefully. The door opened outward and I fell slowly backward, apathetically. Then Dick had come to help and they had more or less carried me to Arnold, whom I hardly knew. At that point I had seen him only twice, and we hadn't touched on anything particularly difficult, but had mostly kept to the surface of my emotional life. But now I was deposited in his armchair in a state where I was completely powerless and defenseless. All my suppressed fear, rage and grief had floated up to the surface and was lying there waiting; all he had to do was help himself, or at least that's how it seemed to me—as if he were lapping up my feelings with his big, rough, psychologist's tongue. And he had succeeded in getting me to talk about death, about when someone dies or disappears, like Majken, like Siv, like my parents and other people I had known who no longer existed.

Afterward I had actually felt better, it didn't feel as if he had taken something away from me at all; on the contrary, it felt as if he was there for me. I wasn't completely sure that this was actually true, for real, but the main thing was that it felt that way.

And so this time, a week to the day after Majken's final donation, he thought we should talk about life.

"The meaning of life?" I said. "That's a difficult question. I don't think I can answer it."

"Try," said Arnold.

"Do you mean my life, what's the meaning of my life? Or do you mean life in general?"

"You're free to interpret the question as you wish."

Normally, if I'd been out in the community, that would have put me on the defensive. Experience told me that whenever a doctor or a psychologist or a boss or a teacher or a policeman or a journalist says you are free to interpret a question as you wish, that usually means you are being tested in some way. If you interpret the question like this and respond like that, then you are seen as belonging to a particular category, and if instead you interpret it like that and respond like this, then you belong to a different category.

But here in the unit, I thought, it didn't really matter how you interpreted questions. There was only one category here after all, and however I might choose to respond, that was the category I belonged to. I didn't need to try to work out how I ought to respond, but could relax and answer however I wanted. I could allow myself to babble and ramble and feel my way, roughly the way I did when I wrote.

"I suppose I used to believe that my life belonged to me," I rambled. "Something that was entirely at my disposal, something no one else had any claim on, or the right to have an opinion on. But I've changed my mind. I don't own my life at all, it's other people who own it."

"Who?" asked Arnold.

I shrugged my shoulders. "Those who have the power, I suppose."

"And who are they?"

"Our rulers, of course."

"And who are our rulers?"

"Well," I said. "We don't really know. The state or industry or capitalism. Or the mass media. Or all four. Or are industry and capitalism the same thing? Anyway: those who safeguard growth and democracy and welfare, they're the ones who own my life. They own everyone's life. And life is capital. A capital that is to be divided fairly among the people in a way that promotes reproduction and growth, welfare and democracy. I am only a steward, taking care of my vital organs."

"But is that your own opinion, Dorrit?"

"Certainly. Or—maybe not entirely. But I'm working on it."

"Why?"

"To get through this, of course. I live for the capital, that's a fact, isn't it? And the best I can do with this fact is to like the situation. To believe it's meaningful. Otherwise I can't believe it's meaningful to die for it."

"Is it important to you to feel it's meaningful to die for what you call 'the capital'?"

"Yes."

"Why?"

"Because otherwise I would feel powerless, which essentially I am, but I can cope with that as long as it doesn't feel that way too. I'm here now, aren't I? I live here and I'm going to die here. I live and die so that the gross national product will increase, and if I didn't regard that as meaningful, then my existence here would be unbearable."

"And you want to have a bearable existence?"

"Doesn't everyone?" I asked.

Arnold didn't reply. His lack of response provoked me, and I said acrimoniously:

"Perhaps that's the meaning of life. Perhaps that's the answer to your question: the meaning of life is that it should be bearable. Are you satisfied with that answer?"

"You're angry," he said—I couldn't work out whether it was a question or a statement.

"Of course I'm bloody angry!" I said. "Wouldn't you be?"

"Yes," he said, "I probably would be."

He didn't say any more about it. And he didn't ask any more questions about the meaning of life, so I didn't say anything either, and we sat there without speaking for quite a long time, almost a whole minute I think, and all the time I was very angry, so angry that tears came to my eyes. But I didn't cry, even if there was something in my throat that had tied itself in a knot and was stuck there throbbing and burning. I was what I used to call "politically angry," and above all I was feeling boundlessly sorry for myself.

In the end Arnold said:

"Do you know who received Majken's pancreas?"

I had to clear my throat before I was able to reply: "No. Or rather yes: a nurse with four children."

Arnold leaned over to one side, picked up a folder from the little table next to his armchair, opened the folder and took out a photograph. He was just about to pass it over to me when he stopped himself:

"Of course it isn't only this person who's got their life back thanks to Majken. Her heart has probably gone to someone, her lungs to someone else, her kidney—I assume she only had one left—to someone else again, and her liver too. And a great deal of other material will have been removed and stored in our organ and tissue banks. A single brain-dead body can save the lives of up to eight people. The removal and transplantation of these other organs and tissues is a bonus, you could say, when a specific organ, in this case the pancreas, from a specific donor with the right blood type and other criteria goes to a specific recipient in a planned and carefully prepared transplant. And this"— he leaned forward again and passed me the photograph—"is the specific recipient of Majken's pancreas."

He leaned back in his chair.

The photo in my hand showed a woman with four children of preschool age, two of whom were twins. The woman looked old and tired, her face unhealthily bloated and worn.

"She's on her own with the children," Arnold explained. "Her partner—the children's father—died in an accident two years ago. She has no brothers or sisters, and her elderly mother has some kind of dementia and needs constant care. The picture is comparatively recent; the oldest child will soon be six, the twins have just turned four, and the little one wasn't even born when the father was killed. The woman has type 1 diabetes, so it isn't something self-inflicted, and—I don't know all the medical details, but the pancreas has two functions. It produces normal insulin, as you perhaps know, and it also produces another fluid that helps to break down food. The production of insulin has never worked normally for this patient, and some time ago the secondary function of the pancreas also stopped working. Therefore the digestive process does not work properly either. She can neither eat nor drink normally, but lives on a nutritional drip. Since you don't have children you perhaps can't imagine what it must be like to look after four children on your own, while worrying about a senile parent and at the same time dragging round an IV stand, giving yourself injections and taking medication, under constant medical supervision."

I could actually imagine all that very clearly, and I would have loved to be in her shoes. I would have gladly swapped places with this sick, worn down, fairly ugly woman, old before her time. I missed my mother; it wouldn't have mattered how confused and helpless she got, just as long as she had been around to grow old, just as long as she'd lived. And I would have happily lived, sick and exhausted and constantly worried with four small children and an IV stand. Because that was at least a life, even if it was sure to be hell. I would have liked a hell, just as long as it was a life.

But then Arnold said:

"And the most important point: without the transplant she wouldn't have had long to live. It would have been a matter of months, a year at best. Now, however, she has a very good chance of seeing her children grow up. She might not live long enough to have grandchildren, but she will probably have time to fulfill her role as a parent. And that is thanks to the pancreas from a person who had no one to live for."

I said nothing. Just looked at the picture. The eldest child, the six-year-old, was wearing glasses and smiling at the camera. It was a big, innocent, open-mouthed smile; there were gaps where milk teeth had fallen out. The twins looked a little more serious; they were sitting on either side of the six-year-old, but were leaning their heads toward each other as if there were an invisible magnet between them. The smallest child was on its mother's knee, waving a chubby hand in the air—perhaps he or she was waving at the camera—but was looking up at the mother's face. Its expression was steady, secure. Full of trust. The woman was smiling wearily at the camera, her head tilted slightly to one side.

I looked at the photograph for a long time. There was something about the eldest child in particular that got me; something about her—I thought it was a girl—her open smile, something in her eyes behind the glasses, a kind of self-confidence, the sense that everything would be okay, the kind of spiritual strength that we only have at that time, when we are five, six, perhaps seven, or which is at its peak then at least; from then on it is destroyed, bit by bit, until it remains only in the form of shards and fragments.

Arnold cleared his throat. "What do you think about when you look at that picture?"

"Is it a girl, the eldest child?"

He looked at me, then picked up the folder, opened it, flicked through the papers, read, looked up:

"Yes," he said. "It is." Then he was silent for a moment; he seemed to hesitate, but added:

"Why do you ask?"

"I would have liked a girl," I replied, and my voice was—involuntarily—so quiet that I wasn't sure if Arnold had heard what I said.

He didn't comment, nor did he ask me to repeat it.

My hour was over. I took a last look at the six-year-old, then handed the photograph back to Arnold, got up and went toward the door. With my hand resting on the handle, I turned back and asked:

"Did Majken get to see that picture?"

"Yes, of course."

"Does she—the recipient, the woman—know anything about Majken?"

"No."

"Why not?"

Arnold spread his hands. "That's the way things are done. It would be unethical."

I nodded. "Of course," I said. Then I said good-bye and thanked him, pressed down the door handle, opened the door and left.

8

As long as Majken's exhibition was still up I visited the gallery every day, standing for a long time in front of the paintings; I often went along the dark corridor and into the sacred, cavelike room with the dripping water hollowing out the stone. It became something of a ritual, it became like visiting a gravestone, honoring Majken's memory.

When the exhibition eventually came to an end and everything was taken down, I went to see the director of the gallery to ask if I could possibly have the small picture of the deformed fetus. That was fine, he said, just some formalities to be dealt with first, some papers to be signed by him and Petra Runhede and me, but a few days later I was able to collect the picture from the office inside the gallery. I took it home and hung it on the wall above my desk, where the fetus grinned scornfully at me, its eyes unseeing, or writhed in agony—or both. "To be or not to be . . ."

Then I took the handwritten pages out of the plastic folder where they had been lying upside down since the day Majken made her final donation. I switched on the computer, and there in my new and definitely very expensive desk chair, with support for my lower back, my shoulders and my arms, I finished the short story about the woman who gave birth to a deformed child. It ended with the death of the child three days after it was born, whereupon life went back to normal; no questions remained, no "if," apart from the fact that the woman had about five years left to become needed.

In the middle of March, six new dispensable individuals arrived in the unit. There was another welcome party with dinner, entertainment and dancing. I made some new friends, both among those who had just arrived and among the older residents, and my relationship with those who were already my friends deepened. I hadn't had so many friends, such a wide social circle, since I was in my twenties.

I spent most of my time with Elsa; we talked about childhood memories, and gossiped endlessly about what became of this or that old school friend, some former teacher, or others who lived in the little community where we grew up.

I also grew very close to Alice. She was easygoing and funny, without being superficial. She was beginning to look and sound more and more like a man, a short man with small hands, a broad bottom and ample breasts, but the planes of her face were becoming more angular, she had graying stubble (when she couldn't be bothered to shave), and a dark, booming laugh. She seemed to be taking it all very cheerfully. "Better to be both sexes at once than dead!" she would say if anyone felt sorry for her or sympathetically asked how she was feeling. And I think she meant it. I think she really did prefer to be living as both a man and a woman than not to be living at all.

I wrote intensively for five hours every morning. Then I had lunch in the Terrace restaurant, after which I relaxed for an hour or two, either by going swimming or for a sauna with Elsa or Alice or both or someone else, or I took a walk in the winter garden or lay on the lawn gazing at the sky and the clouds, or sat down on a bench to read or just enjoy the greenery, the scents, the birdsong and the warmth. Once a week I went to see Arnold or the masseur. From time to time I treated myself to a pedicure, massage and manicure, and I regularly visited the hair salon to have my hair trimmed and colored. I got myself some new clothes: expensive silk shirts, linen pants, jackets in different colors and styles. Expensive Italian shoes. Jewelry.

Every afternoon at two o'clock I took part in the scientific fitness and strength training tests. It was completely safe, apart from the fact that I ended up with periostitis and suffered from a lack of vitamins and minerals (this was one of the things they were measuring), felt dizzy and overexercised, with aching muscles and extreme fatigue, and had to be careful to eat and sleep a lot in order to cope. But I wasn't complaining, quite the opposite, as long as I was participating in this particular test I was safe from operations and donations, I didn't even have to give blood or plasma—thanks to my fatigue. I came to love this exhaustion, as if it were a loyal friend or even a guardian angel. During my first two months in the unit most of the people I knew donated at least part of some organ or tissue: Erik, the animator, donated a section of his liver, Alice the cornea from one eye, plus eggs for the production of stem cells (paradoxically, her ovaries were still functioning), Elsa also donated eggs as well as skin, Lena a kidney, Johannes a little bit of the small intestine—this was something new that had hardly ever been tried before. And Vanja, who was with Erik, went in to donate her heart and lungs, and of course didn't come back. Erik was devastated.

Our everyday life in the reserve bank unit really revolved around scientific humane experiments. That was what we were mainly used for, in reality. They tried to keep us alive as long as possible, in fact, and some individuals who were very fit had lived in the unit for six or seven years before they were taken in for their final donation. Those who are dispensable constitute a reserve, and those who are needed and are seriously ill are first of all given organs produced from their own stem cells, and if that doesn't work, they go on a waiting list for organs from younger people who are pronounced brain-dead after an accident. They don't use the dispensable until it is obvious that no other method and no other material is available for a particular patient with a serious illness, or in those cases where it is extremely urgent. This whole thing—"this whole free-range pig farm" as Elsa angrily called it—is in other words significantly more humane than I could have imagined at first.

9

It was another new month, April this time. It was Saturday morning, and nine new dispensable individuals were expected. One of them was to have Majken's room, I had heard. I was sitting in my pajamas and robe on the sofa in the lounge, drinking my morning coffee and reading a book when she arrived, accompanied by Dick and Henrietta.

She was very tall and fine-limbed, strikingly feminine in her stance and her movements; she had the palest skin, black, shiny, shoulder-length hair, almost unbelievably red lips and big, watchful eyes. Henrietta was carrying her two suitcases, Dick her thick, bulky winter coat. I thought it must either be unusually cold for April out there, or she felt the cold a great deal. Or perhaps the coat meant something special to her. Because here in the unit there is no need for winter clothes, and she must have known that; it's one of the positive things they highlight in the information packet. My own peacoat and the heavy winter boots I had been wearing when I arrived two months ago were still in the top part of my closet, and I hadn't given them a thought until now.

When Dick caught sight of me he introduced us. Her name was Vivi. I got up, tightened the belt of my robe and went over to shake hands. Her hand felt cold and slightly clammy. I looked up at her face and saw her terrified expression. I said:

"If there's anything you're not sure about, or if you just need to talk to someone, or if you simply don't want to be alone, then I'm here on the sofa or in my apartment for the next few hours. It says Dorrit Weger on the door. Don't hesitate, you mustn't think you'll be disturbing me, because you won't."

"Okay," she muttered, then she and Dick and Henrietta carried on through the lounge, past the laundry and the kitchen, and disappeared out of sight into the hallway.

The same evening, during dinner at the welcome party, I sat with Vivi, Erik, and Alice, which wasn't exactly the best combination in the world: Vivi, tense, introverted and terrified, Alice with one cloudy unseeing eye, stubble, a deep voice and her Adam's apple bobbing up and down when she came out with her loud laugh, and as if that weren't enough: Erik, who was so deeply depressed after the loss of Vanja that he could barely speak or eat. He sat there, alternately stammering or completely silent, poking at the food on his plate. Fortunately Alice was in a good mood as usual, exuding warmth and confidence, and gradually Vivi seemed to relax a little.

When dinner and the entertainment were over I took her to the bar, where we tried out different colorful drinks with umbrellas in them, tasting of fruit and sweets. The bartender was

new; he had arrived the previous month, and he was now showing what he could do. I ordered a banana and lime drink that
was served in a cocktail glass. It was called a Green Banana and
was a cold, yellowish green in color; the umbrella had green and
yellow stripes and there was a slice of lime perched on the side
of the glass. The drink was cloyingly sweet and sharply fresh at
the same time; the sharpness balanced the sweetness and vice
versa. It was delicious. Vivi chose Raspberry Rock, which consisted of freshly squeezed orange juice mixed with raspberry juice,
with frozen raspberries in it. The umbrella was red, blue and
orange, and there was a frosting of blue sugar around the rim of
the glass.

"Food coloring?" I guessed, but Vivi tasted the frosting with
the tip of her tongue and shook her head.

"Blueberries," she said.

She didn't say any more after that, she just sipped slowly, in
silence. A raspberry kept bumping against her top lip. I didn't
know what to say, so I just gave her a little smile and smoothed
down an invisible crease in my dress, which I had put on for the
first time since arriving at the unit. It made me feel elegant and
sexy, but a bit unsure of myself at the same time. So we were
standing there, Vivi shy or scared or both, me unsure about my
outfit and about my self-appointed role as supporter, when Elsa
turned up, cheerful and sweaty from dancing, and exclaimed:

"Oh, what fantastic drinks! If there's alcohol in them the
evening will be perfect!"

"Unfortunately not," replied Vivi, looking amused—for the
first time I saw her smile.

I introduced her to Elsa, they shook hands and immediately
started chatting. They seemed to like each other straightaway. I
felt relieved. Elsa ordered a Black Night, and it really was black.
It was served in a tall, narrow glass with a black-and-red-striped
straw, and something red, perhaps a candy, at the bottom. She
bent over the glass, and as she placed the straw between her lips

and took the first careful little drink, Vivi and I stood on either side watching her reaction. She let go of the straw, swallowed, looked thoughtful.

"Not bad," she said. "Strange, but delicious. Recommended."

Vivi put her half-finished orange and raspberry drink to one side and ordered a Black Night. And I probably would have done the same if Johannes hadn't just elbowed his way through the crowd to us. After a friendly but brief nod to Elsa and Vivi, he turned to me, took my hand, and said:

"Dorrit, you look lovely tonight," at which point he bent forward and kissed my hand.

"May I have the pleasure of a dance?" he asked.

I accepted, and without a word we sailed out onto the dance floor.

It was a rock ballad. The singer in the band had a hoarse voice. Johannes led; I followed, the hem of my dress brushing my calves. He was holding me around the waist, I had one hand on his shoulder, the other in his hand. Our joined hands formed a point, the prow of a ship; he was port, I was starboard. When I closed my eyes he was Nils.

10

We left the party together and walked slowly through the winter garden. I liked to take this diversion late in the evening or at night, when everything was still and quiet, the artificial dew glistening on the greenery, the air full of different fragrances. I liked to remember Majken here in this stillness and among these scents.

Johannes had his arm around my shoulders, and when we reached the patio with the fountain and the marble benches, he said:

"Shall we sit for a little while?"

We sat down on the cool, slightly damp marble and peered up past the branches of the palms and through the glass dome to the night sky. It was full of stars.

"There's Ursa Minor and the North Star," said Johannes.

"Where?" I had never been particularly good at constellations. I could just about make out the Dipper.

Johannes pointed, describing Ursa Minor as a smaller version of the Dipper, and then I saw it in the angle between two palm leaves.

"And the North Star is the big one there right at the front, the one that's shining so brightly. It's always in the north," he went on, and showed me the easiest way to find it: it's along the line between the two stars right at the back of the Dipper.

"But how can that be?" I asked. "How can it always be in the same direction? We're spinning around, after all."

"Yes . . ." Johannes sounded uncertain, a little hesitant to start with. ". . . but we're spinning around our own axis. And whatever is in the north is always in the north. Although the important thing in this case is not how it gets to be that way, but how it actually is. If you can just identify the North Star you need never get lost on a starry night."

I didn't laugh. Normally I would have, because the likelihood of any of us running the risk of getting lost at any point during the rest of our lives was, as far as I could determine, negligible. But Johannes's tone was so totally sincere that it felt as if the information he was giving me was extremely useful and worth remembering, and instead of laughing I nodded thoughtfully. Then we sat there in silence among the palm trees in the darkness. It was like a mild, still summer night. I felt young. My thoughts wandered here and there: from this feeling of youthfulness to the North Star to Majken to Siv to my family—and from my family to the novel I was working on, which was about a family not unlike the one I grew up in, and from there to something I'd been wondering about recently. And now I broke the silence to ask Johannes:

"What do you think happens to the things we write here that are politically incorrect or taboo? Do you think they're destroyed?"

"No," he said firmly. "Everything is kept and archived."

"How can you be so sure?"

"Partly because we live in a democracy, and freedom of expression is one of the cornerstones of a democracy; without the freedom of expression it would collapse. Therefore it is unthinkable to destroy literary or artistic works because the content does not agree with the norms and values of society. So even the politically uncomfortable is taken care of and archived, presumably in some underground vault beneath the Royal Library in Stockholm. Partly because man is a collector, a fanatic when it comes to documentation, with a compulsion to preserve everything that can possibly be preserved for posterity. Life and existence have no value in themselves. We mean nothing; not even those who are needed mean anything. The only thing of any real value is what we produce. Or to put it more accurately: the fact that we do produce something—exactly what it is that we produce is actually of lesser importance, as long as it can be sold or archived. Or preferably both."

What he said sounded convincing. But I wasn't completely sure he was right; I wasn't completely sure that works of art weren't destroyed. However, I did think that we probably had to assume they were not destroyed, that we had to live as if we believed everything people created was permitted to exist, somewhere.

We stayed for a little while longer, until the air began to feel slightly damp and chilly. Then we got up and left the garden, emerging into the light of the Atrium Walkway. Johannes walked with me to elevator H.

"Will you have dinner with me tomorrow evening?" he asked.

I accepted. He kissed me softly on the cheek, and we said goodnight.

That night I dreamed of Jock. We were on the beach. It was autumn, and windy. The clouds were sailing across the sky like fluffy ships. Between them the sun stretched out its golden arms to us, glowing, dazzling, warming, suddenly disappearing behind a racing cloud ship, popping out again and just managing to lay its warm hands on my head before disappearing once more. The sea was roaring and hissing. We were running along the beach. I stopped. The wind nipped at my cheeks with ice-cold teeth, tugged at my hair. Jock was capering and dancing around me, barking and looking up at me with those brown eyes. He was happy, playful. I bent down, picked up a stick from the sand, shouted "Fetch!" and hurled it away from me. He barked and raced after it, picked it up and came back, dropped it at my feet, looked up at me, panted, snorted, ears pricked forward, tail wagging like mad. I patted him. "Good boy, Jock," I said. "Good dog." And I picked up the stick and threw it again. And Jock shot after it, the sand whirling up around his paws, his ears flapping in the wind, he picked it up, came back and dropped it at my feet, and I patted him and praised him again. And we did it again, and again, the same thing over and over again, hour after hour, while the sea roared, the clouds sailed by, and the sun, slowly sinking toward the horizon in the southwest, stained the clouds pink and the sky orange. That's all it was, the dream was just Jock and me and the stick and the beach and the sea and the sky and time passing by, and that was all, there was nothing else. And that was happiness.

11

Johannes had cooked fish with saffron in a cream sauce, accompanied by crushed potatoes; I could already smell the aroma when I stepped out of the elevator, and all I had to do was follow it through the door into section F2 and down the hallway to his door, where the nameplate announced that Johannes Alby lived here.

I knocked. He opened the door. He had an apron knotted around his waist and a wooden fork in his hand. He kissed my cheek and said:

"Welcome—you look lovely! Dinner won't be long. Have a seat while I finish up."

I sat down at the table, which was already set for two: blue stoneware plates, glasses with a stem, blue napkins folded into triangles beside the plates, two candles in brass holders, a box of matches.

A stone—grayish pink, about as big as a medium-size cell phone, and containing a white, cone-shaped fossil—lay next to one of the candle holders as a decoration. Johannes disappeared into the kitchen with his wooden fork; I could hear the sound of clattering and banging, and he was whistling and humming. I picked up the matches and lit the candles. Johannes came in with two placemats and a carafe of something that looked like white wine, but turned out to be grape juice. He smiled. "It's ready now," he said, placing the mats and the carafe on the table before disappearing and returning with a big frying pan, a saucepan and two ladles. Before he sat down opposite me, he switched off the overhead light.

And so we sat there, just the two of us, in the glow of the candles. The food was very good. I complimented him. We didn't talk much while we were eating, just looked at each other from time to time; for some reason I was feeling shy, and it's possible that he felt the same. At one point toward the end of the meal, when the fact that he was looking at me made me feel embarrassed, I looked down at the table and at the pink stone with the fossil.

"Where did you find that?" I asked.

"On a beach. On the south coast. Between Mossby and Abbekås, to be more precise."

I put down my knife and fork, looked up at him. "When?"

"When? Er . . . let's see . . . More or less exactly two years before I ended up in here. Just about five years ago. Why?"

"Because that's my beach!" I said. "Well, when I say mine . . . I used to go there with . . . with my dog. At least two or three times a week. What were you doing there? We might have bumped into each other."

He looked at me.

"Yes," he said. "Indeed we might."

Then he told me what had happened when he found the stone, and why he had kept it:

"It was autumn. I was working on a novel—probably my last—and I'd hit a block, and was on the point of chucking the whole thing. But to clear my head and avoid doing something too hasty, I borrowed a car from some friends and took a trip to the south coast; the sea is more open there than it is around Öresund, and I wanted to be by the open sea, I wanted to know that it was a long way to the next shore. So I walked there, along the beach, hour after hour, from Abbekås harbor to Mossbystrand and back again, several times. It was quite late in the autumn, so the twilight came early and it was steel blue, as the autumn twilight can be by the sea if it's cloudy. Anyway, as I was plowing along through the sand and it was beginning to get dark, I was looking at the stones and shells and driftwood and all the garbage the sea had washed up. And that was when I caught sight of this stone. It was lying by the water's edge. The fossil was chalk-white in the dusk."

Johannes fell silent. The stone was still lying in my hand, resting palm upward on the table, and he placed a finger on the stone and caressed it with his fingertip in my cupped hand as he continued talking:

"It was lying there at the water's edge glowing at me, or so it seemed. So I stopped and squatted, and at the very moment when I touched the stone, everything became clear. All the pieces fell into place. It was as if a ravine had opened up in front of me, and in the widening gap I could see the resolution to my novel—with absolute clarity. I put the stone in my pocket and drove home, and finished the novel in a couple of days. Since then I haven't wanted to part from that stone."

After dinner I went to sit in an armchair, Johannes on the sofa. We were drinking tea.

"Tell me about your dog," said Johannes.

I hesitated, feeling the tears weighing heavy and twisting in my throat at the mere thought. I presume he could tell, because he added quietly:

"Only if you want to, of course, Dorrit."

But I did want to, and so I told him; I told him about Jock and my love for him. Johannes didn't seem to find it at all amusing that I was talking about love in connection with a dog, not even when I talked about the fact that the dog loved me; he listened with understanding and respect. And I went on talking, about my house, my garden, and a little bit about Nils too, once I'd got going.

Then Johannes told me about a woman he had loved when he was my age. They had lived together, and he had been very happy with her. But as soon as she got pregnant by him, she left him.

"One evening she told me we were expecting a baby, and I was so happy. I was so proud that I was going to be a father. But a couple of days later, when I got home from jogging, her shoes and coats were gone from the hallway, and her closet was empty, and her shelf in the bathroom, and her books, her photographs, her laptop, everything that belonged to her was gone. After that I became cold. I was incapable of loving. I couldn't even have sex. Couldn't get close to anyone. And time just passed. Suddenly I was sixty and ended up in here, on the glass mountain. Or rather *in* the glass mountain."

"So how are things now?" I asked.

"What do you mean?" he asked, although I could see from his eyes and from the softening of his mouth that he understood what I meant.

"Would you be able to now?" I said.

"Be able to do what?" he said, and now there was something teasing in his expression.

It made me embarrassed.

"Oh, you know . . ." I mumbled.

My cheeks felt hot, and I realized I was blushing. I looked away.

There was silence for a little while. Then he said:

"Dorrit. Come and sit here."

His voice was soft, not at all peremptory. But it was also firm and determined, like the voice of someone who knows exactly what he wants, and it made something tremble inside me, shooting and throbbing. This was just the way things had been with Nils; he also used to sound as if he knew what he wanted, and he could also make me tremble just by expressing a simple wish in a gentle but firm voice.

I have always had a tendency—far too much of a tendency— to be turned on by people who know what they want and are able to express themselves without yelling and shouting and blustering. I have always been turned on by people who sound as if they are in control of a situation. So I sat there in Johannes's armchair, trembling and throbbing like a heart that has just been cut out of one body and is about to be inserted and stitched into another, and I could feel myself pulsating down below, the sensation spreading along the inside of my thighs, and my cheeks were burning and my eyes felt hot and shiny, as if I had a temperature. But I said nothing and did nothing, I just sat there in the armchair being all those physical reactions and feelings.

"I want you to come and sit here on the sofa next to me," said Johannes in that same gentle, firm voice, and I didn't look at him, but I could feel him looking at me, my whole face could feel his eyes searching for mine.

"And I want you to do it now," he added.

"Why?" I croaked.

"You know the answer to that," he said. "Come over here."

And I tried. I tried to get my legs and arms to work and heave myself out of the armchair to walk the two or possibly three steps over to the sofa, but I had become a helpless simpleton with no will of her own—no, that's not true, I did have a will of my own, because I wanted to move, I wanted to move so much it hurt—and couldn't control my limbs, let alone make them move. I gave up.

"I think you'll have to come and get me," I whispered.

And he did. Without a word he got up from the sofa, came over to the armchair, lifted me in his arms, and carried me over to the sofa. And I did nothing. I just lay there limp in his embrace, allowed myself to be laid down on the cushions. I did nothing when he kissed me, I just kissed him back, hungrily eating my way in between his lips, sucking on his tongue as if it were a teat and I were a starving lamb. I did nothing when he unbuttoned my shirt and my pants and undressed me, one item of clothing at a time; nothing when he looked at me as I lay there undressed in front of him, just parted my legs a fraction before his gaze. I did nothing when he took hold of me, when he caressed my skin with his hands—everywhere, searching, as if he were looking for scars and other traces of incursions, attacks, accidents—nothing when he caressed my hands, my arms, my neck, face, breasts, stomach, thighs, bottom, vagina. I did nothing, I didn't move a muscle when he bent down between my thighs and pressed his tongue against me, nor did I do anything when he tensed the muscles in his tongue and began to stimulate my clitoris with it; I did nothing but let myself come in warm waves, flooding and flooding through me. After I had come, the second after, before I had even managed to catch my breath, he plowed into me, from the front, from above, supporting himself on his arms, his thrusts sometimes slow and teasing, sometimes hard and deep. He screwed me—this really was being screwed. He took me, he took me the way a veritable male chauvinist and oppressor of women, a caveman, a Neanderthal, a male animal with a reptilian brain would have taken a woman. And I did nothing, absolutely nothing, just allowed myself to be taken, and it was . . . no, there are no words to describe how it was.

12

I hadn't thought it would be possible to have sex in the reserve bank unit. I didn't think anyone would want to or would be able to, partly because of anxiety and stress, partly because of the surveillance, which made any kind of private life impossible in the true sense of the word. But I didn't feel as if I lacked a private life. We were all monitored everywhere all the time, whatever we were doing, but by this stage I had stopped attaching any importance to it. I never really managed to ignore or forget the cameras, but they just became a part of life, almost something natural. It was presumably similar to the old days, when religion had a clear place within daily life, and people were convinced that God was keeping a constant, watchful eye on them, that he saw and heard everything they did and said and thought and felt, and that there was no point in trying to hide anything.

So we made love, Johannes and I, we made love with no modesty, physically, quite openly. We made love for the rest of that evening after the saffron fish, and more or less all night. And the next evening and night, and the next, and the next—and so on. We simply became a couple. We became a loving couple. And we made love in the old-fashioned way without the least trace of embarrassment. He was the seducer, the one who took the initiative, the active one. He took what he wanted from me, and I accepted, allowed myself to be passive. It was like making love with Nils again, but better, freer. Johannes and I were living our lives locked away, outside the community, and therefore had nothing and no one to be ashamed of.

Nor did we need to part over and over again because Johannes had to go home to his partner; I was his partner. We couldn't move in together—that wasn't allowed in the unit—but we could spend the night with each other as often as we wished, and I wasn't "the other woman." I was simply The Woman. And I enjoyed it, I enjoyed the fact that we could walk along openly holding hands, the fact that everyone knew we were a couple and accepted it. We even had mutual friends that we spent time with: Erik, Elsa, Alice, Lena and many others. Sometimes we would meet up with other couples. We would go out to dinner with couples. It was something completely new and fantastic, to be invited to dinner by a couple along with other couples, and to be part of a couple, not always the fifth wheel on the wagon, but regarded and treated as someone who belonged with someone else.

With Nils (as with a number of other men before him) everything had happened in secret. We never met up with other people together, no one in his family or circle of friends knew of my existence, and none of my friends knew about him. And that wasn't only because he was someone else's partner, but because much of what we were doing was taboo.

Nils was actually breaking the law. He could have gone to prison over and over again for both the oppression of a woman and the improper use of male physical strength. When we got together he would often spend time chopping wood for me, or mowing the lawn or cutting the hedge or pruning trees, while I was in the kitchen preparing lunch or dinner for us. He also sometimes changed the tires on my car, fixed a leak in the roof, put up new guttering and mended cracks in the facade of the house. And I showed my gratitude by dressing sexily and cooking something really delicious and making the table look particularly nice.

It was a very special feeling, standing there in the kitchen with an apron over my dress, which in turn hid my silky lingerie, cooking for myself and my big strong lover—my big strong man— as he stood out in the cold and the wind, swinging the hickory ax and splitting one log after another just as easily as if they had been made of wax, and at a speed I found hugely impressive. Nils could chop as much wood in an hour as I could in two. And whenever he changed over to winter or summer tires on my car, he did the whole job in the time it usually took me just to loosen the wheel nuts. Not having to do these heavy and often dirty jobs myself—not having to get sweaty, filthy, to end up with strains and pains in my arms, shoulders and back—and still to get the work done was of course very satisfying in itself. But it was much more than that. When Nils came in after his hard work I would get out a clean bath towel for him, and while he showered and changed into clean clothes (which he always brought with him from home in a briefcase) I would finish cooking and setting the table. And then, at the very moment when I could hear the splashing of the water and Nils singing in the shower, I would sometimes stop and kind of taste the whole scenario, drink it in, fill my mouth with it and hold it there, and at those times I felt so alive, so involved, almost as if we belonged together, Nils and I. Almost as if we were needed by each other.

There was also a sexual dimension, of course. I was seething with lust as I stood there busying myself in the kitchen with my apron knotted around my waist, like an obedient little house-wife as I heard the logs being split against the chopping block outside, or the constant hum of the lawnmower or hedge clip-pers, the pounding of the hammer or the churning of the ce-ment mixer. There was an infinite bubbling expectation in preparing food with housewifely care, not to mention the satis-faction of seeing Nils eat it later with the hearty appetite that comes from physical exertion. Yes, it was all sexual, it was sex, it was part of our foreplay. And it was—or it could have been—a lifestyle. If we had been a proper couple we would presumably have lived by this division of roles. Not openly, perhaps, but when we were alone. When we were alone we would have allowed our feelings and our bodies, not our thoughts, to decide who did what.

I think it's beautiful when men show their physical strength openly without being ashamed of it or apologizing. And I think it's beautiful when women dare to be physically weak and ac-cept help with heavy jobs. I believe there's a kind of courage in that, and courage is beautiful. If I can choose between mind and body, I choose body. If I can choose between brain and heart, I choose heart. With Johannes I could make that choice without being forced to hide it.

13

The exercise experiment was over. I had a few days off, then it was time for me to make my first organ donation: one of my kidneys was to go to a young medical student. I was very frightened.

The night before I was due to go in, Johannes stayed over with me. We made love, then I wept. He tried to calm and console me.

"I've only got one kidney," he said. "It's fine, I can't tell the difference."

"It's not that," I said. "I'm afraid I won't wake up from the anesthesia. I'm afraid I'll never see you again."

He was quiet for a moment. He looked at me, his expression serious. Then he said:

"That day will come, you know. We both know that, and we have to live with it. But it won't be now. It won't be tomorrow."

Not now. Not tomorrow. That thought calmed me, and I fell asleep straightaway.

When the morning came I walked on relatively steady legs to department 4 in the hospital, which was part of section K. On the lower ground floor were the nursing center, the pharmacy, massage therapists, the podiatry and physical therapy clinics, a hairdresser, restrooms, and the elevators to different departments. Department 4 was on the fourth floor. My room—to my surprise I had a single room—had a window looking out over the Atrium Walkway, and through the glass walls I could look down over Monet's garden.

This was the first window I had seen in the unit, and I stood there entranced, gazing down at the people moving about in the Atrium Walkway, some walking, some jogging. And I looked up and gazed out through the glass wall and across the pond, at the bridges with their rose arbors and at the wisteria, the copper beech, the weeping willow, the bamboo grove and the narrow paths where people were walking. I recognized Lena by her short, tousled white hair. She was moving quickly, loose-limbed, she looked like a little troll in a hurry. She stopped and exchanged a few words with someone I didn't recognize who was sitting on a bench by the pond reading a newspaper.

"Dorrit Weger?" I turned around; a nurse in white pants and a light blue shirt was standing in the doorway.

"I'm Nurse Ann," she said, coming into the room and shaking my hand. "I'm the head of department here on 4."

Nurse Ann started to tell me about what was going to happen and what I had to do over the next few hours: take a shower using Hibiscrub, put on a hospital gown, have a sedative injection, be taken down to the operating room on level K1 on a gurney, be anesthetized.

□   □   □

The operation went well. I came to, felt sick, and threw up via a tube in my nose. It was disgusting, but at least I was alive. The young medical student had received my kidney, and things seemed to be going well there too, I heard. After just a few days I was discharged. Johannes came to pick me up with flowers and a box of chocolates; he took me home and looked after me, cooked for me and served up my meals, made coffee and tea and fed me chocolates. He even read aloud to me: Somerset Maugham's short story "The Ant and the Grasshopper," among other things.

I needed a little while to recuperate, but I was strong and was soon more or less back to normal: working on my novel, going for walks, swimming and going to the sauna—the last often with Elsa and Alice, who had both recently had surgery as well. Elsa had donated part of her liver, Alice had donated a kidney, just like me.

"If I'd known what a relatively simple procedure it was," said Alice one afternoon when all three of us were sitting in the sauna, she and Elsa in opposite corners of the top bench and me on the middle level below Elsa, "I might well have considered donating a kidney voluntarily, just like that, out in the community."

"Would you?" said Elsa, sounding really surprised. "To some needed stuck-up bitch with five splendid kids and a job that supports economic growth? Voluntarily? Are you serious?"

"Yes, but of course it wouldn't have gone to somebody like that! Then again, why not? Everyone has the right to live. Even stuck-up bitches."

"Oh yes?" said Elsa. "That's what you think, is it? How noble!"

"Absolutely. Just call me Saint Alice." She pressed her palms together as if she were praying, while at the same time crossing her eyes, her expression deeply serious and saintly, and from the depths of her lungs she intoned in her baritone voice:

"Aaamen . . . !"

It was impossible not to laugh, and that wasn't such a good thing because it hurt to laugh, and Elsa and I clutched our scars from the operation.

Then we started comparing our scars. There was no one else in the sauna just then, except the surveillance cameras and the invisible microphones, of course. Alice's scar was bigger than mine, but mine was uglier, bumpier, and in shades of blue, green and pink. Elsa's was the biggest and extremely bumpy, almost like a lump, and the area all around it was inflamed and purple, but then it was also the most recent. When we'd finished discussing our scars, Elsa said:

"Dorrit, I have something to tell you. I've been trying to find the right time, but . . . Anyway, this is as good a moment as any. It's about your sister."

"My sister?"

"Yes. Her name was Siv, wasn't it?"

I nodded.

"She was here," said Elsa. "She lived in B4."

I remembered the wall hanging down in lab 2; I'd been right, then—it was Siv who had made it. I wasn't surprised. I felt completely calm.

"How did you find out?" I asked Elsa.

"When I was in for my operation, I met a nurse. Clara Gransjö."

"Gransjö? Is she related to Göran Gransjö?"

"She's his daughter. Göran Gransjö was the principal of our school," she explained to Alice before she went on. "Clara recognized my name, and I recognized hers, so we got talking about people at home in the village and checked to see whether we had any mutual acquaintances, and I was just about to mention you when she exclaimed: 'Siv Weger! Did you know her?' 'No, but I know her sister,' I said. 'She's in H3. We see each other every day.' You don't mind my saying that?"

She looked down at me anxiously.

"Of course not," I said, climbing up to the top bench in between her and Alice, so that we were on the same level. "But tell me what you know about Siv."

"Well," Elsa began, "she came here when she was fifty, like most of us, and she was evidently involved in lots of medical and other experiments; she also went through three organ donations and a number of egg and bone marrow donations. The quality of her eggs was apparently as good as those of a twenty-five-year-old, and she was regarded as a real superwoman. And then she found love here, just like you. She met a woman called Elin or Ellen, Clara couldn't remember which, and they were together until it was Elin or Ellen's turn to donate her heart."

I felt a stab of pain in the region around my own heart, and had to gasp for breath in the humid air of the sauna. I was thinking about Johannes, who was so much older than me and who had been in the unit for so much longer. I closed my eyes, thought "not today, not tomorrow," and at the same time felt Elsa's hand clutching mine.

"Are you okay?" she said. "Do you need to go out for some air? To cool down? Water?"

"No, no, I'm fine." I said. I opened my eyes, met her gaze and nodded to her to carry on.

She pulled her hand away and leaned back cautiously against the hot wooden wall. Her whole body was shiny with sweat, mine too, and Alice's. Alice was sitting in silence with her knees drawn up and her arms around her legs, listening earnestly to Elsa's story.

"After she had lost her Ellen-Elin, she applied to make her final donation."

"Can you do that?" said Alice.

"Didn't you know?" Elsa replied. "Well, anyway, now you do. Her application was approved—I think they always are—and just a week or so later there was someone with Siv's blood type who needed both a heart and lungs. And . . . That was four years ago."

By this time I was no longer calm, by this time I was seething, and it had nothing to do with the heat of the sauna. As I said, I wasn't surprised. As I've already mentioned I hadn't thought it very likely that Siv would still be alive. I would have been surprised if she had been, if I had bumped into her here, for example during a walk in the winter garden, large as life, just older than when I last saw her. Nor was I upset, not primarily at least. I was angry. The fact is that I had worked up a real rage, little by little, while Elsa was telling us what she had found out. And the knowledge that Siv's heart and lungs lived on inside someone who needed them more than she did—someone who perhaps had five splendid kids to provide for—didn't make me less angry in the slightest.

"But what about me?" I burst out, slamming my hand against the wall. "Perhaps I needed my sister, why doesn't anybody care about things like that? That brothers and sisters might need each other? I needed my big sister, I still need her, she was my family, my closest relative, why doesn't anybody care about that?"

I punched the wall, over and over again, the sweat pouring, almost gushing out of me, splashing as I banged and punched, until Alice and Elsa moved in close to me from their respective corners, grabbed my arms and held me, stopping me from punching and flailing. They enveloped me, they rocked and soothed me as if I were a little child, and our warm, damp bodies slipped and stuck together.

"You know that relationships between siblings don't count," said Alice after a while. "It's only new constellations they approve of. People who make a new home and produce new people. You know that, Dorrit; you know that everything has to move forward."

14

Sometimes at night I dreamed of Jock. We were usually on the
beach or on our way home from there, tired and hungry, me with
cold red cheeks, Jock with his breath steaming, and we went into
the house, I put some wood in the stove and lit it, gave Jock some
food and cooked something for myself. The seasons in the dream
varied, but mostly it was autumn or winter. We were on the beach,
I would throw a stick, and Jock would dash off barking with joy
to fetch it, place it at my feet whereupon I would praise him,
pick up the stick and throw it again. It was like a film, a loop,
and I was very contented in those dreams, it was as if everything
important was contained in that everlasting loop, as if everything
else was unimportant, small, worthless. Sometimes I would wake
up with the word "cycle" going around in my head, and I would

stretch, then creep close to the still-sleeping Johannes and caress him or simply press myself against him until, half asleep and grunting slightly, he would begin to feel for my body with his hands, and before he was even fully awake he would part my legs and push inside me.

The night after Elsa told me about what happened to Siv, I dreamed the beach dream. This time it was unusually intense, the colors and contrasts unusually clear and sharp, almost like a film in Technicolor, and the sound of the waves, the wind, the gulls, the terns, the herons and Jock were clearly distinguishable. I could even smell the sea and the seaweed.

I was happy in the dream, but when I woke up it was with a feeling that I was falling apart, that I was cracking up from the inside and slowly falling to pieces. My heart was jumping and grating like a cold engine that doesn't want to start, my skin was crawling and I couldn't manage a single clear thought, it was as if all my thoughts were crushed to bits just as they began to take shape.

I didn't get much done that day. After Johannes had gone home to write—reluctantly, because of course he noticed that I wasn't feeling too good, but I told him I had to work—I sat for a long time, first in bed with my notepad on my knee, then in front of the computer, but I was incapable of writing one single syllable.

Around eleven o'clock in the morning I gave up, took a shower, got dressed and went out. Restlessly I meandered along the paths and tracks in the winter garden, did a circuit of the Atrium Walkway, then went back into the garden, the Monet part this time, but I felt kind of suffocated, shut in, almost as if I was about to have an attack of claustrophobia in there. So I turned and left via the nearest air lock, and did another half circuit of the Walkway until I reached the galleria and took the elevator up to the Terrace restaurant. Up there, closer to the glass roof, closer to the sky, it was lighter, and it made me feel slightly better to be looking out over the tops of the trees rather than being beneath them. I sat there for a long time in the middle of the lunchtime rush with my back to those who were eating, looking out over the garden without doing anything, just sitting and trying to breathe normally, until I felt a hand on my shoulder and turned my head. Alice.

"How are you, my friend?" she asked.

"I don't actually know," I replied, and I really didn't know. I couldn't understand myself: I had Johannes, after all; I loved him and everything pointed to the fact that he loved me in return. And I had friends who I cared about and respected, and who cared about me, and with whom I felt secure. And the information that Siv was dead had come as no surprise. I had assumed as much long ago and accepted it.

But there is a difference between assuming something and having it confirmed. There's a big difference. They're two completely different things.

And then there was Jock.

Alice went and got a chair, sat down beside me and put her arm around my shoulders.

"I miss my dog," I said.

"Your dog? I didn't know you had a dog."

"But I did."

"Poor you," said Alice. "Poor, dear Dorrit."

I leaned against her. I don't remember if I cried, but I think so.

That same afternoon and evening I attended an information meeting about a medical experiment in which I was to participate. The experiment was to do with a new kind of psychiatric drug, a kind of antidepressant that was intended to work immediately, not like earlier versions that were fully effective only after several weeks of increased depression and fatigue. There were thirty of us at the meeting, including Erik, Lena and Kjell. Kjell was in a bad mood, claiming he had been misled; for some reason it seemed he had believed that his role of librarian within the unit exempted him from medical experiments. I didn't really follow his argument, but it had something to do with the service at the library.

"It's only for now, Kjell," said one of the orderlies involved with the experiment, a heavily pregnant woman with greasy hair and a double chin, "it's only during this particular meeting," she clarified, "that you can't be in the library. But Vivi Ljungberg is standing in for you, and she's supposed to be an excellent librarian, so . . ."

Kjell snorted. "Vivi Ljungberg is *not* a librarian. Vivi Ljungberg is a *library assistant*. And what's more she's not familiar with this particular library. And besides . . ."

And he went on and on and on in his monotonous, whining voice. I got really irritated with him, and felt not a little uncomfortable. I thought he was making himself look ridiculous.

After the meeting, as I was standing in elevator F on my way up to Johannes, I became aware of how anxious I was about these happy pills I was due to start popping the next morning. There was a risk of certain side effects, and we had been asked to be on the lookout for symptoms such as dizziness, nausea, vomiting, disturbed vision, numbness in the hands and feet and loss of feeling in the face. This would be the second experiment with the drug, after an adjustment to its composition. The side effects I mentioned had, in the first experiment, affected 90 percent of those taking part, and in certain circumstances they had been extremely serious, developing into bleeding stomach ulcers, strokes, and a dementialike state. There were rumors that a couple of people had actually died. Because of these risks and rumors the team leaders had decided it was necessary for us to take our pills under their supervision. They were afraid that otherwise we would wreck the whole project by not taking them.

When I knocked on Johannes's door I was very tired. I felt heavy and old. But when I heard his footsteps approaching the door I felt lighter, it was as if I were being filled with helium or laughing gas; I felt happy and giddy.

"Here you are at last!" he said when he opened the door.

And he more or less pulled me into the apartment, into his arms, closed the door behind me, kissing my forehead, the tip of my nose, my cheeks, my mouth. My hands fumbled and grabbed and tore at his back, his upper arms, his back again and his buttocks, and he ran his hands through my hair, over my face, my neck, my breasts, forced one thumb into my mouth and made me suck it while he ordered me to look into his eyes. And with the other hand he found his way under my shirt and un-buttoned my pants, pulled them down, then my panties—not far down, just enough so that he could get at me. Then he slowly took his thumb out of my mouth and got hold of the hair at the back of my neck instead and held my head so that it was impos-sible for me to take my eyes off his face, while at the same time alternately rubbing my clitoris with his middle finger and push-ing one, two, three, four fingers inside me. At the moment of orgasm my knees gave way, and if he hadn't held me firmly I would have fallen forward onto my knees; instead I stayed there in his grasp, supported by his upper body and the hand massag-ing my pussy, and I heard myself uttering gurgling, whimpering noises of pain and pleasure mixed together.

Afterward he allowed me to slide slowly to my knees, and I stayed there, panting, sobbing, and watching his coarse yet at the same time soft hands with the raised lilac-blue veins float-ing in a sparse forest of white hairs, as they unbuttoned his pants and his cock emerged in front of my face, and I opened my mouth, closed my lips around it, hard, like a sphincter. He breathed out with a slow "aaah . . ."

Later we lay in bed naked. I still hadn't told Johannes what Elsa had found out about Siv—I hadn't actually mentioned Siv or the rest of my family at all—so I told him now.

"Superwoman Siv!" he exclaimed before I'd even finished telling him. "Was Superwoman Siv your sister? I didn't know her name was Weger."

"Did you know her?" I sat up in bed.

"No. But when I arrived here three—or what is it now, three and a half years ago—people were always talking about her and Ellen, her partner. Majken had time to get to know her, though. Just about. I think Superwoman Siv might have been to Majken something of what Majken was to you."

"Do you really think so?" I said. "You're not just saying that to make me feel better?"

"Now you're being stupid, Dorrit! Why on earth would I do such a thing? I'm saying it because that's the impression I got about the contact between Siv and Majken: a short friendship that made a deep impression and helped Majken to achieve a kind of balance pretty quickly, to get on an even keel and be able to cope with the circumstances of life in here."

"She seemed to cope very well."

"Presumably thanks to your sister, to a certain extent."

"I wonder who was a friend like that to Siv," I said.

Johannes didn't reply, he just looked at me, and it seemed to me that his expression was suddenly sorrowful and slightly distant.

"Are you sad, or just serious?" I asked.

"I don't really know," he said.

I lay down again, took hold of his hand. We lay there on our backs, hand in hand, gazing up at the ceiling.

"The generations are very short in this place," I said.

"Yes," said Johannes. "They are."

After a while I could tell from his breathing that he was struggling with tears. I turned over onto my side facing him, and placed my hand on his slightly rough cheek. He turned off the light—perhaps he didn't want me to see his face when he was crying, or maybe he just thought it was time to go to sleep now—then he turned to me in the darkness, pulled me close, one arm around my shoulders, the other holding my head against his chest, and I pressed myself against him with my arm around his waist, my forehead against his breastbone and one leg wrapped around his thighs, almost as if I were climbing him.

In the morning when we woke up we were in the same position: like two drowning souls who have clung to each other in a final fruitless attempt to save themselves—or simply to avoid dying alone.

15

The experiment involving the antidepressant drug forced me into new routines. Three times a day—morning, afternoon, and evening—I took the elevator down to lab 3 on K1 to swallow a little yellow pill. It upset my schedule, especially in the mornings when I had to interrupt my writing, or to put it more accurately: because I was always aware that at some point between eight and nine o'clock I would have to break away to get dressed and take the elevator and swallow that pill, I found it difficult to achieve the peace and concentration I needed to be able to write at all. So instead I would usually spend the time sitting and reading through what I'd already written, making the kind of notes and corrections I would have preferred to leave until I had the whole thing printed out.

This was irritating enough, but what upset me considerably more was the feeling of not being trusted, of being treated like a difficult child, a cheat, a rebel. I found it offensive to have to stand there and open my mouth in front of Nurse Karl or the brisk, naive Nurse Lis or one of the other nurses who handed out the yellow pills then looked in your mouth as if you were a horse at a horse fair back in the olden days, before carefully ticking it off from a list and chirruping smugly: "Well done, Dorrit. We'll see you between two and three."

My dignity shrank by several inches every time I had to go through this procedure.

On the other hand, I had more time to write, more time generally during this medical experiment than during the exercise experiment, because my only obligation was to make sure I was in the right place three times a day. That took up about half an hour per day in total, and it should have outweighed the disadvantages, but it didn't.

During one of my many conversations with Arnold I took up this question of my dwindling dignity, and the fact that I found it difficult to settle down to work because of having to break away. I had hoped that he might manage to say the right thing and give me some idea how I should handle the problem, but he just nodded and listened, made notes, and asked questions like: "What kind of feelings do you get when you can't write?" and "How would you define the term 'offensive'?"

So I started to talk about my concerns regarding the side effects instead.

"Have you experienced any?" asked Arnold.

"No, but I haven't felt any positive effects either. If anything I'm more anxious than I was before. These pills are supposed to have a direct effect."

"Direct doesn't always have to mean immediate," said Arnold.

"Oh really?" I said. "And what does it mean when it doesn't mean that?"

He didn't reply. Just sat there opposite me in his armchair with one leg loosely crossed over the other, his elbows resting on the upholstered arms, pressing the tips of his fingers together as he contemplated me with a thoughtful expression. I changed the topic of conversation again, started talking about Siv: about how I had almost fallen apart when what I already knew about her was confirmed.

This clearly interested him, because his expression came alive, he placed his hands on his knees and began to ask questions about Siv and my family and the relationships when I was growing up. I answered dutifully and almost mechanically, rattling off my thoughts and theories on why Siv and I were the only two out of the five of us who hadn't succeeded in establishing a family of our own, and had chosen professions with an uncertain income.

It would definitely have been more useful to talk about my recurring dreams involving Jock, or about what was happening between Johannes and me, because these were new phenomena and new feelings that I didn't really understand, while my relationship with my family was old and already made sense. But I couldn't bring myself to change the topic of conversation yet again, and when I left Arnold's office it was with the feeling that I had wasted a whole hour of my life.

16

One afternoon after I had been downstairs and swallowed the second pill of the day, I took the elevator up to the library to return some books, and found Vivi behind the desk. There was no sign of Kjell, and as I turned my books over with the bar code facing her, I asked where he was.

"Did he get fired?"

It was meant as a joke, but Vivi's expression was serious.

"Haven't you heard?" she said. "He's sick. Serious side effects. He's really dizzy all the time. And completely disoriented when it comes to time and space. He can hardly get out of bed or feed himself."

"What?! How long has this been going on? I'm in the same experiment, so I mean I'm wondering . . ."

". . . if it's going to happen to you too? It won't."

"Really . . . ?"

"If you haven't had any side effects by now, then you've been given sugar pills. And if you're wondering how I know, well of course I don't. But all the indications would suggest that. Some of you became very happy at first, then confused and completely out of it. Up like the sun, down like a pancake, you could say. Kjell was like a completely different person for the first few days—I was here at the time, helping to unpack new films and clear out some of the old magazines and newspapers. He was in an excellent mood, joking and carrying on, and so intense that it was almost unbearable. Then all of a sudden, from one day to the next, he became listless and tired. Then it just went downhill; he found it difficult to judge distances, walked into things, tripped and fell over and dropped things left and right. And he got so forgetful, he hardly knew where he was after a while. In the end he couldn't carry on here, it just wasn't working. And, as I said, he isn't the only one. That man who's always so sad, for example, the one who sat opposite you at my welcome party—he's the same. Bedridden."

"Erik?" I said. "You mean Erik." I felt my heart sink and I had to lean on the issue desk for support; my head was spinning. "How do you know all this?" I asked her.

Vivi said with a little smile that when you work in a place like a library, you find out all kinds of things about all kinds of things. And she went on telling me what she had heard about a couple of other people who were involved in the same experiment as me. But I wasn't really listening, I was thinking about Erik. I was thinking about how low and lost he had been since Vanja's final donation. He would have needed her now, he would have needed the love and solicitude of another person.

□ □ □

I gathered together a little group: Elsa, Lena, Johannes, and
Peder, and we went to visit Erik. It was around eight-thirty in
the evening, after I had been to the gym, had dinner, and been
down to lab 3 to take the final yellow pill of the day.

Erik was in a worse state than I had thought. He didn't recognize any of us. And it wasn't only because he had problems with
his vision and was shaking so much that he couldn't keep his head
still. Something had happened inside his head as well, something
to do with his awareness and his memory. He just didn't know
who we were, not even Peder, whom he'd known the longest.

"Oooh!" said Erik in a strange, singsong voice, and smiled with
his whole face when we walked into his bedroom after being let
into his apartment by a young orderly wearing big, round glasses
with black frames, who was looking after him and helping him
to eat and wash and go to the bathroom. "Wel-wel-wellllcome!"

His huge smile was the only redeeming feature about his
condition; at least he was happy, and for the first time in weeks.
But he called Peder Uncle Jonas, Johannes Grandpa, and Elsa
Mommy. And he called me, with a certain amount of contempt,
the Snork Maiden and Mademoiselle. He didn't speak to Lena
at all, but he was very shy around her, blushing and giggling and
looking away every time she spoke to him or glanced at him.

We were all very low when we left. As we were walking through
the living room on the way out, Johannes said so quietly that
only I, walking next to him, could hear:

"It's only a matter of days."

I looked up at him but said nothing. Instead I went over to
the young orderly, who was sitting on the sofa watching TV, and
asked:

"How serious is it?"

"What do you mean?"

I sat down next to him on the sofa. POTTER read the name badge on his shirt.

"Will Erik be . . . normal again?" I asked.

Potter looked me in the eye, his expression behind the glasses strangely distant yet sympathetic at the same time.

"I don't think anybody really knows for certain. But personally, I don't think so."

And after a while, in a very low voice—and protected by the noise of the television: "I've seen the X-ray plates."

Then he leaned forward a fraction, coughed, cleared his throat, and at the end of the throat clearing he spat out, so quickly and hoarsely that I only just managed to get it: "Abnormal atrophy." And another cough: "The brain . . . ," and a final throat clearing: ". . . has shrunk."

I knew very well what abnormal brain atrophy was; it's the cause of Alzheimer's, and simply means that the brain becomes vestigial, that it shrinks inside the skull until nothing remains, just a big space between the ears and a despairing expression on the sufferer's face. I had seen this a lot when I was young and working in geriatric care.

After his brief coughing attack Potter placed, very properly, a hand on my shoulder and said in a friendly, conversational tone:

"But you mustn't worry. He's getting very good care. And you could see how cheerful he is."

I nodded, well aware that patients with Alzheimer's are unhappy far more often than they are happy. As if Potter had heard what I was thinking, he added:

"He's actually cheerful like this most of the time. He seems contented. Strangely enough."

Of course I don't know whether what he said was true, he might have said it just to console me.

"Have they stopped the experiment?" I asked.

"No, it's still ongoing."

"No, but I mean in Erik's case. Is he still having three pills a day?"

"Of course. The experiment is still ongoing, as I said."

Potter smiled—his expression now considerably more distant than sympathetic—and I realized that the audience was over, so I got up, asked him to take good care of Erik, and went to join the others, who were sitting in the lounge, pale and silent.

"What did he say?" asked Peder, who was palest of them all.

"He didn't know much," I lied, because I couldn't abuse the young orderly's trust and speak openly about the information he had been kind enough to cough at me. I just added: "But things don't look too promising, he did say that."

A few hours later, as soon as Johannes and I were inside my apartment, I pulled him to me and began kissing and caressing him, and as he moaned and grunted loudly I whispered in his ear what I had found out about Erik's brain.

17

Erik and Kjell and thirteen others were sent to make their final donation. Officially the residents weren't told much more than that. The unofficial information—the information that was whispered and coughed and spread among various sources—was patchy and, presumably, mixed with rumor and speculation. What we did eventually manage to establish as being reasonably reliable was this:

During the manufacture of the antidepressant drug an accidental mix-up had occurred between different components, and traces of a kind of nerve poison of the same type used in some chemical weapons had found their way into the pills. When the pharmaceutical company, late in the day and by pure chance, discovered this lamentable error, those responsible informed the leadership team in the reserve bank unit immediately; they in turn decided it would be best to eliminate the fifteen participants in the experiment who had been affected, since their brains were irrevocably destroyed and there was no point in drawing the whole thing out. They therefore chose to act quickly and effectively, to save what could be saved from the bodies of those involved, then to return to the normal way of things without saying any more than necessary about the matter—and to allow collective amnesia to play its part.

The account didn't state to what extent the demand for organs and tissues matched this sudden flow onto the market, but I know that certain types of tissue can be preserved for a long time until a recipient is found, and I'm sure dead bodies are always welcome in research and teaching. So I hope and believe that the remains of Erik and the others were of use in some way.

The other fifteen of us involved in the experiment were called to a meeting led by the unit's director, Petra Runhede, herself. As she allowed her gaze to glide over us, serious and sympathetic as always, lingering for a second or two on each person, she expressed her regret at what had happened and confirmed what Vivi had told me: that those of us who had not suffered side effects had been given sugar pills.

"Of course the experiment will be canceled with immediate effect," she went on. "You will be allocated new tasks very shortly."

Naturally we were all shaken, and overwhelmed by powerful, conflicting emotions. It is in the nature of things to feel conflicting emotions when you realize that you belong to a group of survivors, selected purely at random. Some people wept, some laughed hysterically, a couple sat staring blankly into space, shivering, their teeth chattering—of course they were taken care of and treated for shock—and two collapsed and had to be more or less carried out for emergency sessions with their respective psychologists. Lena and I kept calm, but we sat there holding hands throughout the entire meeting.

□ □ □

After Kjell's death Vivi took over responsibility for the library. She seemed very happy with the arrangement, and unfortunately I have to say that not many people missed Kjell. He was a miserable complainer but didn't make much noise apart from that, and he didn't exactly have any friends in the unit, even if he didn't have enemies either. He was mourned by no one, left no one behind, and Vivi slipped into his shoes just as if she had always been the one padding around between the shelves, putting the books, films, CDs, magazines and daily papers in the right place, noting down and sending off orders for distance loans, signing out readers, downloading e-books and exchanging a few words with the borrowers as they came and went. After just a few weeks it was as if Kjell had never existed, and if it hadn't been for the fact that his life had come to an end because of a scandal and a tragedy, I don't think anybody would ever have given him a thought.

10

After the incident with the failed antidepressant experiment, Elsa
and I ended up for the first and only time in the same scientific
experiment, a psychological study where the researchers wanted
to find out if there was a biological or genetic parental instinct,
and if so, whether it was the same in women and men. As dispensable people we were the perfect target group, since none of
us had the physical or emotional experience of caring for and
bringing up our own children, as mothers and fathers have.

For the first few days we each sat with our head inside a brain
scanner, which measured and registered the reactions of the brain
as we were exposed to a series of visual, audio, and olfactory
impressions. There were pictures of children at different ages
and in different situations, the sound of babies crowing, children

laughing, newborn babies crying, tantrums, the smell of baby rice, talcum powder, baby feces, wet diapers and baby vomit. There were also pictures, noises, and smells that signaled different kinds of threat or danger: hot stoves, the screech of a car's brakes, fire, smoke, swimming pools, steep staircases, buzzing wasps, growling dogs baring their teeth, sharp and pointed objects, guns, different kinds of poisonous items, nasty old men offering children candy, images of child pornography and lots of other things.

After these introductory days the experiment continued with a series of different tests. There were multiple-choice questionnaires, there were discussion groups, there were sessions when different scenarios were acted out for us and our reactions measured in different ways. The experiment lasted for two weeks and on the penultimate day we got—or at least I got—a small shock when we arrived in lab 2, where the majority of the work had taken place, to find the place crawling with real live children. There were something like twenty of them, aged between eighteen months and six years, and we were to play with them, talk to them and, if necessary, feed them and change their diapers and their clothes.

Elsa and I spent several hours playing with a girl aged four and a boy aged two and a half. We built a cabin using a table, some blankets and some cushions, and we had a tea party with some dolls and were attacked by extremists and had a battle with the terrorists and died and we were dead until the girl decided it wasn't actually that serious, we were just badly injured and needed Band-Aids and bandages, and then we could carry on eating cake and conversing with the dolls. Although after a while we were interrupted again, because the boy needed to pee so urgently and so badly that we didn't quite make it to the bathroom before he wet his pants a bit, so he had to change into a pair of dark green pants that he didn't like instead of the red ones he'd been wearing, which he liked much better. And he wept, furious and desolate, for a while until Elsa came up with the idea that he was actually wearing a pair of green military pants, and that it was time for a new war on terror, and everything was fine again. The boy was called Olav and the girl was called Kristina; I thought they were a delight.

The following day we were interviewed, one on one in separate little rooms, about how we had felt and how we had reacted to our time with the children. The room was equipped with a very basic desk, two chairs, a DAT recorder, a TV and a DVD player. The person who interviewed me was a woman of roughly my age, quite powerful and with a calm, steady gaze. Under normal circumstances I would have found her reassuring, but not this particular morning.

During the previous evening and night I had been very low, and had felt the same kind of ache in my stomach and chest that missing Jock had caused during my first months in the unit. I had fought back the tears and turned my back on Johannes in bed; he had noticed that something was wrong and tried to comfort me, but hadn't really succeeded. Naturally I didn't want to talk about this during the interview. But the psychologists running the tests had access to our journals, and therefore the woman interviewing me knew that I had had an abortion when I was young. And—as if that weren't enough—when she asked how I had experienced the contact with the children in light of the fact that I had had an abortion early in life and then not had any children, and I refused to answer, she said:

"Look at this, Dorrit," and she pressed PLAY on the DVD.

Something greenish that looked as if it had been filmed with an underwater camera appeared on the screen. I was automatically expecting to see fish, starfish, corals, and billowing seaweed, and perhaps a diver in a rubber suit with an oxygen tank on his back. But after only a couple of seconds I realized this was no film recorded at the bottom of some ocean, not even at the bottom of some lake, or even an aquarium, it was a room, a greenish bedroom, with two greenish people in a greenish double bed filmed with a thermal imaging camera. At first the two people were lying there still and silent, one with their back to the other, but then there were some muffled sounds, then a murmur, and the murmur had words: "Dorrit . . . ? Darling, what is it?"

And I saw, from above and at an angle, how Johannes turned me to face him with gentle force, and I heard my own muffled sounds transformed into words and sentences, at first chopped about by sobs and incomprehensible, then a little unclear but perfectly audible. I was surprised—and horrified—at the sound quality.

The interviewer stopped the film, turned to me, looked at me, calmly waiting, without saying a word. It lasted quite a long time. We sat there in silence, she with her hands on her knee and her gaze fixed on my face, me as stiff as a corpse. I was silent and stiff for so long that it finished me off completely, it was as if everything inside had shut down, I was empty, and when that happened I was able—mechanically—to begin to explain how I had felt about the events of yesterday and what I had felt and thought afterward.

19

Time passed. Time flew. The days flew like balloons, filled with
hours at the computer beneath the picture of Majken's deformed
fetus, hours spent on experiments and humane tests, hours of
walking, stamina training, swimming, appointments with the
psychologist, massages, pedicures and saunas. The evenings came
and went with visits to the cinema, dinners, conversations, time
spent with friends. And the nights came in to land, only to drift
away again filled with hours of lovemaking, whispering, sleep
and dreams. And the days and nights turned into weeks, the
weeks into months, and at the end of each month five, six, seven
or eight new dispensable individuals would arrive in the unit,
and a new welcome party would be held with dinner, entertainment and dancing. And each month a number of residents would

disappear from the unit and would not come back; more and more often there would be someone I knew among them. And for a while the time just flowed into one for me. Or to put it more accurately: in my memory the time flows into one. And that probably isn't only due to the fact that our memory is selective and mixes things up and picks out what seems right at the time. Under normal circumstances, in the real world out there, our memory can usually support itself by the seasons; a certain event is linked with a particular time of year. For example, I know that my father died and was buried in the fall, because the maples in the churchyard were red and orange, and the weather was crisp and clear and cold. And my mother died the following summer, right at the beginning, when the oilseed rape is in flower and the schools are letting out. I also know that it was early spring when Nils came home with me for the first time, because I remember showing him the hepatica that had just come into flower behind the compost, and at first he didn't believe they really were hepatica, because for some reason he thought they were extinct, and I had to go in and get my flower book and look it up and show him. I had moved into my house in the late fall when the trees were bare and the fields muddy and heavy. And Jock became mine that same winter; I had to clear the car windshield of freshly fallen wet snow and clear the garden path before I drove, slowly and carefully, through the slush to the animal rescue to collect him. But when I think back over my time in the unit my memory has no such assistance from the seasons, because the seasons never change. In the unit there are only days and nights, that's the only thing that changes: darkness and daylight. In the winter garden everything is in bud or in flower, but nothing shrivels, withers or dies. It is never winter in the winter garden.

After lunch one day, during one of my more or less daily walks in the garden, I arrived at the citrus grove just as the petals were falling. I went in among the low trees, into the Impressionist pattern of white dots, and stood there thinking of Majken and Jock—Majken because she liked the Impressionists' way of portraying the world, Jock because I knew he would have loved this white blizzard of petals. I turned my face upward and watched the little petals as they drifted down toward me slowly and with dignity, like perfumed snowflakes that would never melt on this windless day, landing in my hair, on my forehead, on one eyelid, on the other eyebrow, on the tip of my nose, on my upper lip. I blew the last one away, then looked down again and gave myself a shake. Then I saw that I was not alone in the grove. A person wearing round glasses was standing a little way off in his pale green staff shirt, watching me through the white-dotted air. Potter.

"Hi there!" he called out, raising a hand in greeting when he realized I had seen him.

He started walking over, and when he got to me he asked: "How are things?"

"Good," I replied. "And how are you?"

"Fine . . ." Then he seemed to hesitate, looking down at the ground, then up again before taking a deep breath and saying:

"It was terrible, what happened."

"With Erik and the others, you mean?"

"Yes. Mistakes like that just can't be allowed to happen, and it just doesn't matter whether the drug in question is being tested on those who are dispensable or on rats or amoebae or on those who are needed. It's a completely indefensible . . ."—he searched for the right word—". . . waste."

"Yes," I agreed. "They could just as well have thrown their research funding in the sea."

"A waste of people, I mean," said Potter. "Not money."

"People are money," I replied. "Just as time is money."

He shook his head.

"People are people," he said seriously. "Life."

"Yes, yes," I said. "Of course."

"I nearly resigned," Potter went on, clearly needing to unburden himself. "It's difficult, seeing the way you're treated here."

"We're treated very well," I said.

"Do you think so?" He was genuinely surprised, and perhaps a little disappointed.

"Yes," I replied. "If you compare it with the way we're treated out in the community. In here I can be myself, on every level, completely openly, without being rejected or mocked, and without the risk of not being taken seriously. I am not regarded as odd or as some kind of alien or some troublesome fifth wheel that people don't know what to do with. Here I'm like everybody else. I fit in. I count. And I can afford to go to the doctor and the dentist and even to the hairdresser and the podiatrist, and I can eat out and go to the movies and the theater. I have a dignified life here. I am respected."

"Are you?"

"Yes. In comparison, I mean."

Potter looked at me.

"Okay," he said. "I understand. I think."

I changed the topic of conversation.

"So why didn't you resign, then?"

"Well . . . I don't think I can afford to be out of work right now. My partner and I are expecting. Twins. We need a bigger place to live."

"Right," I said. "I understand. I think."

He laughed. I smiled. Then we parted company. I carried on through the citrus grove. It was like walking through a landscape veiled in fresh snow, and suddenly I felt an intense longing for winter and wind, biting cold and steaming breath, mittens, a scarf and hat, and a little white dog with brown and black patches racing through drifts of powdery snow, tail wagging like mad, snuffling with his nose at the porous covering so that the white snow flew up ahead of him like little whirlwinds.

And I got an idea.

I had three things on my agenda for the rest of the afternoon: give blood at the central blood bank at the hospital, go down to the labs for a chromium injection—I was participating in an experiment where high doses of chromium were being tested as a means of raising the blood sugar—and go for a massage. Later, in the evening, Johannes and I were going to the theater to see a new play everyone was talking about.

While I was giving blood, and during the full body massage that followed, I had plenty of time to work out carefully my idea for a plan, and as soon as I got home I set the wheels in motion:

I opened my door and went into the living room, yawning and stretching lazily—a massage always made me sleepy—then ambled into the kitchenette and poured myself a large glass of water. Turned back to the living room with the glass in my hand, yawned again, then wandered across to the sofa, where I sank into a half-lying position and tried to drink my water. Then I put the glass on the table next to the remote, which I picked up and fiddled with absentmindedly. Turned onto my side with a sigh, pointed the remote at the TV and selected a channel at random. Watching television was something I had rarely done since I became dispensable, so I tried to make it look as if it were a spur of the moment impulse. The image of a hilly, lush landscape burst onto the screen: a valley with meadows and terraced vineyards scrambling up the slopes, the blue tones of distant mountain ridges in the background; then I lay there watching, apparently relaxed, a soap opera that was set in some French wine region.

I waited until a commercial break, and until the second advertising slot, which was for diapers; then I pretended that I'd had an idea, an idea for my writing, sat up quickly and put my feet on the floor, grabbed the notepad and pen that were always on the coffee table, placed the pad on my knee, bent over and scribbled feverishly. But my handwriting was much smaller than usual, and I had worked out what I wanted to say in advance, while I was giving blood:

I have a Danish-Swedish farm dog called Jock. He is white with brown and black patches; his left ear is white, the other black, and on his back he has a bigger brown patch that looks like a saddle that has slipped to one side slightly. He lives with Lisa and Sten Jansson, Verkholma Farm, just outside Elnarp, the second farm on the right just after the speed limit sign if you're driving toward Kasstorp. Please, if you possibly can, find out how he's getting by, and let me know!

When I had finished I read through the four sentences, said, "No, no!," ripped the page from the pad, screwed it up and threw it on the coffee table, then slumped down on my side on the sofa again and finished watching the soap.

A while later, after a quick shower and a change of clothes, I was tidying the room while I waited for Johannes, who was being a gentleman and picking me up for our visit to the theater. I picked up the glass and the crumpled piece of paper, and as I walked toward the kitchenette with the glass in my left hand, I pretended to straighten my pants with my right hand, and took the opportunity to slip the piece of paper into my pocket. I put the glass down on the counter, then just to make things look right I opened the cabinet under the sink and pretended to throw something in the trash.

Then all I could do was wait. For Johannes, first of all, and then for the moment when I might bump into Potter again. I sank back down on the sofa, and half lay there wondering what might have come first: the name or the glasses. Was Potter a nickname he had acquired since he got those glasses with their round black frames, or did he go for glasses like that because he was called Potter? But who calls their child Potter—as a first name? If he'd been a girl, what would they have called her? Longstocking?

Johannes arrived. Kissed me on the mouth. His lips were cool, as if he had just come from the real outside world, from an outside world where the temperature was below freezing, or almost. I closed my eyes and pretended that was the case.

"You look happy," he said.

"Yes, you taste of winter. That's why. You taste as if you've just come in from a storm."

He laughed. "It almost feels that way. I feel as if I've been running against the wind all day. I'm shattered."

Johannes had started on a new experiment involving drugs that lowered the blood pressure; perhaps his blood pressure was a bit too low. I frowned in concern:

"They are carrying out regular checks on you? Pulse, blood pressure, and so on?"

"Sure," he said. "Don't worry. Shall we go?"

The play was long and not particularly entertaining, but its premise was interesting: it was about a couple who had one miscarriage after another, and how their love grew stronger and stronger through this constant blossoming of hope that was dashed every time, how grief and yearning and their common goal bound them closer and closer together into a single unit. But when, roughly halfway through the play, they managed to carry and give birth to this longed-for child, they began, slowly but surely, to drift apart, only to end up as two strangers who didn't speak the same language—quite literally; they spoke different languages and were unable to understand each other—and all communication was carried out through the child, who had to act as an interpreter between the parents. All very strange.

Johannes slept through most of the second act, which meant he was wide awake when it finished.

"A beer would be just fantastic right now!" he said, stretching as we came out into the square after he'd just woken up.

"A proper snowstorm and a good strong beer!" I said, because that was exactly what I felt like right then.

"You seem really into all this winter stuff. How come?"

"Oh, the petals were falling in the citrus grove today."

Then we went back to my place. When I got undressed I was careful to fold up my pants so that the piece of paper wouldn't fall out of the right-hand pocket.

"My, you've gotten very tidy all of a sudden," said Johannes from the bed; he was already undressed and under the covers with one arm behind his head.

"I just don't want them to get creased."

"They already are."

"Well, even more creased then."

"Since when did you start worrying about that kind of thing?"

I wanted to change the subject.

"Since I met you," I said, and quickly took off the rest of my clothes—folding them neatly if quickly and draping them over the chair on top of my pants—then lifted the duvet at the foot of the bed to make a gap and crept up the bed alongside one of Johannes's legs, with its soft, curly hairs, its slightly rough skin that smelled of man, that smelled of precisely this man who smelled of sunshine and something that reminded me of cumin, coriander and cinnamon, the calf muscles pressing down against the mattress, the lower part of the kneecap particularly coarse and slightly knobbly and rough like a cat's tongue, and the thigh—the huge thigh muscle at the front, tensing and swelling as my hands found their way further up.

□ □ □

That night I dreamed of Jock and the beach and the stick I picked up and threw over and over again, and which he brought back to me over and over again. But the dream was different this time. Sometimes it wasn't Jock who came back to me with the stick in his mouth, but Johannes running toward me with his arms outstretched and his hair standing on end in the wind. And sometimes it wasn't me throwing the stick but Johannes, and when Jock brought it back we both praised him. And then suddenly we were in the car outside the house, my old car and my old house. We got out of the car and went into the house and all three of us lived there. Johannes was hanging pictures on the walls, framed photographs. I asked him:

"What are those photographs?"

"Can't you see?" replied Johannes. "Those are our children, of course."

"Our children?" I said, and then I woke up and the dawn light was in the room.

I didn't tell Johannes about the dream, not then. It frightened me. It was beautiful and we were very happy in it. And yet—or perhaps that was exactly why—it felt threatening in some way. During the rest of the day I tried to forget the dream, shake it off, the way you try to shake off nightmares. But I couldn't do it, it had fixed itself in my consciousness and it sat there all day, coloring everything I did and everything that happened and everything that was said. Everything was colored by the feeling that I had a man and children and a house and a car and a dog.

20

Another day at lunchtime when I was out walking, I caught sight of young Potter in the winter garden again. This time he was sitting on a bench on a patio reading a book. It had been several weeks, or maybe a month or so, since the day when we had chatted in the citrus grove, and of course I had worn several different pairs of pants during that time. Each time I had carefully smuggled the little piece of paper from the right-hand pocket in one pair to the same place in the other, so that I always knew where it was, and when I saw Potter in there among the palms, half hidden by the little fountain, I pushed my hands into my pockets, wandered onto the patio, stopped and said hi.

He looked up absentmindedly from the book.

"Well hi there," he said when he recognized me. "How are things?"

"Absolutely fine," I said. "How about you?"

"Yes. Good." He adjusted his glasses with his index finger, his gaze flickering up and down slightly; he clearly wanted to get back to his book, but he was polite and made an effort to give me a friendly smile. I didn't want to give the impression that I was the kind of person who would insensitively impose on people who wanted to be left in peace, so I made as if to continue my walk, but then stopped and asked, as if in passing:

"And how are you getting on with finding a new place to live?"

It worked; he brightened up and closed the book with one finger keeping his place as he decided to take a break.

"Good," he said, "we actually went to look at a really nice apartment yesterday. Four rooms with a little garden. It's really close to the neighbors, but the garden is pretty mature and you can't see inside. And it's on two floors with a view over a park from the top floor. A big playground just outside, a day nursery and school close by, and lots of families with children in the community."

I shuddered involuntarily at the very idea of living in a place like that, hemmed in between families noisily spreading themselves out, practically spilling over like rising bread dough, around and on top of people who were on their own and who neither wanted to make themselves heard nor were able to do so, who didn't want to spread themselves like that, and thus became invisible and annihilated—crushed to nothingness. But Potter was feeling chatty now and in full swing, so I steeled myself and tried not to let it bother me as he told me in detail about the lovely, child-friendly residential area, and I pulled my right hand out of my pocket with the piece of paper pressed between my palm and my little finger, ring finger, and middle finger. Potter carried on explaining: about the apartment, its practical design, how they were going to decorate the children's room, about an ultrasound scan of the twins in his partner's stomach.

"Would you like to see it?" he said. "I've got it here." Without waiting for a reply he pulled a wallet out of his back pocket.

Normally I would have hesitated and perhaps even refused, made some excuse and said that I was in a terrible rush—I had already had my fill of blurred ultrasound images of the developing babies of those who were needed—but of course I realized I couldn't let this opportunity slip through my fingers just because of that.

So I sat down on the bench next to Potter, who held out the unclear little picture to me. I feigned interest and took it between the thumb and index finger of my right hand, with the other fingers still holding the piece of paper. He pointed at two paler kidney-shaped areas among all the lines and shadows on the picture, and I nodded and said something about how fascinating it was and asked how old they were now, the twin fetuses, and whether he was looking forward to being a parent, and he replied and explained and chatted, and somewhere in the middle of all this pointing and asking and explaining, while we were still sitting there leaning over the little photograph, I managed to pass the little crumpled piece of paper from my hand into his. When I had done it I glanced quickly up at his face. He didn't look surprised, but just nodded, briefly, almost imperceptibly and with a tiny wink—I got the impression that he realized my interested questions had been nothing more than a kind of camouflage— and then, when we had finished looking at the picture, he put it into his wallet along with the crumpled piece of paper, and put the wallet back in his pocket.

It was several weeks before I bumped into Potter again, this time one evening in section E4. Alice lived there. She had borrowed a DVD from the library and invited me and Elsa and Lena and

Vivi to watch the film and to have some homemade fruitcake
and tea. The film was a romantic comedy, a frothy story full of
mix-ups and misunderstandings that ended with a wedding. As
soon as the titles rolled Elsa and Vivi left. They had begun to
spend a lot of time together lately, just the two of them, and I
was slowly starting to realize that there was something going on
between them, that they were falling in love. I wanted to get back
to Johannes, so shortly after Elsa and Vivi left I thanked Alice
and went on my way. And that was when I caught sight of Potter
in the laundry room as I was on my way out of the section. He
was doing something to the drain in the floor.

"Is it blocked?" I said and stopped, hesitated in the doorway
and then leaned on the door frame.

He looked up.

"Yes," he sighed. "And it's the third time in a week."

And so we stood there for a little while—or rather I stood,
while he was on his knees—and chatted about blockages and
how to sort them out. As the former owner of a house with old
drains and narrow pipes that often got blocked, I was able to give
him some tips on how to solve the problem, and clever ways to
help avoid it in the future.

When he had finished, at least for this time, as he said while
replacing the grid over the drain, he got up and walked past me
on the way out, and we said good-bye, and a neatly folded piece
of paper was slipped into my hand, which I smuggled into my
pocket.

Despite the fact that it wasn't particularly late, Johannes was
already asleep when I got back. He had left the light on above
the sink in the kitchen. From the bedroom I could hear the sighing noises he made in his sleep; it wasn't really snoring, but it
wasn't ordinary breathing either. He sounded like a dreaming
child. He sounded like my brother Ole, when he was four and I

was nine and he and Ida and I shared a room during a vacation in a cottage. He sounded like the wind whispering through a field of corn in late summer. It made me feel at peace. Safe.

I sat down at the dining table in the half darkness. From time to time Johannes would smack his lips in his sleep, half whimpering and muttering something in a thick voice (which didn't sound like Ole at all). Then he would go back to the regular sighing, and that was the only sound apart from the faint, even hum of the air-conditioning. Apart from that the silence was complete. On the table lay the fossil Johannes had picked up on the beach. Beside the stone lay a magazine, I can't remember what it was. I touched the stone, running my index finger over the contours of the cone-shaped fossil that had once been an animal, or at least part of an animal. I picked up the stone, weighed it in my hand, closed my fingers around it, turned it round and round in my cupped hand. It felt good; the stone was cool and smooth. Then I put it down again, pulled the magazine toward me, opened it, flicked through the pages and pretended to skim an article here and there while fiddling in my pocket with my hand—I was trying to make it look as if I were scratching my thigh—and fumbling for the piece of paper Potter had given me. I got hold of it and pulled it out as silently as I could, holding it between my index and middle finger, then carefully unfolded it under the table. Then I quickly slipped it in between two pages of the magazine, which I had positioned right by the edge of the table. Then all I had to do was leaf through until I got to the right place. When I got there I leaned forward slightly with one elbow on the table and my chin resting on the palm of my hand, so that I was hiding as much as possible.

I don't see particularly well in the dark, and it took a while before I realized what the piece of paper was. It wasn't a message, or a letter, not one single word was written or printed on it. It was two pictures. Two photographs, color photographs, printed next to one another in the middle of the piece of paper. I moved a fraction so that the light from the kitchen would shine down on the pictures.

They were taken in Sten and Lisa's garden. In the left-hand picture Jock is with their youngest child, a little girl with round cheeks and curly black hair, big brown eyes and a funny little turned-up nose. Jock has a blue ball in his mouth—at least it looks like a ball—and is running toward the girl with his head up, proud, fearless. She's wearing jeans, Wellington boots, a blue knitted sweater with a big red car on the front, and a gray scarf, and she's laughing and clapping her hands above her head. She had grown, she seemed taller and slimmer, more sturdy—the previous autumn her brother, two years older, had been wearing that sweater. On the lawn, where she and Jock are playing, lie red, brown, and yellow autumn leaves. A few yellowish white mushrooms are sticking up out of the ground. Windfalls: red and pale green apples, half eaten by the birds, rotting. In the background you can see the chicken coop and two of the speckled hens. Sten's red bicycle with child seats at the front and back is just visible on the far side of the chicken coop.

In the right-hand picture Jock and Lisa are sitting on the bench in front of the house and the flowerbed, where a few roses and marigolds are still hanging on, glowing along with the deep red ivy scrambling up the wall. Jock and Lisa are facing each other, one of her hands is resting on his back, level with his shoulder blades. His ears are pointing forward, her eyebrows are raised just a fraction, both of them have their mouths slightly open. It almost looks as if they're singing a duet. It's an amusing picture—and I laughed out loud. Inside me was a different kind of laughter, a kind of huge relief mixed with grief, exploding and bumping at my chest, just inside my breastbone, trying to get out. But it was impossible. I didn't dare let it out. It was too big, this relief, it hurt too much to be set free.

I folded up the piece of paper with the pictures on it, smuggled it back into my pocket, got up, went and turned off the light in the kitchen, then fumbled my way back to the bathroom in the darkness, had a wash and brushed my teeth, crept into the bedroom, got undressed, and slipped under the covers close, so close to Johannes, who was still sighing in his sleep.

I never did find out how it had come about, that business with the photographs—whether Potter had been there, met Lisa and the girl and Jock and taken the pictures himself, or whether Sten and Lisa, or someone else, had sent them to him. I would bump into Potter from time to time in the future, but never had the opportunity to ask him; all I could do was thank him with a nod and a smile for the trouble he had gone to on my behalf. However, judging by the season and by the girl, who had grown since I last saw her, the pictures had been taken recently. And that was all I needed to know.

21

Out in the community it was Christmastime. If you switched on the television or radio or opened a newspaper you were instantly aware of it. There was the sound of bells and there were Advent calendars and news reports of record sales and articles about the stress of it all and commercials for this year's Christmas gifts and tips for Christmas dinner and Donald Duck and dancing around the tree and stories about the Virgin Mary and baby Jesus and the star shining above the stable.

But the unit itself was a blessedly Christmas-free zone. Everything carried on as normal, both before, during and after this holiday, which otherwise swallowed up everything in its path; no glitter, no Advent candles, no Christmas Muzak in the stores, no reduced opening hours at the sports center, no Santa hats on the instructors at Friskis & Svettis and no special gym classes with only Christmas music. The restaurant, art gallery, cinema, theater and stores were open exactly as usual and with no frills; no special Christmas menu, no film matinee for children on December 26, no sales between Christmas and New Year, no New Year celebrations and no Twelfth Night, which would loom up in front of you with a scornful grin just when you thought the whole thing was over for this year.

It was, however, a new year; it was impossible to avoid or ignore that fact; the number at the end of the year changed. Time was passing, inexorably. I would soon be fifty-one. Johannes had just turned sixty-four, which was old for a dispensable person. But he certainly didn't feel old. And I actually felt younger than I had for many years. Presumably it was because I was desired, and because I loved and was loved in return.

My novel was more or less done; I was just putting the finishing touches on it. I read it and made small changes, read it again and made more small changes, didn't really want to let go.

Johannes laughed at me, called me "a mother hen." It was evening. We were lying in bed, naked.

"But don't you get like that too?" I asked. "When you've almost finished something and you know you'll soon have to part from it and start something new?"

"Yes."

"Well then! Why are you laughing at me?" I pinched one of his nipples playfully.

"Because it's fun," he replied, pinching me in return.

"Ouch!" I said.

"That can't have hurt," he said.

"No."

"So why did you say ouch, then?"

"Because it's fun," I replied, and the next second he was on top of me.

Afterward, when we'd fallen asleep, I dreamed the dream about Jock and the stick and the beach, the dream where Jock sometimes turns into Johannes, running toward me in the wind with his arms outstretched as the sea crashes and roars, the dream where Johannes sometimes throws the stick and Jock brings it back and we both praise him, the dream where we get back to my house and Johannes is hanging framed photographs on the walls and I ask him: "What are those photographs?" and he replies: "Can't you see? Those are our children, of course."

It was clearer this time, Johannes's voice was very close, very real, as if we were dreaming the same dream at exactly the same time and the conversation were really taking place, as if we were talking about those photographs in our sleep.

The next day I stopped tinkering with my novel and decided that it was finished now; I burned it onto a CD and put it into a cardboard sleeve with the title of the novel and my name on it. Then I didn't know what to do with it, so I just left it lying on the desk.

And straightaway I started sketching out some ideas for a new story. It was slow going, but that's the way it often is when I start something new: slow, heavy and uncertain, like laboring up a steep hill on a bicycle with a rusty chain that's threatening to break at any moment.

On top of that, I had started to get so tired recently; worn out and dizzy. At first I thought it was because I was involved in another physical training program—something I was very grateful for, of course, because it was far more healthy and pleasant than having to take pills, have injections, or undergo experiments involving different solutions or gases. This time they were measuring muscle volume and the capacity to take in oxygen. After the first preliminary tests on those of us who had been selected to participate, I was told I had the physical fitness of a twenty-year-old. But now, a few weeks into the project, I was feeling weak, sometimes really run down, and I was afraid I wasn't getting enough vitamins and minerals, or that I was dehydrated. I made a real effort to eat better and drink more, but it didn't help.

Then one morning I woke up feeling nauseous, and had to rush to the bathroom. I threw up. After a sandwich and a glass of milk, I felt a little better. I was tired and slightly woozy, but I didn't feel really ill again until the evening. And as before I felt better when I'd eaten, but the next morning I threw up again.

It carried on like this day after day, and it was only after a couple of weeks that one afternoon, after I'd finished my training session, I got the idea of swinging by the hospital and going into the pharmacy to ask for a pregnancy test.

The assistant looked surprised.

"I'll see if we've got any," he said, and disappeared. He was gone for quite a while, but eventually returned with a little box containing a do-it-yourself pregnancy test, complete with instructions.

I went home. Spent the night alone, and in the morning tested my urine. And it was true. However unbelievable it sounds. I really was pregnant. Johannes and I were going to be parents.

I didn't get much done that morning, just wandered around my apartment; into the bedroom, out again, around the dining table and easy chairs, over to the desk, fiddled around on the computer for a while, gave a start when I caught sight of Majken's picture of the deformed fetus, turned my back on it, went into the kitchenette, opened the door of the refrigerator, closed it again, poured myself a glass of water, walked around the dining table again, put down the glass without having drunk any of the water, ambled back into the bedroom and out again. If there had been a window I would have stood by it, to gather my thoughts, to calm myself. But there was no window, so I didn't manage to calm down.

In the afternoon I had physical training as usual, then went home and ate and tried to sleep for a while, which didn't go all that well. I was too overexcited. I was too dizzy, I felt too sick. I was too happy.

As soon as I got through the door of Johannes's apartment that evening I said:

"Now I know why I've been feeling so bad. Or am feeling bad."

"Oh . . . ?" Johannes frowned anxiously, and I almost shouted as I said:

"I'm pregnant! You're going to be a daddy!"

At first he thought I was joking, of course. When he finally realized that my seriousness and agitation were genuine, and that I was telling the truth, he took my hand between both of his and kissed it. Then he kissed me on the forehead and whispered:

"My love."

He held me, my forehead against his collarbone, his cheek against my ear, and he whispered the same words over and over again: "My love. My love."

When he let me go and I looked at his face, his eyes were shining. I interpreted it as a sign that he was moved.

Later, when we had made love and were lying in bed in the darkness, just about to go to sleep, I heard him crying, quiet and suppressed. I turned on my side, stroked his cheek and asked him what the matter was, didn't he feel well? He replied that he was fine, it was just that he was happy.

"I'm crying because I'm so happy," he said.

But he didn't sound happy.

Then I told him about my dream, about him and Jock and me on the beach, and how we went into my house, which in my dream was our house, and how he was hanging pictures of our children on the walls.

"How wonderful," he said. "Such a beautiful dream."

"Now it can become a reality," I said.

In response he put his arms around me and pressed me so tightly against his body that I could hardly breathe.

22

The following afternoon when I arrived at my training session, I was told to go straight to the clinic. I realized it must have something to do with my pregnancy. Naturally both the listening devices and the surveillance cameras would have registered my visit to the pharmacy and my conversation with Johannes the previous evening.

I reported to reception, and was shown into a small office. Dr. Amanda Jonstorp was waiting there along with Petra Runhede, the director of the unit. They were sitting next to each other behind a desk, Amanda in a white coat, Petra in her dark red suit.

"Sit down, Dorrit," said Petra with a friendly but serious expression on her face.

I sat down opposite them.

"It has come to our attention," said Petra, "that you have had a positive result from a pregnancy test."

"Yes, I have," I said.

"You will have to undergo a gynecological examination."

"Of course," I said.

"We might as well get it out of the way right now," said Amanda, getting up with a strained grimace that I assumed was an attempt at a smile—and I suddenly felt uneasy, but not about the examination; I had stopped worrying about gynecological examinations, or finding them embarrassing, a long time ago.

No, it was something else, something to do with Amanda's attempt at a smile and Petra's forced friendliness, it was something about the atmosphere in the room.

"This way," said Amanda, and I followed her into an adjoining room with a gynecology chair in one corner, flanked by a low table with a computer, and a high stainless steel table with medical instruments on it. There was a screen in the opposite corner.

"If you go over there and undress up to the waist, I'll go and fetch the nurse," said Amanda.

I was lying in the chair with my legs up in the stirrups, spread wide apart. Amanda had one hand inside me, pressing the lower part of my stomach with the other hand. She pressed from both sides, very gently—I imagined that she was cupping the fetus in her hands—while muttering words and phrases in Latin to the nurse. Then she removed her hands and said to me:

"Yes, it does appear that you're pregnant. Have you been involved in any experiments with hormones?"

"Not as far as I know," I replied.

"In that case this really is something quite extraordinary, I can tell you. Normally, even if menopause doesn't kick in until around fifty-five, in practice it's impossible to become pregnant beyond the age of forty-five or forty-six."

"I know," I said.

"In normal cases, that is," she added.

"I know," I repeated, wondering how long I would have to lie here in this chair.

"In normal cases," Amanda went on, still standing between my legs, as if she were lecturing my womb, "the body simply stops producing eggs—even if you are still menstruating after forty-five."

"I know that," I said. "Can I get dressed now?"

"Of course. Come next door to see me and Petra when you're ready, then we can have a chat."

They were sitting behind the desk again. I sat down opposite them again. Petra looked me in the eye with her sincere expression.

"Perhaps you can understand that this has come as a shock to us," she began.

"Yes. It's come as a shock to me too." I tried to smile.

"You have . . ." Petra cleared her throat. "You have a choice of two courses of action, Dorrit."

"What? What do you mean, a choice?" I said. "If you think I'm going to have an abortion, you're wrong. I will never kill my child, never!"

One of my friends out in the community had gotten pregnant when she was forty-seven, and an abortion had been recommended to her. Her name was Melinda, and when she told me this she explained that all women who become pregnant after the age of forty, irrespective of whether they already have children or not, are advised to have an abortion, "to cover all eventualities," which isn't that strange when you think about it, since the risk of various deformities and disorders in the child increases with the mother's age, as does the risk of premature birth and other expensive complications. If the man providing the sperm is also older, there is an additional risk that the child could be affected by schizophrenia when it becomes an adult.

These increased risks are actually very small for the individual, percentagewise; Johannes's age, for example, carried with it a 0.5 percent higher risk that our child would become schizophrenic, and the situation was more or less the same with regard to the link between my age and Down syndrome, for example. But the doctors' recommendation to have an abortion is not primarily about the individual. Children who are born prematurely, or with some form of mental handicap, or who develop schizophrenia as adults, cost society enormous sums of money, and if the overall number of defects and complications can be reduced to a minimum, there are significant financial gains to be made. There must be a couple of hundred children per year in total who end up becoming a complete financial loss to society.

Melinda had been informed—in black and white—how much a decision to give birth to her child would cost society if the child had this or that functional impairment. She showed me the calculations, and they certainly told a very clear story; it was a case of tens of thousands of millions in losses—and that was just for one functionally impaired individual from the age of zero to fifty. Melinda was in despair. She said:

"It's not that I want to be a burden on society. Of course I want to be needed in every way, and I want my child to be needed—not to be a drain on the community all its life. Everybody wants to live a life of dignity, don't they? Everybody wants to be respected, and we want our children to be respected too. But I want this child. It's been created, and it's living inside me; there has to be a meaning in that. And irrespective of whether it's born prematurely and might be blind or have some other functional impairment, it's still a child. It's still a person. And we live in a democracy; I do actually have the right to give birth to my child."

But Melinda had had an abortion after all. She already had two healthy children. She was already needed.

But I wasn't. And I was absolutely determined to give birth to my child, to care for it and raise it—regardless of what condition it might be in. I wanted to live as a family with Johannes and the child. I wanted to live a proper life with deep, interwoven relationships for better or worse, which only death could separate. I wanted to feel real, to feel part of things, and to be honest I couldn't give a shit whether it was dignified or respectable or whether it cost the taxpayer a whole lot of money. To hell with the taxpayers! I thought. Just as long as I can have my child, my family, my life! That's why I was immediately on guard with Petra, and why I said that I would never, ever kill my child.

But that wasn't what she meant; abortion wasn't one of the choices I had to make.

"You're not going to have an abortion," said Petra. "At least not until we've taken a sample of the amniotic fluid, which we do have to do, as you will understand. And various other tests— these days it's possible to detect many different defects and difficulties with the child through relatively risk-free tests. Isn't that right, Amanda?"

Amanda nodded. Petra went on:

"And we ought to make the most of that opportunity. In view of your age, I mean."

We, I thought. What we? The only "we" I could see in all this was Johannes and I. But I said nothing, I didn't want Petra, or Amanda either for that matter, to get the impression that I was somehow unbalanced.

Petra now got to the point, and she was talking quickly, as if to get it out of the way as rapidly as possible:

"Your choice is whether to donate the fetus for transplantation, or to carry it to full term and then have it adopted. The latter is of course the safest option, for the child that is, but it might also be the most painful for you, so think it over carefully. Whatever choice you make, you will be allowed to know something about the people who adopt the child, as with any donation, and if you wish I'm sure we can arrange it so that you continue to receive information about how the child is getting on in its family."

My mouth dropped open. I thought: Is she stupid? I sat up straight, cleared my throat, and said, clearly and lucidly:

"You don't understand. I have no intention of giving up this child. It's mine. Mine and Johannes's. We are the child's parents. It is not going to be transplanted or adopted. I mean, we're no longer dispensable, are we? We've become needed."

"No, Dorrit. *Your child* is—at best—needed. *You* are and remain dispensable. And as for Johannes Alby . . ."

She broke off. Stared at me—she looked absolutely terrified, all of a sudden, which confused me. Was she afraid of me? I didn't understand. She took a deep breath and approached the issue from a different angle.

"You must understand," she said pleadingly. "At your age, Dorrit . . . how suitable do you think you would really be as a parent?"

"I can't see that I'd be any less suitable than any other parent. Surely age can also be an advantage? I have considerable experience of life, and self-awareness. I've had my fun, and all trace of youthful egoism and self-obsession is gone. And I'm strong and healthy, mentally as well as physically. Not so long ago I was told I was as fit as a twenty-year-old."

"It's not just about fitness," Petra interrupted.

"I didn't say it was."

Petra now had red patches on her neck—otherwise she was noticeably pale—and she turned to Amanda, as if seeking help.

But Amanda was no help, not to either of us; she sat there in silence, her lips pressed together, looking down at some papers in front of her on the table. Petra turned back to me.

"First of all," she said, "the lifespan of a human being is limited. For many centuries the average lifespan increased, but it has now remained virtually static for several decades. It seems as if we have reached the ceiling when it comes to how long we can live naturally, and the health risks associated with the drugs available to slow down the aging process have so far proved to be far too great for them to be launched on the open market. And secondly . . ."

I interrupted her. "This child will have plenty of time to grow up before either Johannes or I fall off our perch."

Amanda glanced up from her papers and Petra opened her mouth to say something, but I raised my voice and carried on:

"We might not live long enough to see our grandchildren, but we'll damned well have time to fulfill our role as parents. Both of us. Because even if Johannes is thirteen years older than me, he's still as full of life as a thirty-year-old."

By this stage Petra's face was the color of ivory, her mouth a thin, ashen pink line, her neck as red as if someone had poured boiling water over it. I interpreted her expression as a mixture of intense annoyance and the kind of panic that can affect those in a position of power when they feel they are losing their authority. In other words, I thought I had the upper hand in our discussion, and that Petra was losing her grip and was about to collapse in the face of my solid reasoning. She looked pleadingly at Amanda once again, but Amanda looked away again, down at her papers. Petra looked at me. She swallowed, and then she answered me quietly and slowly, as if feeling her way forward:

"But Dorrit. Have you thought about the fact that you—that both of you—would be the same age as the grandparents of the child's friends? There is a significant risk that the child would feel different and would be rejected, perhaps even bullied. Besides which, dispensable parents are hardly a good example for a child."

"There are no dispensable parents, Petra," I said smugly. "That equation doesn't add up."

"The dispensable stamp would remain," she said.

"What stamp? I haven't got a stamp. Can you see a stamp?" I spread my hands wide.

"You wouldn't be good role models," said Petra, her face still as white as a sheet, still speaking quietly, but now with a slight quiver in her voice. "You would . . ."

She seemed to respect me, that was undeniable; she definitely seemed to be in an inferior position. I leaned back in the chair and let her talk for a while. But as she talked without being interrupted, her voice became less shaky and muted, and she gradually regained her composure, became herself again:

"You would—in one way or another—become a burden to your child, Dorrit. Something to . . . be ashamed of. It's true. It is of course extremely . . . praiseworthy that you have both created this child. And if *you* can bring yourself to carry it throughout your pregnancy—provided it goes to full term, that is—then all credit to you. Naturally you will not be expected to go through the process of giving birth. A date will be set for a C-section, when you will be completely anesthetized so that you will not have to see or hear anything. The reserve bank authority will thank you in every possible way you can think of. There will be . . . you will receive certain favors, to put it simply. But—and this is and will remain a very definite 'but'—we cannot allow you to act as a parent. Unfortunately that is completely out of the question. And when it comes to Johannes Alby . . ."

She broke off once again, and this time I reacted.

"What?" I said, slowly sitting up straight in my chair again. "What's going on with Johannes?"

Petra was noticeably nervous. Or was she distressed? Or upset? In an almost breathless voice she said:

"He . . . he hasn't told you, then?"

"Told me what?"

She stared stupidly at me. Stupidly and desperately.

"It's been decided for more than a week," she said.

"What has? What are you talking about?"

By this point I should have understood what she was trying to say—what she had been trying to say all along. I'm not stupid, I should have realized. But there are certain things that, despite the fact that they are looming so clearly in front of you, like enormous waves, are just too overwhelming, too huge, too crushing for us to grasp.

Petra said:

"I . . . I really am sorry that you have to find out this way, Dorrit, but at this stage it's presumably too late for him to . . ."

She broke off again.

"*Out with it, woman!*" I yelled.

Then Amanda Jonstorp looked up from her papers, and after a quick glance at Petra she turned to me, opened her mouth and said:

"What Petra is trying to tell you is that Johannes Alby was taken in this afternoon to donate his liver to a carpenter with three children and six grandchildren. We're very sorry."

23

I ran. I ran along the hallway into the clinic, past one consulting room after another, past nurses, doctors, patients, cleaners and others who stepped aside, shocked. I ran through the waiting room, past reception, tore open the fire exit door—the elevators were too slow—and raced down the spiral staircase. My footsteps echoed in the empty stairwell; the echo bounced off the walls and hammered into my head, where it got mixed up with the echo of those words: *hasn't told you then . . . been decided for more than a week . . . that you have to find out this way . . .* And I ran along another corridor, down another spiral staircase, a third corridor—alongside the swimming pool this time—and a third staircase: round and round and the words went round and round—*too late for him . . . donate his liver . . . carpenter . . . six grandchildren . . . We're very sorry . . .*—and the words and the echo and the stairs made me dizzy, and I staggered out into yet another corridor, down one last winding staircase, out into the culvert on the upper basement level, and finally in through the heavy metal doors of the surgical department.

There I was met—of course I was met, the cameras had been following me, obviously, and Petra had naturally understood where I was heading and had rung down to warn them—by two sturdy young nurses in green scrubs. They blocked my way, forming a human barricade, like the riot police but with masks and protective headgear like shower caps instead of visors and helmets. One took off his mask, revealing a large birthmark on his upper lip. He said:

"It's already happened, Dorrit. Johannes Alby is already on the operating table. We're very sorry."

I stared at him. I stared at his birthmark; it was dark, like dark chocolate, about a quarter of an inch in diameter, and perfectly round. It looked unreal, as if it had been painted on, and in his place I would have had it removed—particularly as he was surrounded at work by surgeons and scalpels. When I had finished staring I tried to force my way through the two-man wall, the living riot shield, by quickly ducking and diving in between the two nurses, but of course I didn't succeed; they were too big, too strong, too well-prepared, and the second one—who hadn't yet had time to take off his mask—grabbed me, gripped my arms firmly behind my back, and held me tightly from behind so that I was forced to lean forward. All I could see were my own legs and shoes and the dingy green floor. I struggled to free myself, but then the grip tightened so that it hurt my upper arms.

His voice was strangely gentle against the back of my neck as he said: "It's already happened, didn't you hear?" As if he was trying to sound calming, as if he was trying to console me—a stark contrast to the police hold he had on me. He carried on, in the same gentle voice:

"There's nothing you can do. The narcotics specialist has already caused his brain to die. Johannes Alby is gone. Clinically dead."

I made a final effort to free myself, but realized that I was only wearing myself out, and gave up. He must have felt in my limbs that I'd given up, because he let me go. I smoothed my shirt and turned to the two men, rubbing my upper arms, and said in as controlled a voice as I could manage:

"I want to see him anyway."

"There's no point," said the one with the gentle voice and the police hold, as he took off his mask to reveal a pointed nose and a pair of thin lips. "He isn't alive," he went on, "even if it looks as though he is. His breathing is being supported by the respirator, his heart is beating and his blood is being oxygenated, but there is no real life there, and you know that perfectly well. He has no perception of anything. He can't hear or feel anything."

"But I can," I said. "Let me see him."

"They're operating right now, they're getting ready to remove the liver, and a team is waiting in a helicopter outside the building to take it. It's impossible for you to go in there now. It's too late. I'm sorry. You need to go back, go home. If you want we can book an emergency appointment with your psychologist. Who do you see?"

"I don't need any psychologist. I need to see Johannes. That's the only thing I need, the only thing I want, and the only thing I'm going to agree to. If I don't get it, I shall kill myself. And I can assure you that I know how I'm going to do it, and it will be so quick and effective that nobody will have time to stop me or save me."

Irrespective of whether they believed my threat or not, I knew it was an argument they had to take notice of. It's just like when the police get information about a bomb threat in a department store, for example; they have to evacuate the building whether or not they believe there really is a bomb. I knew I was valuable as a dispensable person; I was in perfect health, had excellent readings, was very fit, still had almost all my organs, and on top of that I was carrying a child—fresh human capital—beneath my heart. I was, literally, worth my weight in gold. They couldn't afford to risk losing me.

The nurse with the birthmark on his upper lip said:

"Perhaps we might be able to arrange it. It's possible they might agree to let you in for a short while when they've finished with the liver."

"But then they're going to take . . ." began the one with the police hold.

"Yes, but there's no real hurry with that," interrupted Birthmark. "Most of it's only going into the banks anyway."

The banks, that's where they keep the organs and tissues that can be preserved; the other parts of Johannes's body were going to be kept there, the parts they always take if they are medically viable: some of the remaining vital organs plus corneas, cardiac valves, bone and other tissue. Everything that can be used is removed and placed in a nutritional fluid or deep frozen and preserved. It's purely routine, and naturally applies also to needed individuals who are brain-dead as a result of accidents or violent crimes.

The nurses showed me to a small break room, closed the door behind me and tried the handle from the outside, presumably to make sure it was locked.

The room was furnished with a bed, a chair and a desk. And it had a window. Yes, a window, a real one. A real window looking out over a park. There was snow in the park. It was winter. There was a frozen pond with a gap in the ice in the middle, with ducks, grebes and other waterfowl walking to and fro, taking a quick dip like winter swimmers. The pond was partly surrounded by bushes and tall trees, the snow lying on the bushes like little caps, and like a soft, shimmering mattress on the ground. A gust of wind shook the treetops, and the snow drifted from the branches like sifted powdered sugar.

Something didn't add up; I was on level K1. In the basement. But now it turned out that this upper basement level was above ground. There was no doubt that this was a real window and a real view—when I went right up close I could feel the draft through the gaps, a draft that was cold and smelled of winter. In a pure reflex action I grabbed hold of the handles on the window and tried to lift it upward, but it was locked, and I let my arm drop and remained standing there, upright, gazing out at this whiteness, this reality. This outdoor space.

In the end I managed to tear myself away from the window and allowed my eyes to travel slowly over the walls, the ceiling, the corners, the furniture, the light, and it was as I'd thought: no cameras. At least I couldn't see any. Unless they were as tiny as the head of a pin, there were no cameras. Clearly the two nurses were more afraid that I would run amok in the operating room than that I would kill myself, despite everything.

Birthmark came back.

"That's fine," he said. "But it'll be about another hour, and you'll have to wait in here. And we've been ordered to lock the door. I hope you understand."

I nodded.

"Would you like anything while you're waiting? Coffee? Tea? A sandwich?"

"No."

He had backed out and was about to close the door when I changed my mind.

"Actually, yes. One of those application forms, you know the ones."

"What kind of application form?"

"One of those you fill in when you want to make a final donation as soon as possible."

An expression of dismay appeared on Birthmark's face.

"Are you sure?" he said. "You're . . . you're expecting a child, aren't you?"

I didn't reply, just gave him a long stare. He looked away, slightly embarrassed I thought; he looked as if he felt stupid.

He went away, came back with an application form, and left me alone once again. I sat down at the desk. The first question was:

1.

This application comprises

☐ A. a request to be moved to another section. (Proceed to question 2)
☐ B. a request to be moved to another unit. (Proceed to question 5)
☐ C. a request to make a final donation. (Proceed to question 8)
☐ D. a request for postponement of a final donation (Proceed to question 9)

I ticked box C and went on to question 8, where I ticked box A:

8.

I wish my final donation to be carried out

☐ A. as soon as possible
☐ B. with effect from this date: year _____, month _____, day_____.

Right at the bottom on the other side of the form, under "Further information," I wrote: *I am six weeks pregnant. Request transplantation/abortion of fetus to be carried out in conjunction with final donation.*

Then I signed my name, wrote my ID number and the date, then turned my chair to the window. While I was waiting I looked at the pond, the trees, the snow, the birds. Watched a male wild duck as he emerged from the water, shook himself so that the droplets of water formed a ring around him, then began to waddle across the ice, up over the uneven and obviously slippery bank where he stumbled and slid several times before he managed to get up onto the flat, snow-covered ground where he stopped for a few seconds, as if to catch his breath. Then he waddled off across the snow on his orange duck's feet which seemed to work extremely well as snow shoes, because he didn't break the surface once, not until he began to run, clumsy and without any real rhythm, as he flapped his wings, flapped and flapped, and took off. He flew in a wide, shimmering green arc above the pond, then in among the trees where he disappeared from view.

24

Johannes was breathing. Or to be more accurate: the respirator was breathing for him. The respirator was an air pump with a thick plastic tube going into a mask that covered half his face. The respirator hissed and clicked and sucked, hissed and clicked and sucked, at regular intervals. Meanwhile the heart frequency wrote its monotonous message on a monitor next to the respirator, accompanied by a mechanical beep, also at regular intervals.

I was sitting next to the operating table on a high stool, wearing a protective lab coat, plastic gloves, a hairnet, and a mask. Most of Johannes's body was covered with green surgical sheets, with only his head, neck, shoulders and arms visible. His skin had a yellowish tone. From beneath the covers snaked various tubes containing different-colored fluids, attached to different machines.

There was another tube running between a needle inserted into the back of one hand and a drip behind the headboard.

I ignored the instructions I'd been given, took off the plastic gloves and placed one hand cautiously on the green sheet above the left side of his chest. His heart was beating as usual. Exactly as usual, just a little more evenly, the rhythm as steady as a drumbeat, and it was not affected by either my presence or my touch; no increased pulse rate, no surprised or happy double beat, no short, breathless pauses. Just this sucking noise followed by the hissing, the clicking, and the monotonous little beep.

I wished I had lived at the time when people still believed in the heart. When people still believed that the heart was the central organ, containing all the memories, emotions, capabilities, defects and other qualities that make us into specific individuals. I longed to go back to an age of ignorance, before the heart lost its status and was reduced to just one of a number of vital but replaceable organs.

The fact that Johannes's heart was beating, that I could feel the warmth of his body and a steady pulse against my hand meant nothing more than that the blood was being pumped around the body that had been his. He was alive, but he no longer existed. And yet I leaned over, took off my mask and whispered in his ear:

"Why? Why didn't you say anything? Why did you say you were happy? Why didn't you let me grieve with you? While we still had the chance."

I got no reply, of course. I straightened up, slid my hand up from the covered chest to his bare shoulder and the area around his collarbone. The skin was so warm, and the throbbing veins beneath made it feel so alive that for a fraction of a second I expected him to raise one hand and stroke my cheek gently, consoling me, just as he had done that first evening at the welcome party, exactly a year ago. I closed my eyes, caressed the length of his upper arm and lower arm, ran my fingers through the coarse hairs there and on the back of his hand, grasped his hand between both of mine. It was limp and heavy, but otherwise it felt just the way it always did: broad and rough, like that of a person who did physical labor, but with long, sensitive fingers—dream fingers for a pianist, or why not a surgeon. I turned the hand over, touched its cupped shape: the deep lines in the palm, the smooth calluses on the surfaces of the otherwise soft cushions at the base of the fingers—the hand's equivalent of pads. With my fingertips I felt his fingertips, which had so often and so passionately touched the most sensitive parts of my body. Then I bent over his palm and kissed it. As I did so I felt—close, so close—the scent of his skin, his body. I drew that scent into my body.

"Dorrit . . ." The voice made me jump and open my eyes; I hadn't heard anyone come into the room.

I straightened up immediately, let go of Johannes's hand and turned in the direction of the voice. It was Birthmark.

"I'm sorry," he said. "But the team needs to carry on. You'll have to . . ."

"Yes," I said. "I know." And without either looking at or touching Johannes's body again I slipped down from the stool and followed Birthmark out.

Outside the operating room he stopped, turned to me and looked at me with the same sincere expression that Petra Runhede favored.

"What is it?" I asked crossly.

"You're very pale," he said. "You look completely worn out. You look as if you need to talk to somebody about what you've just been through."

I didn't feel at all worn out, oddly enough. But life had taught me that reactions after traumatic experiences are sometimes delayed, and perhaps Birthmark could see something reflected in my face that I was not yet aware of. However, I had no desire whatsoever to talk to someone right then, particularly as I suspected he meant that the someone should be him. Because what could someone like him do for someone like me in a situation like this?

As if I had spoken out loud, he said:

"As you are perhaps aware, all unit staff are trained in trauma management. Let's go back to the break room."

I didn't know that, in fact, but said nothing, merely shrugged my shoulders and allowed myself to be escorted back to the little room with the view over the park.

The light had altered slightly outside. A bluish twilight was falling slowly over the whiteness.

"Sit down," said Birthmark, closing the door then checking the handle to make sure it was locked. I presumed this was a reflex action, just like when I had tried the window.

I sat down on the chair, he sat on the bed. I threw him a venomous look—at least I hoped it was venomous—and wondered whether I should tell him that the birthmark on his upper lip did nothing for him at all, that he would be doing himself—and those around him—a favor if he had it removed.

He smiled, a serious smile, then said:

"Don't worry, Dorrit. I have no intention of trying to get you to talk to me about your feelings and experiences. I just wanted to get away from cameras and microphones—this room is a free zone, where the staff can come to relax, knowing that nobody is sitting and studying what we do and what we say. The reason I wanted to come in here with you was to give you this."

Out of a pocket in his short green jacket he took a small plastic card, which he handed over to me. It had the unit's logo on the front and a black magnetic strip on the back. It looked like a credit or debit card.

"What am I supposed to do with this?" I asked.

"I . . ." he began, but then he stopped, looked away, out of the window—a streetlamp was just coming on out there, and an orange glow blended with the ever-deepening blue twilight. He cleared his throat, started again:

"I presume that you, like other dispensable individuals, have already lost everything once. And now it's happening to you again. And I feel . . . well, I can't just stand and watch. Yes, you are dispensable, and no doubt you could have avoided that situation if you had just made enough of an effort. But you're also a human being. And now you've succeeded in getting pregnant as well, and if that had happened just a year ago you wouldn't even have ended up in here. And whatever happens, you ought to have the right, in the name of democracy, to your own offspring—both you and Johannes Alby ought to have had that right."

Birthmark paused, cleared his throat.

"This," he went on, pointing to the plastic card in my hand, "is a key card. It opens all staff areas and all the rooms and areas that are locked to residents at night. And above all, it opens all exits."

What exits? was my first thought. I stared at the card. The idea of trying to get out, away, escape from here had never crossed my mind. Not even during the very early days when I had missed Jock so much, not even a couple of hours ago when I had tugged at the window, not even when I discovered shortly afterward that the room had no cameras, not even when I watched the wild duck flying away through the trees. Not even when I had felt Johannes's pulse and at the same time realized that he no longer existed.

Birthmark continued:

"I didn't send your application form through the internal post. Instead I actually took the liberty of putting it in the shredder. To give you time. Time to think this over. You can always fill out a new one; it's never too late. But if you don't, and instead agree to give birth to the child so that it can be adopted, then you will have seven or eight months with no experiments or any kind of interference that would put your health or that of your child at risk. And during that time you can think things over, you can plan an escape, and you can carry it out."

He paused again, as if to give me the chance to say something. But I didn't know what to say; I only knew what I absolutely must

not say, which was that he ought to have that unnaturally perfect birthmark removed. After a silence he said:

"The card is personal. It's a duplicate of my own key card.
When, or if—it's your decision, of course, I only want to give
you the chance—when or if you use the card, then you swipe it
through the reader at the edge of the doors in question. This
one, for example."

He got up from the bed, took the card from me, went over to
the door and swiped the card through a reader mounted in the
edge of the door frame, so discreetly placed that you would never
have noticed it if you didn't know exactly what you were looking for and where to look. A small opening in the door frame
silently appeared, revealing a keypad. Birthmark punched in a
code at lightning speed, and the door gave a barely audible *click*.
He pushed down the door handle, opened the door an inch or
so and immediately closed it again. He walked over to the bed
and gave the card back to me.

"Right," I said. "So where do I find these doors, then? I've
never seen any—apart from this one just now. And how do I know
which of them are exits and which just lead to staff areas?"

"All the doors of this kind in the large communal areas, for
example the square and the Atrium Walkway and the big party
room, lead to stairwells. In these stairwells are identical doors
leading to break rooms, staff rooms, changing rooms, washing
facilities and so on. Those you need to avoid, obviously. All you
have to do is take the staircase down to the main door. And you
haven't seen these doors because you've never looked for ways
out, have you? You've never looked for escape routes, never even
given it a thought. You've never had the motivation."

I gave an embarrassed snort and muttered:

"Are you a mind reader or something?"

"No, I'm not a mind reader. But I've done my training and I
know what psychological methods and power games they use to
control the dispensable residents. I know how it works, how they

make sure you have no motivation to escape. But if you do manage to get motivated, if you really do want to survive, then you will find those exit doors. I know it sounds crazy, but that's just how the human psyche works: we generally see what we are prepared for, what we expect to see."

"But what then?" I said. "If I do decide I want to survive and I manage to get out without being discovered. Where do you imagine I could go? Without money. Without anywhere to live. Without friends. How would I manage? Where would I give birth to my child? How would I support it?"

"I don't know," said Birthmark. "But you'll think of something. If you have the courage and strength to get out of here, then I'm sure you also have the courage and strength to do what's necessary for yourself and your child once you're out. You're strong. I know you'll cope."

I'd heard that before; I'd heard it until I was completely sick of it. People had often told me I was strong, and I regarded it as something dismissive rather than a compliment—or whatever it was meant to be. Because I knew, and I know, that there are no strong people. All people are weak. Some are certainly more independent than others, but that doesn't mean they're strong.

But strong or not: I was holding a key in my hand, and, I thought, perhaps it will act as a substitute for strength.

We were silent for a long time, both Birthmark and I. The room grew dark, at least as dark as it can be in a room with snow and streetlamps glowing outside. I could still see Birthmark's face. I could still see his birthmark.

"The code," he said at last, "is 98 44. I want you to memorize it, don't write it down anywhere, don't tell anyone about it. Don't tell anyone about this conversation either. Ever. Whatever you decide to do, or not do. Wherever you end up in the world."

I nodded to show that I had understood, then said perfectly calmly:

"I don't know what to say. You're taking an enormous risk, perhaps even putting yourself in danger. What if I happen to drop the card? What if I'm suddenly taken ill or have an accident and they have to cut my clothes off and they spot the card? It wouldn't take many minutes to trace it back to you. And then you'd be up shit's creek."

"Yes, I would," he admitted. "That's one of the reasons why I'm begging you to be careful. It's for my sake as well as yours. Learn the code by heart. Never take the card out so it's exposed to the cameras, and never take it out or look at it in a way that could make anyone curious or suspicious. Be silent, quick, and discreet. If anything beyond your control should happen, well, that's the way it is, that's fate. I would never blame you for that."

I fingered the card, turning it this way and that. Then I pushed it into my pocket.

"Did you say 98 44?" I asked.

"Yep!" he said with a smile. "And if you forget the code . . ."

"I won't," I said.

"Good," said Birthmark. "Now go home and rest. And by the way—my condolences on your loss."

This last comment was made with a different sort of sincere tone than the professional one, a tone of voice that sounded genuinely honest.

Together we left the break room; the cold neon light in the supposedly underground corridor stabbed at my eyes. Shooting pain seared up into my head, and my eyes began to run. Dazzled and with tears in my eyes I thanked Birthmark for the helpful conversation he had found the time to have with me. Then I left the surgical department, my eyes still running, came out into the green culvert, took the first elevator up to the Atrium Walkway, then changed to elevator H.

When I reached H3 I hurried through the lounge to my apartment, into the bedroom, where I sank down on the bed, my cheek against the pillow, my legs drawn up in the fetal position, my arms around my knees. Eyes tight shut.

25

When I woke up it was because I was freezing. I was so cold I was shaking. It was night, the clock on the bedside table showed 2:18. I got up and felt the radiator; it was warm, almost hot. I went over to the other end of the room where there was a thermometer hanging on the wall. It was showing seventy-five degrees; so the fact that I was freezing had absolutely nothing to do with the temperature in the room.

This is the delayed reaction, I thought—and was amazed at how the human brain works: you can be at the mercy of your emotions to the extent that your teeth are literally chattering, while at the same time in another part of your brain you can calmly work out "here comes the delayed reaction." And as if that weren't enough, you can sit there being amazed at how the brain works.

I had fallen asleep with my clothes on; I put my robe on over my clothes, turned up the collar and pulled it tightly around my body, knotting the belt around my waist. But that wasn't enough, I was still frozen, I was so cold I felt sick. Shivering, I pulled out a chair and placed it in front of the closet, climbed up and opened the cabinet above the closet, took out my old peacoat—100 percent wool—and put that on as well. Then I went into the living room and through to the kitchenette to make myself a cup of tea with warm milk and honey.

I curled up on the sofa, my hands wrapped around the warm mug. I sat cross-legged, with a blanket over my legs. The steaming drink smelled of bergamot and milk, and I raised the mug to my lips, taking big, deep gulps as I gazed at my blurred gray-green reflection in the blank television screen. I looked like an apparition. Or like an old American Indian. I thought I looked like the ghost of Sitting Bull in the lotus position.

I didn't get any more sleep that night. It turned into a kind of vigil, but without a body to watch over, during which I did nothing and thought nothing—I didn't even think about Johannes, or about our child, growing in my stomach, or about the key card in my pocket. I just sat there and drank my tea, and when I'd finished it I sat there with the empty mug in my hands.

Gradually I became aware that the room had grown light. The clock on the DVD player showed six, then seven, then eight, then nine. Just after nine I heard a series of loud rapping noises; I jumped, looked around me. What the hell is he doing? I thought.

"What are you doing, Johannes?" I asked. But when three more loud knocks echoed through the room I understood someone was knocking on the door, and I remembered that I had spent the night alone, that Johannes wasn't there, and I realized that despite everything I had been in a kind of slumber with my eyes open, somewhere on the shifting border between sleep and wakefulness. I realized that and yet I believed, for a fraction of a second, that since Johannes wasn't there with me then it must be him knocking on the door, wanting to come in to say good morning. But as I said, that was only for a fraction of a second, the idea simply flickered through my mind, and then I was right back in reality, where Johannes no longer existed, and I tried to get up, but it was as if the lower half of my body had suddenly become incredibly large and heavy, and I had to gather myself and drag myself off the sofa as the knocking started again, louder this time, and in three series of three knocks each, and when I at last got to my feet I felt dizzy and had to lean over and support myself on the coffee table for several seconds, black dots spinning before my eyes. And the knocking went on and on, nonstop, six, seven, eight, nine impatient knocks.

"I'm coming!" I shouted, then finally managed to straighten up, shrug off the peacoat, which now felt clumsy, and open the door.

Outside stood Petra Runhede, her head tilted slightly to one side, gazing sympathetically into my eyes as she said, her voice respectfully muted:

"*May* I come in?"

At this point three things happened simultaneously. The first was that I took a step to one side to allow Petra to go past me into the apartment. The second was that my emotions woke up, just as I took that step to one side they woke up, and they woke up like a cat, going from a deep sleep to full awareness in no time at all, and the emotion I felt was a searing hatred toward this polite woman with her artificial intimacy, her professional empathy. And at the precise moment when I took a step to one side and my hatred came to life, nausea welled up inside me, like a volcano.

"Excuse me," I managed to blurt out before I rushed into the bathroom with my hand to my mouth, slammed the door and lifted the toilet seat. And with the vomiting came the crying, a howling, gulping sobbing that hurt my throat and filled my nose.

I stood there for a good while, bent over the toilet bowl with tears and snot pouring out of the orifices in my face and cold sweat pouring out of all the pores in my skin.

When it was all over, I blew my nose several times. Flushed the toilet. Got to my feet with difficulty; I had a new kind of soreness in my lower back, stiff and yet porous at the same time, as if I were crumbling just there at the base of my spine, and I had to hold onto myself, press one hand against my back as I grabbed hold of the sink with the other and pulled myself to my feet. Then I turned on the cold water, washed my hands, cupping them under the stream, leaned forward cautiously, bathed my face with the cold water, lapped at the water, rinsed my mouth. Then I straightened up once more, panting with pain and with one hand pressed to my back again, and brushed my teeth, but very quickly and only at the front of my mouth so that I wouldn't risk making myself gag again when the toothbrush went farther in. I spat and rinsed quickly, turned off the faucet, dried my mouth and face with a towel. I stood there, contemplating my reflection above the sink: my skin grayish white, eyes red-rimmed and bloodshot, nose swollen, cheeks puffy, hair standing on end, clothes creased and sweaty beneath the dressing gown, which had fallen open. I smoothed down my hair and ran my hands over my clothes in a vain attempt to smooth them down as well. As my hand passed over the right-hand pocket of my pants I felt the rectangular key card through the fabric and I thought, There it is, there's my secret. I didn't think, There's my way out, my ticket to freedom, to survival, to a life with my child; I just thought, There's my secret. Then I pulled my dressing gown around me and knotted the belt at my waist.

Petra had made coffee and two cheese sandwiches. I sat down at the table and allowed her to pour me coffee and place the plate of sandwiches in front of me.

"Do you mind if I sit down opposite you?" she asked, almost submissively, and I had the urge to answer yes, I do mind, you can go out into the hallway and wait there until I call you and then you can come in and clear the table and wash the dishes and then you can discreetly disappear again. But of course I didn't say that, I just shook my head and made a feeble gesture toward the chair on the other side of the table. She pulled out the chair and sat down on it, sat there without saying anything for a long time, while I drank the coffee and took small bites from one of the sandwiches and chewed slowly.

My newly awakened hatred was now under control. It was lying beneath the surface, awake but resting. It had woken like a cat and it was resting like a cat: with its eyes half closed and its ears acting like periscopes, picking up the slightest movement, the slightest hiss, whisper or sigh.

When I had slowly forced one of the sandwiches down, Petra cleared her throat. I ignored her, looking down into my coffee cup before picking it up and drinking the last drops.

"Dorrit," she said in that quiet, intimate voice that was her signature. "I am sorry. Really. I'm sorry about everything."

"Everything?" I glanced at her, skeptically, before putting the cup down.

"Everything you're going through," she clarified. "And everything you've *been* through. I think that those of you who are dispensable are often subjected to an unnecessary amount of suffering. You're not criminals, after all, you haven't done any harm to anyone or anything. You have simply lived your lives, without thinking too much about the future or the world around you, it has to be said, but on the other hand you have often lived on very little money and for the most part you haven't made a great deal of fuss. Presumably you all had neighbors who didn't even notice you existed, and very few of you have actually been a burden to society—I know you haven't. And you have all lived in a headwind, a social headwind. Then you end up here, and things are often really good during the time you have . . ."

She broke off.

". . . left," I supplied, whereupon a dark red flush flooded her face. She cleared her throat again and went on:

"But sometimes some of you are struck by tragedies. Like what you're going through now. I wish you didn't have to suffer like this. I wish there was another solution. That there could be a different policy, one less driven by economic considerations, one that was a little . . ."—she fell silent, leaned across the table, glanced covertly at me, then went on in a quiet voice—". . . one that was more of a *planned economy*, in fact."

I raised my eyebrows. What in the world was she talking about? What was she up to?

She stopped talking. The flush was still visible on her cheeks, just a little more faint than when it had appeared, and there was something glassy about her eyes, a kind of feverish eagerness, as if she were sharing secret desires with me, forbidden values.

But there are no forbidden values. Anyone who lives in a democracy has the right to wish for whatever they want, and to express any views and feelings whatsoever, as long as these do not offend, threaten or persecute. And if there did perchance happen to be any limitation to this right, then Petra, director of the Second Reserve Bank Unit for Biological Material, would hardly have been sitting there expressing her views in my bugged room. Besides which I knew perfectly well, from my own experience, how sensitive the microphones were and how crystal clear the sound quality was. But Petra obviously wasn't aware that I knew, because she went on, in a whisper now:

"I would like to see a more . . . socialist-oriented policy, one where not everyone has to be profitable all the time."

She really was very good. I didn't understand what she was trying to achieve with all this, but she was certainly good. If it hadn't been for the surveillance and for the fact that she was the director of the unit, I'm sure I would have believed her. But as I didn't, I said:

"Stop talking crap, Petra. Tell me why you're here."

She gave me a hurt look, then replied in her submissive voice:

"I just wanted to see how you were."

"Right. Thank you so much."

"And to let you know that you're being given a week's sick leave."

"Very kind of you," I said.

"And then I thought I'd take the opportunity to ask you to decide—when you feel up to it—what you're going to do. How you want things to be. Whether you . . ."—she cleared her throat again—". . . whether you want to donate the fetus or carry it to full term and—"

"I intend to give birth to my child," I interrupted her.

She laughed out loud, relieved, and said that was fantastic, before adding:

"Then I'll let Amanda Jonstorp know. You'll have a series of regular checks and ultrasound scans and amniotic fluid samples and all the other tests. And when—or if—we know that every-thing is as it should be with the child, you can decide on a suit-able time for a C-section. And I'll get in touch with the Adoption Commission. I can tell you, Dorrit, that in cases like this—which are very rare, for obvious reasons—the adoptive parents are more or less handpicked. There will be very, very thorough investiga-tions before they decide who will be considered as parents for the child you are carrying."

"Surely that's always the case," I said, and it was more of a statement than a question, because I knew perfectly well how thoroughly those who applied for permission to adopt were in-vestigated. On those occasions when I myself had applied I had been rejected for a whole range of reasons, from my low and uncertain income to the lack of suitable male role models in my social network. The last time I had applied I had also been deemed too old.

It struck me now that if I had been granted permission to adopt and had managed to scrape together the necessary funds for all the fees and possible journeys involved, then I might well have ended up with a child that a dispensable woman had given birth to and been forced to give up.

Petra didn't reply to my question, which was more of a statement, but placed her hands on her knees and made a move to get up. But then she stopped:

"By the way. Is there anything I can do for you, Dorrit? Is there anything you need?"

"Yes," I replied, and I was surprised at my own quick thinking. "If they haven't already emptied Johannes's room, I'd like access to it before they do. There are things in there that belong to me."

This was only an excuse, of course; in fact I just wanted to be there for a while, alone, and Petra seemed to understand that, because she said:

"I'll arrange it. I'll also make sure the surveillance unit doesn't monitor Johannes's apartment while you're there."

"Why?" I said.

She sighed mournfully. "Because in my opinion you have the right to be completely on your own for a while."

What did she want? Either she was expecting me to return the favor somehow, or she thought I would be eternally grateful and thus particularly cooperative and pliant. Or she really did have a bad conscience, felt genuinely guilty about her part in this whole luxury slaughterhouse—which was one of Elsa's descriptions of the place.

And I suppose Petra was only a human being after all. She probably had children of her own and a man or woman of her own with whom she shared the children. Or perhaps she'd also lost a partner at some point—perhaps she'd lost the man or woman she shared her children with. Or perhaps she'd actually lost a child.

I never found out how things stood in that respect, I didn't ask, of course, and actually I didn't want to know what her reasons or motives were, but I was very keen to keep my distance from this undoubtedly very gifted individual. She obviously had considerable talent as an actress—even if she overplayed things slightly sometimes; she could have done with honing her exaggerated sincerity and her sympathy—perhaps she was a former wannabe actress who had chosen security and normality over her youthful dream. Such people are, in my experience, rarely entirely kindly disposed toward those who have chosen to follow their youthful dream—like me. They despise our almost childish sensitivity, still intact after all these years, and our unwillingness—or inability—to compromise and fit in. They call us bohemians, oddballs, aliens or divas. They envy those of us who achieve some success, and rub their hands with glee when they see the rest slowly going under.

No, I had no desire whatsoever to get close to Petra, to ask personal questions or even to pretend to believe that her goodwill was genuine. I said:

"There is absolutely no need to switch off the surveillance cameras, from my point of view; it would give me no pleasure whatsoever. I have no intention of doing anything that would be better unseen or unheard. And in any case I have no way of checking whether the surveillance is switched off or not, so it makes no difference."

But she didn't give up:

"Irrespective of what you believe or think or feel might give you pleasure, I will personally ensure that the apartment is blocked to the cameras between . . ."

She looked at her watch, then glanced up at me:

"Is two hours enough?"

I shrugged my shoulders.

"Let's say three," she said. "Shall we say between one and four this afternoon?"

I nodded.

"Okay, so you have free access to room 3, section F2 between thirteen hundred hours and sixteen hundred hours today."

"Thank you," I said.

"During that time the surveillance will be switched off."

"Whatever you say," I said.

She got up and came around the table on her way to the door. As she was passing me, she stopped and pressed her hand lightly on my shoulder.

"And let me know," she said, "if there's anything else I can do for you."

Then she removed her hand and left.

26

The only sound was a faint humming from the air-conditioning. No sounds penetrated from outside, the silence was compact— like in a padded cell, where any risk of an echo or other sound effects has been removed. I had never experienced this kind of silence in Johannes's apartment before—or any other apartment in the unit, for that matter.

I had closed the door behind me, turned the bolt, and was now standing with my back to the door, looking at Johannes's living room and the wall he had built around his kitchenette. If I had placed my hands on my back I would have touched the door, I was standing so close to it. You might have thought I was afraid of something in the room, you might have thought I was afraid to go in, that I was unsure whether I really wanted to be there, or whether I ought to be there. But it wasn't that. I wasn't afraid, or uncertain, just slow; perhaps it was the stillness in the room that was making me that way.

On the dining table stood two empty coffee mugs, a bread basket containing a forgotten slice of whole-grain bread, and two plates with crumbs; one of the plates had on it a half-eaten sandwich with a shiny slice of cheese, the edges turning upward. The remains of yesterday's breakfast. The half-sandwich was mine; I had been hungry, much hungrier than I usually was in the mornings—perhaps it was the knowledge of the child in my stomach that made me suddenly think I needed to eat more than usual. But when I started my third sandwich I had realized I couldn't finish it.

"Do you want half of this?" I'd asked.

Johannes had shaken his head and said:

"No thanks, darling, I'm full."

Then he had sat there looking at me for a long time, his expression serious. In the end I had laughed out loud and asked:

"What's the matter? Do I look funny?"

"Not in the least. You look more beautiful than I've ever seen you."

When we left the table and I was leaving to go back to my room to work, we had hugged exactly as we always did, and I had said:

"See you tonight."

And he had said:

"I love you, Dorrit. I love *both of you*," and he had placed one hand on my stomach and I had replied that I loved him more than I had ever loved anyone, which was true.

And he had kissed me and stroked my hair and whispered:

"You have given my life a meaning, do you know that? The meaning of my life is you."

All morning he had been a little more serious than usual, a little less flirtatious, slightly less playful and naughty. But then he had just found out he was going to be a parent, and it wasn't unusual for him to say serious, loving things to me—for *us* to say serious and loving things to each other—when we went our separate ways after breakfast. So how was I to know that this talk of the meaning of life was his way of saying good-bye?

Was it cowardly of him not to say anything? Or was it thoughtful? I don't know. I only know that whether he was cowardly or thoughtful or both, he did it out of love.

How long I stood there just inside the door I don't know, but when I finally began to move I was stiff, and my legs felt numb and swollen, just like when I was really young and I was at high school and worked in the book department of a big store in my spare time, or later on when I wasn't quite so young and I supported myself by posing as a life model for art classes, standing still for twenty minutes at a time with a five-minute break, day in and day out for several weeks sometimes; I would feel numb and swollen just as I did now, and in this state I moved through the room, over to Johannes's desk, where I found a CD in a clear plastic case beside the computer. *Blue Whale*, Johannes had printed on the disk with a black marker pen. His collection of short stories. I left it where it was, I didn't even touch it; partly because I had already read it, partly because I was quite sure that the work of dispensable authors was well looked after by the unit staff who, unlike us, had contact with the outside world. During the past year I had read a small number of new books written by "unusually driven authors making their debut," who later turned out to be authors who were, or had been, here in the unit.

Between the computer and the printer lay all kinds of things that are typically found on a desk: pens, an eraser, a ruler, paper clips, and Post-it notes in different colors and sizes. Among these bits and pieces lay the pink fossil stone. I picked it up and weighed it in my hand, closing my fingers around it. It was cool and smooth and had a distinct weight, without actually being heavy.

In the bedroom the bed was unmade. I had always slept on the inside, next to the wall, when I spent the night with Johannes. Now I lay down on the outside, in his place, and drew the duvet up to my chin. The scent of him was here, acrid and subtle at the same time, like nutmeg or cumin, and on the pillow where his head had rested lay odd white hairs that had been his.

I lay on my side, inhaled the scent and clutched the fossil stone in my hand.

If he had driven to the south coast on a different afternoon, I thought. If he had driven there on one of those afternoons when I was there with Jock during the autumn and winter, instead of one of the days when I wasn't there. And if we had walked toward each other and caught sight of each other, and I had thought, Oh look, there's Johannes Alby, and he'd thought, Oh look, there's Dorrit Weger with her little dog. And if we had stopped and chatted, and if I had invited him back to my house for a cup of coffee or a bowl of soup or some pasta. If it had started like that. If it had started then.

PART 3

1

The aroma of chervil and freshly baked bread hit me as Vivi opened the door. I was late. I had hesitated for quite some time before I had actually walked out of my apartment and taken the few steps down the hall to Vivi's door and knocked.

I had been feeling so tired. I had been so tired for so long, I just hadn't had the strength to socialize, to turn up at parties or dinners or other gatherings where you were expected to have fun, to be interested in other people and to talk to more than one person at a time. I had withdrawn, been passive, at times even apathetic, and I would probably have cut myself off completely if it hadn't been for Elsa, Alice, Vivi and Lena. They had been there the whole time. During the first weeks after Johannes's final donation they had even taken turns to stay the night with me.

Every time I woke up because I was upset or angry or felt sick or whatever, there was someone there to support and console and fetch water and make tea and listen and hold my hand until I went back to sleep.

But they were there afterward as well, after those first few days when I was presumably in shock. Quiet. In the background. On standby. And they were here whenever I needed them—or needed anyone at all—to talk to, or just to have around. And they did it without asking anything of me, without expecting me to be grateful or even pleasant. This had gone on for over two months.

When Vivi finally said one day that she was thinking of inviting some friends to dinner, and then, very cautiously, added: "It would be really lovely if you came too, Dorrit," I felt that yes, perhaps I ought to try. And after a lot of dillydallying, here I was.

"You came!" said Vivi, taking my hand and pulling me in—as if she was afraid my courage would fail at the last minute, and I would run away if she didn't grab hold of me and give me a helping hand.

She led me over to the table where the other guests were already seated and were just helping themselves to newly baked whole-grain bread and a steaming carrot soup with fresh chervil, because they had just given up on the idea that I might turn up. There was Elsa, Alice and Lena, and two people I'd never seen before. Vivi introduced them to me and we shook hands. They were called Görel and Mats.

Mats had arrived last month, Görel just a week ago, and she still had that expression newcomers always wear: horror and grief and rage—or whatever it might be. The fear of death, perhaps.

I sat down between Alice and Elsa, who hugged me from their respective sides. Alice took the opportunity to plant a noisy kiss on my cheek, and everyone laughed. When I turned and looked at her up close for the first time in ages, I noticed that she had changed. The coarseness of her facial features had been replaced by a kind of fragility, to a certain extent. She looked

soft in a way I had never seen her look before. I thought perhaps the male hormones were finally beginning to leave her
body. But she looked so tired as well, slightly hollow-eyed,
slightly haggard. But then who isn't haggard? I said to myself,
pushing aside the stirrings of a sense of unease, and helped
myself to the carrot soup.

During dinner the conversation moved through a range of
topics. I didn't take much part in it, I just sat there listening most
of the time. Eventually they started talking about the outside
world. The community. Things were changing out there. The
number of childless fifty-year-old women and sixty-year-old men
was dwindling significantly, and dispensable individuals were
now being taken from professions that had previously been completely protected. It no longer mattered if you were a school-
teacher or a day care teacher or a welfare officer or a nurse or
any other profession that involved caring for people; not even
midwives were given a dispensation now; if you were childless,
you were childless, end of story.

"And as if that weren't enough," said Mats, "there's talk of
reducing the age limit. People are really stressed out. Kids are
getting pregnant at seventeen or eighteen, just to be on the safe
side. The queues at the fertility and IVF clinics are getting longer
and longer. The same with the adoption centers. Some people
don't make it to the front of the queue before it's too late. And
cases of HIV and chlamydia are increasing rapidly, because
women are just going out and picking up one stranger after another and having unprotected sex."

"And the number of small children being kidnapped has increased as well," added Görel. "People are desperate."

"There don't seem to be any guarantees about anything any
longer," said Vivi. "Not for anyone. It makes everyone feel so
insecure."

"Yes, but why didn't we think of that?" said Elsa. "Stealing a
kid. The way these needed individuals spread themselves out with

their strollers and carriages and little ones running around all over the place, they can't possibly keep an eye on them all at the same time. I think it would be easy just to pick a sleeping baby out of its stroller in passing, while the parents are trying to watch the rest of the kids."

I thought: So that's the reason! That's why Petra had so obstinately maintained that I was an unsuitable parent: because there was a shortage of dispensable individuals. The demand for organ donors and candidates for various experiments was no doubt as great as ever—perhaps even greater. I thought. But I didn't say anything. Because I hadn't yet told my friends I was pregnant. I hadn't found the right opportunity yet.

Suddenly I realized that this was as good an opportunity as any, right here and now. So I opened my mouth to say: "Speaking of children, I've got something to tell you . . ."

But Alice beat me to it. Although she didn't say "speaking of children," she just came straight out and said, apropos of nothing at all:

"I've got something to tell you." And she went on: "I've got something I *have* to tell you. And I have to do it as quickly as possible because I might not have much time left so I'll do it now. I've got a brain tumor."

There was silence. Not a cough, not a gasp, not even the slightest clink of glass, porcelain or cutlery. Just silence. Everyone froze, everyone turned to look at Alice as she sat there beside me, so small all of a sudden, it seemed to me, so old all at once. Just silence, just endless stillness, until she herself spoke again:

"They think it's the radiation." She turned to Görel, the new arrival, and explained: "You see, I'm involved in an experiment with some kind of radiation. Something radioactive."

"But why?" asked Görel.

"Why? Because I'm a dispensable person and a lab bunny, of course!" said Alice, screwing her mouth up and chewing like a bunny rabbit.

Nobody laughed. Not even Alice.

"No, no," said Görel. "I mean: what are they going to use the radiation for? What's the point of the actual experiment?"

"The point?" said Alice, waving one hand dismissively. "My dear friend, I haven't the faintest idea!"

2

The longer a person remains in the reserve bank unit, the more risky the experiments he or she is expected to participate in, while at the same time he or she moves closer to donating vital organs.

Now, knowing that there was a shortage of dispensable individuals, I could see that the situation in the unit had changed somewhat: fewer new arrivals came in each month—now it was usually two or three, whereas earlier it had been between five and ten. People were used up more quickly, and the generations grew shorter. Alice, for example, who had presumably been exposed to experiments involving chemical weapons, had only been in the unit for a year and a half. And during the time immediately following the dinner with Vivi, my closest friends had to undergo the following:

Elsa took part in a series of short but debilitating humane experiments, interspersed with donations. First it was a test involving some new super cleaning fluid, then an experiment with cigarettes and other tobacco- and nicotine-based products. Then her respiratory organs were exposed to vapor and gases from various chemical solvents. And between these experiments she donated part of her small intestine, the cornea from one eye, and the auditory bone from one ear. These operations just meant that she couldn't see or hear as well, and that she got very tired, but the experiments gave her a horrible, itchy eczema on her hands and arms, bronchitis, and even asthma. Her general fitness and overall condition worsened. She was no longer the same athletic woman she had been just a year earlier; she got out of breath very easily and often had to rest. She stopped diving, and instead contented herself with quietly swimming the breaststroke in the shallow pool.

During the same period Vivi donated one kidney and a section of her liver; she also participated in all kinds of medical experiments, mostly involving psychiatric drugs that, as well as making her either listless and calm or euphorically high, also caused side effects including dizziness, palpitations, swollen limbs, rashes and hair loss. Within a very short time she and Elsa became old ladies, slowly hobbling along, arm in arm, as they went for their daily walk in the winter garden, stopping every few minutes to cough, catch their breath, or clutch their chest.

Lena, who by this time was one of the seniors, having spent three years in the unit, was taken in to donate her pancreas, liver, kidney and intestinal system. She did what Majken had done: told us that she was going to make her final donation, but not when, so that one day she simply wasn't there anymore. The same thing happened to Elsa and Vivi as had happened to me: they went to Lena's room to look for her just as the section orderlies were busy clearing everything out.

But in my opinion Alice was the one who had suffered most because of the increased demand for dispensable material.

Meanwhile I was safe, protected like a sea eagle, and was sent for regular checks, given tried and tested dietary supplements, and went to yoga and dance and Friskis & Svettis. And the humane experiments I took part in involved harmless things like sleep or dream studies, or comparing and charting a person's ability to see in the dark or to distinguish different tastes, smells and sounds.

It was only a matter of time before Elsa, Vivi and Alice would notice that I was being treated completely differently from them, despite the fact that the four of us had been in the unit for roughly the same length of time. It was of course also only a question of time before they would be able to see that I was pregnant. I had already filled out: my hips were broader, my breasts were bigger, and my stomach was protruding under the loose clothes I had started to wear to hide the changes for as long as possible. So far I could just about get away with looking like someone who had just put on weight—at least as long as I kept my clothes on. But at around this time I started to avoid changing or showering in the sports center, I stopped taking a sauna, stopped swimming because the shape of my stomach under my swimsuit was unmistakable.

In other words, it was high time I told the others about my condition. Since I still regarded Elsa as my best friend and confidante, I decided to start with her, and took the opportunity one evening when the two of us were alone together in her room. Vivi was busy with library inventory and wouldn't be there until late—they always slept together nowadays, just as Johannes and I had done.

Elsa was lying on the sofa, breathing heavily and gasping for air from time to time. I was sitting in the armchair across from her.

"Elsa," I said. "There's something I have to tell you, something I've been . . . carrying for a while."

She looked at me, closing her cloudy eye—the one from which the cornea had been donated—and squinting anxiously with the other.

"Don't tell me you're sick too, Dorrit?"

"No, I'm not sick. I'm pregnant."

"What?" Elsa's arms and legs flailed as she struggled into a sitting position, turned her good ear toward me, coughed, cleared her throat noisily, then said hoarsely, almost hissing: "What did you say?"

"I'm pregnant," I repeated.

"Are you joking, have you gone mad?"

"I'm not joking," I said.

Her expression—she had never looked at me that way, I didn't recognize the way she was looking at me, didn't know how to interpret it—disbelief or envy or disgust or what?

"How the fuck did that happen?" she spat out eventually.

I felt as if I'd been stabbed, she'd never sworn at me before. I didn't reply.

"How long have you known?" she asked.

"Since the day before Johannes's final donation," I answered.

"But that was several months ago. Why didn't you say anything?"

"I'm saying it now," I said. "It's . . ." I was stumbling now, a lump in my throat, "it's not unusual to wait for a while before you tell friends and acquaintances; the risk of miscarriage is highest in the early weeks."

"I know that, for fuck's sake! Do you think I was born yesterday, do you think you're the first person I know who's ended up pregnant and started handing out a whole lot of completely superfluous information?"

Once again I didn't reply.

"How far along are you?" she asked, then gasped for air.

"Seventeen or eighteen weeks," I managed to say before her chest started rattling, and it was as if her windpipe was somehow blocked, as if something had gone down the wrong way, but then came a thin, whistling sound. I imagined a very, very narrow, flattened tube through which a minute amount of air managed to filter, down into her lungs. She grabbed her inhaler, which was next to her on the sofa, held it to her mouth, and pressed the button; there was a faint click and she breathed in. After a little while she began to breathe more evenly, more calmly, but the whistling sound was still there as a faint accompaniment when she spoke:

"So you're going to have a child?" she said. "A baby? Here?"

I shook my head.

"No. Not here. Are you going to go out there and live a needed, worthwhile life, showing off with your offspring and spreading yourself out all over the streets and squares and public transportation, pushing everybody else out of the way with your stroller and all the rest of the stuff you'll find it necessary to carry around with you?"

I shook my head again, then told her as briefly and matter-of-factly as I could about the two choices Petra had given me: have the fetus transplanted or have the child adopted. Of course I didn't say anything about the third alternative, the one connected to the key card that was still in the right pocket of my pants; I put my hand in my pocket and touched it from time to time, undecided. So far I hadn't been in any state to make my mind up on that particular question, or even to look for doors that might lead out of the unit.

After my short explanation I expected Elsa to be sympathetic, or at least to politely express regret at the fact that I wouldn't be allowed to be a parent to my child. But she didn't. Instead she said:

"I don't know, Dorrit, but this feels really bad. It feels like shit, to be honest."

"What do you mean?" I said.

"Well, you're not one of us anymore. I mean, how are we going to be able to . . . How are we going to be able to trust you? Now that you've gone and become like them?"

I didn't know how to respond to this. I was completely unprepared for her reaction. I didn't understand it. I understood that she probably, in common with most dispensable individuals, lived with the sorrow encapsulated within her of never having had a child, and that this sorrow had now been activated. But I didn't understand why she was so angry with me; after all, I hadn't gotten pregnant in order to upset her or to hurt anyone.

When I didn't speak, she went on:

"So you're going to be waddling around here, with a big belly like a Buddha, looking smug and important and on a higher plane, just like all those needed stuck-up bitches out there in the community?"

I didn't say anything now either. I just got up and left. Behind me I could hear her having another attack, gasping and panting for air. The faint click of the inhaler was the last thing I heard before I closed the door behind me.

3

Alice went downhill quickly. It had begun with headaches, pains in her jaw, dizziness and anxiety. Just after she had told us about her tumor, she started to get confused from time to time. She would suddenly lose the thread while she was talking, would forget that we'd arranged to meet, would get lost and be unable to find her way home, or would get the day's activities all mixed up. She was often upset, weeping in despair. The unit authorities let her carry on as long as she was no danger to herself or to others, for example as long as she didn't do anything like leaving something on the stove. But we all knew it was only a matter of time before she was sent away to make her final donation.

We tried to spend time together as we used to do, Alice, Elsa, Vivi and I, but we didn't have the same joy, the same healing humor between us. This was partly because Alice's illness increasingly overshadowed everything, and partly because the relationship between Elsa and me was chilly to say the least, which naturally affected the atmosphere too.

I hadn't gone through with my plan to tell Vivi and Alice about my condition as well. I presumed that Elsa had passed the information on to Vivi, and I wasn't sure whether I ought to tell Alice at all. When I noticed how quickly she was deteriorating, getting lost in time and space more and more often, and staying that way for longer and longer periods, I decided there wasn't any point in saying anything.

But even if we couldn't quite manage to socialize like before, we still took care of Alice. When she became bedridden we took turns sitting with her every evening and night. During the day members of staff came and went, made sure that she ate something, washed herself and got dressed—things that at quite an early stage she forgot to do, or forgot that she'd done already. Sometimes she took a shower every hour or so, sometimes she didn't wash for several days, sometimes she ate breakfast several times a day, while on other days she would forget to eat at all. She would go around wearing several layers of clothes because, strangely enough, she didn't notice that she was already dressed when she decided it was time to put some clothes on.

One night when it was my turn to sit with her, I was woken by the sound of her crying as I lay on the sofa in the living room. She was crying like a child, that all-absorbing, abandoned sobbing that is so heartrending you'll do anything in your power to make things right again, and I shot up from the sofa, felt dizzy and almost lost my balance in the darkness, leaned on the wall for support, and tottered off feeling slightly nauseous. In the bedroom I switched on the light and she was lying there in bed, flat on her back with her arms down by her sides, looking up at the ceiling and sobbing so hard that her whole body was shaking.

I sat down and got hold of her shoulders.

"There now, Alice, it's okay," I said. "What is it? What are you sad about?"

She didn't reply, just kept on sobbing as if she could neither see, hear, nor feel my presence. I spoke to her in a calming voice, stroked her arms, her hair and her cheeks, dried her tears with the back of my hand. I tried to reach her, tried to make her understand that she wasn't alone.

"I'm here, Alice," I said. "I'm here. Maybe I can help you. Don't be scared, there's nothing to be scared of."

I just kept talking, as reassuringly and calmly as I could, and after a long time the sobbing slowly subsided and she said:

"I know. I know you're there, Mom, but I can't see you."

For a fraction of a second I considered whether I should tell her that I wasn't her mother, but decided not to bother; when it came down to it, it didn't really matter who I was at that particular moment, and instead I said:

"That's because you're looking up at the ceiling, darling. I'm sitting beside you."

She lowered her gaze then, her eyes flickering around the room, turned her head in my direction and eventually managed, with some difficulty, to focus on my face. She sighed deeply, closed her eyes, rolled over onto her side facing me, curled up, made a few contented smacking noises with her lips, then fell asleep. I pulled the covers up over her shoulder, stroked her hair and went back to the sofa in the living room, and I fell asleep too.

In the morning she knew exactly who I was once again. She was just tired, bone weary somehow—the sort of tiredness, I assume, that sleep doesn't really touch; you just have to work your way through it, and either it disappears of its own accord, or it stays put and becomes a part of you. In Alice's case, of course, the tiredness was due to the tumor, and was definitely there to stay. I helped her to the bathroom then back to bed, an effort so taxing that she went back to sleep for a while as I got breakfast ready.

"Thank you, Dorrit," she said, slurring her words slightly, when I carried in the breakfast tray. "You're an angel."

"So are you," I said. "You've taken care of me plenty of times."

She drew herself up into a sitting position and I plumped up the pillows so that she had some support for her back when she leaned against the headboard.

"Yes, but you weren't ill," she said. "It's harder work with sick people, especially if they're going to die soon."

As I passed her a cup of coffee I said I wasn't sure if I agreed with her. "A person who's physically healthy but in despair can be just as difficult to deal with, surely. Looking after someone who's ill is quite simple, really; at least you know what you have to do, in purely practical terms. But what do you do with someone you can't do anything for?"

Alice smiled.

"You listen, I guess," she said.

"Yes, and isn't that the hardest thing of all?" I said.

"Is it? It doesn't require any special knowledge or skills. Just the ability to hear. And a little calm in your body. The ability to sit still and listen. I don't see why it should be so difficult."

Then she turned her attention to her coffee for a while, taking tiny, tiny sips, closing her eyes for a second after each sip, looking as if she was really enjoying it. Then she suddenly stopped, looked at me and said:

"Try not to be angry with Elsa."

"What?" I said. "So you know we . . ."

I didn't know how to finish the sentence, so I let it hang there, gaping, incomplete.

"I've noticed," replied Alice in that slow, tired tone of voice that had become hers. She added:

"You have told her, haven't you?"

"Told her what?"

"That you're having a baby, of course."

I frowned and glanced down at my stomach.

"Oh, it's been obvious from the start," said Alice. "Ever since . . . let's see, it must have been just before Johannes died, I think. A week or so before that."

I must have looked as if I'd seen a ghost, because she laughed and said:

"Don't look at me like that, there's nothing strange about it, I'm not psychic or anything. I've known so many women who've gotten pregnant and had children that I've learned to recognize the signs straightaway. Something happens to a woman's face when she becomes pregnant; it becomes a fraction broader, somehow, and so does the mouth. And there's something subtle about the posture and the look in the eyes that changes too, but I can't quite put my finger on it."

She put the cup down on the bedside table, her hand shaking; it was as if she didn't have enough strength to talk and hold a coffee cup at the same time.

"What are you going to do?" she asked. "Are you going to give birth to it?"

"Yes."

"And then?"

I snorted. "What do you think?" I said.

"I don't think anything," she said. "You tell me."

"They're going to take it away," I said. "They're going to take it from me and give it to someone else."

Alice looked at me, with absolute clarity, as if she were looking straight through me, but she didn't say anything else; it was as if she knew, or at least suspected, that I had a choice, a possibility, a way out.

There's something strange about people who know they're going to die soon. It's as if their senses are expanded to superhuman dimensions, as if they acquire X-ray vision and become mind readers and can see into the future and suddenly understand everything that's going on inside and between other people. And either that really is the case, or else we just want to believe it is, because it makes dying more attractive and easier to reconcile ourselves with, somehow.

In the end Alice said:

"Anyway, try not to be angry with Elsa."

"I'm not angry with Elsa," I said. "She's the one who's angry with me."

"Try to understand her," said Alice. "I might have reacted like her as well, if it weren't . . . if it hadn't been for this."

She tapped herself on the head.

"Try to understand her," she repeated, and I was afraid she was on her way into a new episode of short-term memory loss. But she went on: "You haven't forgotten how it feels to lose a friend because of a child, I hope?"

"But she isn't losing me," I said. "I'm here, I'm not about to disappear. And if anyone is losing anything it's me, losing my child."

Alice looked at me in that same way again, clear and omniscient. I didn't say any more, and we sat there quietly for a while. She reached for her coffee cup again. I offered her a plate with two cheese sandwiches that I'd made, but she shook her head. She looked even more tired now, and I had the impression that I was literally watching her disappear, little by little, before my eyes. I put the plate back on the bedside table, and all of a sudden I felt inexpressibly sad; it was as if a trapdoor had opened inside me, and I couldn't stop myself from crying. In a vain attempt to hide the fact that I was crying, I turned my head away.

"Dorrit, my dear . . . ," said Alice, putting her cup back down on the bedside table.

"I'm sorry!" I sniveled. "I ought to be strong. Strong for you. But it's just that I can't stand—I hate—the thought of losing you!"

"I know that, Dorrit," she replied calmly. "It comforts me to know that. And that's enough for me. You don't need to be strong."

That was the first time in my life someone had told me I didn't need to be strong.

"Hey," she said next. "How about climbing in here with me for a while? I think it would do both of us good."

I nodded, blew my nose on one of the napkins on the tray, then went around to the other side of the double bed, lifted up the covers and crawled in beside Alice. She was warm, red hot, like a stove.

That was the last real conversation I had with the Alice I had gotten to know. That was the last time she knew it was me she was talking to for more than a couple of minutes at a time. Within a week she had made her final donation. A boy with diabetes received islet cells from her pancreas, and one of the country's most popular television personalities, a mother with two children, received her remaining kidney.

4

My new writing project had remained more or less untouched over the past few months. The only thing I had done was to read through what I had already written: thirty pages or so, a good start—though I say so myself. But a good start doesn't go far, not if you no longer have any idea how you want the narrative to proceed, and particularly if you can no longer remember what you wanted to achieve with the story. It was as if the train had left, the train carrying the theme and my motivation.

I did, however, make one last attempt just after Alice's final donation. I thought perhaps I might find some solace in the project, I thought I might be able to rediscover my motivation through that solace. So I sat down on my fantastic desk chair with support for the base of my spine, my neck and my arms, switched on the computer, opened the file. Then I sat there for a good while, three or four hours or more. Wrote a few lines. Deleted them. Wrote a few more lines. Deleted them again. Took out a notepad and wrote by hand instead. Crossed out what I'd written, turned over the page and tried again, wrote, crossed out, turned the page and tried over and over again, but no, I just got angry and tired. In the end I decisively selected the document on the screen and moved it to the recycle bin, then emptied the recycle bin and shut down the computer. Leaned back in the chair against the headrest. My gaze happened to fall on Majken's picture of the deformed fetus, either grimacing with pain or smiling scornfully. And it was then, at that very moment, that I first felt a movement in my belly. A brief, fleeting movement a bit like an air bubble, somehow, that was definitely not gas or anything else connected with the digestive process.

I looked down at my belly and it happened again: a kick or a push, perhaps even a movement of the head, how should I know, but it was the first tangible sign that something was not only growing but also living—and living it up—in there.

"Hello there," I whispered, and pressed my hand gently against my stomach over my shirt. "Hello, little one."

I did nothing more that day. I just called down to lab 4, where I was currently participating in a safe but irritating psychological experiment to do with living space and territory and so on, and said I needed to rest today. The team leading the experiment was very understanding about that kind of thing. It was partly because they knew I was expecting a child and was tired and slightly nauseous almost all the time, and partly because they were psychologists, so I guess it was their job to be understanding. Afterward I went and lay down on the bed, took the fossil stone out of my left pocket and lay there holding it, turning it round and round in one hand while the other hand rested on my stomach beneath my shirt.

After an hour and a half I felt another bubbling movement in my belly, and at the same time a very, very slight, almost imperceptible pressure against the palm of my hand. I pressed back, carefully. Another movement, almost like a reply. I gasped, then I laughed, then I cried, then I got up and went to the bathroom and had a pee and washed my face. Then I went and lay down again and fell asleep.

If anyone had asked me whether these early kicks or pushes made me happy or unhappy, I wouldn't have known how to answer them. I didn't know whether what I felt was longing or loss, togetherness or loneliness.

A few days later I went for an ultrasound. Amanda Jonstorp herself was doing it. She squeezed out a blob of clear gel; it was cold and it tickled and I giggled a little. She smiled at me, then picked up the wide probe and began to slide it over my stomach, alternating between small movements and broad sweeps. At the same time she stared with concentration at a computer screen that was turned away from me.

"Does everything look okay?" I asked.

"Yes, everything looks great," said Amanda. "Better than expected, to be honest."

"So can I have a look now?" I said.

"What?" she said, stopping abruptly in mid-sweep through the slippery gel on my stomach, and I realized I wasn't meant to see my child on that screen, wasn't meant to carry around a blurred picture of my scan to show everybody I bumped into who wasn't quick enough to come up with an excuse to get out of it.

Amanda had red blotches on her cheeks and something of Petra Runhede about her as she stumbled over her words:

"I . . . I'm . . . really sorry, Dorrit. I thought . . . I thought you . . . realized. I thought . . . You do understand it would be wrong for us to encourage you to . . . to . . . bond with the fetus."

As I was walking toward the elevators in the clinic reception area, I pushed my hand into my pocket and felt the key card. Just as when I had been carrying that little crumpled note with the message to Potter, I had changed pants several times since that day in February when I had been given the card, and by this time I had become very adept at moving it from the dirty pair on their way to the laundry to the clean pair I took out of the closet. I would hold it against my palm with my thumb and make sure I kept the back of my hand angled upward until I had slipped the card into the right front pocket of the clean pants. At the same time I would do my best to distract attention from that hand by doing something with the other: scratching my head, coughing into it, lifting the lid of the laundry basket and putting in the dirty pants, smoothing out a crease or picking off a loose thread. I was silent, quick and discreet, just as Birthmark had advised me to be.

The key card had been constantly on my mind over the past months. I had often slipped my hand into my pocket to feel it as I was doing now, and every time I had done so I had repeated the code to myself: 98 44, 98 44—which I also did now. But I hadn't done any more, not yet; I still hadn't come to a decision as to whether I would use the card or not. I didn't make a decision now either, but this time it was as if everything associated with the key card—the possibilities, the risks and the uncertainty—had moved up into the part of the brain that actually thinks. And I realized I had reached a point where I had to make a decision.

I don't know if it was because of this shift or if I would have seen what I saw in any case, but just as I came out of the hospital lobby with my hand in my pocket and started to walk toward elevator H, I saw, in an alcove next to the row of elevator doors, a staff member fiddling with something, her face turned to the wall. The wall was the color of linden flowers just there, exactly like the uniform shirt she was wearing, and it was quite dark in the alcove. But not so dark that I couldn't see her, and after a moment I also saw that she was actually standing in front of a door, a very narrow one, with no handle; it was the same color as the wall, surrounded by a door frame, again exactly the same shade of green, and she was fiddling with something next to this door frame, but not for long; it only took two or three seconds for her to do what was necessary to open the door, and a second or two more for her to push it open a little way, slip through it and disappear, whereupon the door quickly and soundlessly closed behind her.

5

Vivi carried herself just as beautifully as before, just as fine-limbed and lovely. But she was moving more slowly and more stiffly as she walked around the library pushing a little cart, replacing the books on the shelves. I saw her through the big window facing out onto the square as I came around with two films and a book to return.

For the past two weeks or so I hadn't gone out any more than necessary; I had just spent time with my own thoughts and my steadily expanding belly. It was showing now, my belly, I could no longer hide it, even under the loosest, bulkiest clothes, even if it wasn't yet quite so large that an observer could be 100 percent certain I was pregnant just by looking at me when I was fully dressed. At least that's what I thought. When I walked into the library and Vivi caught sight of me, she stopped short and said:

"Wow! I mean: hi! I haven't seen you for a long time, Dorrit."

She left the cart of books between two shelves and hobbled over to me at the circulation desk.

She had lost great clumps of her thick, shiny hair and nowadays always wore a handkerchief knotted around her head. It made her face look smaller, and her eyes and mouth bigger, and the whole thing gave her a naked, vulnerable appearance.

"How are things?" I asked tentatively.

"Okay," she said.

"And . . . Elsa?"

"Not bad. A little better than she was a while ago, actually."

I placed the book and the films on the counter, and was just about to ask her to give Elsa my best wishes, when she said:

"What's going on with you two these days? You never see each other. She never talks about you. And if I ask her about something to do with you, she changes the subject. What's happened?"

"Hasn't she said anything?"

"No, that's what I'm telling you: she doesn't say a thing."

And that's the way it was: Elsa hadn't told Vivi about our conversation, our quarrel. She hadn't told her I was expecting a child.

"You're joking!" she exclaimed when I told her.

And then she laughed. "And there I was thinking . . . I was thinking you'd started comfort eating or something. Or maybe you were taking part in some experiment that made you swell up, or where you had to eat a load of candy and cookies all day and weren't allowed to exercise or something, these researchers come up with so many dumb ideas. And in fact you're . . ."

She broke off, and said: "But how did it happen? I mean, how is it possible? Have you had hormone treatment? Or fertilized eggs implanted?"

"Why would I have done that?"

"I don't mean on your own initiative, of course," she said. "But it could have been done to you, couldn't it? While you were anesthetized."

"But I haven't been anesthetized," I said. "Not since I donated my kidney, and that's ages ago; only an elephant could be pregnant that long."

"I see," she said. "Well, maybe you were impregnated naturally."

"I think so," I said.

I was about to leave; I was tired and Vivi seemed kind of strained, somehow. But now she said in her usual warm, serious tone:

"Was it Johannes who . . . ?"

I nodded.

"Did he . . . Did he find out before . . . ?"

"Just about," I replied.

She looked at me. It was too much for me, that sympathetic look. I glanced away, swallowed. Then she held out her long arms, pulled me close to her, wrapped me in her embrace and stroked my back. She was almost as tall as Johannes; the top of my head reached her chin, and I closed my eyes, allowed myself to be enveloped by her, leaning my cheek against her breast. The scent of her reminded me of honey and fields of oilseed rape in bloom. I thought about Jock, and my dilapidated house and the farms and meadows around it, I thought about early summer in Skåne, about the wind and the sound of tractors and blackbirds and nightingales and young crows and the neighbors' children playing and the wood stacked up to dry and washing hanging on the line between the apple trees, flapping in the breeze, and I could see my blue-painted garden furniture and there, on one of the chairs, I saw Johannes sitting, scratching Jock behind the ears as I walked toward them with a tray of coffee and cookies. I could see it as if it were a memory, and I didn't cry, but it was as if my throat had been ripped apart, as if I had been crying, and my legs were about to give way.

Vivi led me over to her chair behind the circulation desk. I sat down. She fetched me a glass of water and pulled out a chair for herself, then sat down beside me with her arm around me. I drank a little of the water. Then we just sat there, behind the desk, until some borrowers came along needing Vivi's help.

6

Elsa was lying on the lawn in the winter garden. She was lying on her side in the sun on a blanket. She was resting her head on her arm; an open book lay beside her. But she wasn't reading, she was sleeping. Her rib cage was heaving, long deep breaths, even, almost completely free of that rattle now, but she coughed in her sleep from time to time. I stood in the shade on the gravel path just a few yards away from her. Stood there missing her. Dare I go over? Dare I go over and sit down next to her, be there when she woke up?

I did it, I walked from the crunching gravel onto the silent grass, sat down cross-legged an arm's length away from her, in front of her, so that I wasn't casting a shadow over her.

I had thought a great deal about what Alice had said. "You

haven't forgotten what it feels like to lose a friend because of a child, I hope?" Of course I hadn't forgotten that feeling of being abruptly pushed out of a close circle to some distant periphery. Coming second, third, fourth, last. Being treated like someone less knowledgeable, someone inferior. Being shut out—and yet, paradoxically enough, being taken for granted. The old friends out in the community who had become parents had continued wanting to see me, but when we did meet up they were distant, sometimes condescending and always inaccessible, as if they were wrapped in invisible padding, at least when the children were small. The strange thing was that this only applied to my female friends; the men were certainly very much preoccupied with the child and with the upheaval involved in becoming a parent, and later with the chaos that ensued when they had their second child, which intensified when they had the third, fourth, fifth and so on. The men were absorbed, yes, but it was as if the women were on Valium: they talked and laughed and nodded and smiled, but they weren't really there. It was as if they focused all their energy and all their interest in others on one single entity: the child.

I had always thought this was a deliberate stance, that they actually chose to close themselves off to more or less everyone except the child, who of course was dependent on them for its existence. I had always been convinced that this was a conscious decision to prioritize. But now I wasn't so sure anymore. Now, while I was carrying something that would be a child, I noticed that I was changing; I was becoming self-absorbed in a new way that was hard to define, and I was beginning to sense that the self-sufficiency of those parents I had known was perhaps not a matter of choice. It wasn't that I didn't care about my friends anymore. My senses were heightened as never before, particularly my sense of smell and my hearing, and I was sensitive and easily moved, but at the same time I was becoming less and less receptive to the sorrows and troubles of those around me, and to their joy and happiness as well, when it came down to it. My friends meant a great deal to me—the few who were left. I didn't think any less of them than before, quite the opposite, in fact. I rejoiced in the new ones, Görel and Mats and a couple of others, was immensely grateful that Vivi was such a good friend, and I grieved for Alice and Lena and Erik and Vanja and Majken and all the others I had lost. And Elsa, lying here in front of me on the grass, her head resting on her arm—I missed Elsa so much it felt as if my heart were being ripped out of my body. I enjoyed meeting and spending time with my friends, and when I did see them I registered everything they said and reacted to it, but a second later it slid off me like rain off a newly polished car: rapidly and without friction and without a single drop penetrating the surface. It was strange: in one way I was more sensitive than ever, in another I was more or less closed off.

When I had perceived this change in my own attitude, I couldn't help asking myself if there might be a biological cause, if this might be some form of primitive behavior on the part of the female mammal that women couldn't escape, just as we couldn't escape the fact that if we were to become a parent naturally, then unlike men we didn't have all the time in the world.

At any rate, I had to admit that Elsa was right, and I intended to tell her so as soon as she woke up, which I did. She had just about realized that I was sitting there, when I said:

"You were right, Elsa. I am indeed waddling around looking smug and important and on a higher plane, just like all those needed stuck-up bitches out there in the community."

She sat up, pushed her hair back, yawned, and rubbed her eyes. "Oh yes?"

"But," I went on, "I have to tell you that the smugness has nothing whatsoever to do with human economic growth. It's not that kind of self-sufficiency; it has absolutely nothing to do with what I can do for society or how good and valuable I am. Everything is here—and here." I placed my hand on my midriff, then on my head. "And I can't help it. It isn't something I have any control over, that's just the way it is. I'm at the mercy of my hormones!"

"Okay," she said. "I understand. I understand that's something I don't understand. I don't suppose you'd like to go for a swim instead of sitting here talking in riddles?"

I couldn't help laughing. I stood up, held my hand out and pulled her to her feet in a gentlemanly manner. She picked up her book, Emily Brontë's *Wuthering Heights*, and I folded up her blanket, and we ambled off arm in arm with the book and the blanket along the gravel path toward the galleria, stopping to say hi to Mats who was digging in a flowerbed, dressed only in shorts and heavy boots and a tool belt. On a cart behind him on the path were shrubs in pots, waiting to be planted. In the distance, on a bench, I could see Potter with his round, black-framed glasses. He was munching on an apple and flipping through a magazine. It was lunchtime; people were pouring up and down the staircase to the Terrace restaurant and its groaning buffet. Still arm in arm, Elsa and I emerged into the Atrium Walkway, and took the first elevator down to the sports facility.

We swam, slowly and for a long time, side by side, in silence. Afterward we had a sauna. I sat at the bottom, closest to the door, pushing it open slightly from time to time, unsure what I had actually heard about pregnancy and saunas: had I heard that it was a good thing, or had I heard that it wasn't? Elsa sat right up at the top where it was hottest, on the third bench, and leaned back against the wall. We didn't say much, we mostly just sat there being friends again. From time to time one of us would say lazily to the other something along the lines of: "Have you heard that so-and-so is involved in an experiment with this and that?" or "So-and-so has finished with so-and-so, did you know?" or "Do you remember that guy back home in the village who was like this or that and who used to do this or that?"

But when we eventually decided we'd had enough, and Elsa climbed down, she said:

"Dorrit, do you remember what we promised each other at the start?"

I remembered. Shortly after Majken's death Elsa and I had promised each other that the day one of us found out we were on the list for our final donation, we would tell the other—and not only that it was going to happen, but also *when*. So that the other person wouldn't have to run around looking for someone who no longer existed.

"Yes," I said, looking up at her as she stood there in front of me, the sweat pouring down her wiry body, which was quite scarred by this stage.

"Why?"

"Does it still apply?" she said.

"Yes, I guess it does," I said, and felt the anxiety stab down into my chest and squeeze it, hard. Don't say it's time now! I thought. Don't say we have to part now, when we've just made friends again, don't say that she's going to . . . and my voice was trembling as I repeated, emphasizing the question:

"*Why?*"

"Oh," said Elsa, taking a step toward the door and pushing it open, "I just wanted to check. I just wanted to know that's what will happen. That you won't just disappear. That you won't just be gone one day, without telling me in advance."

Feeling relieved I got up and followed her out. My legs were shaking, I had been so scared and now I was so relieved. In the shower room she turned to me.

"Can we promise each other, Dorrit? Can we promise each other again?"

"Of course, Elsa," I said. "Of course we can."

"Good," she said, and her voice gave away the fact that she was moved. It was trembling, somehow exposed, as she went on: "Shall we shake on it?"

We clasped hands and then we hugged each other, standing there naked and covered in sweat on the tiled floor outside the sauna. A woman with short white hair smiled at us as she passed on the way in. She reminded me a little of Lena, but she had a longer, narrower face and her expression was more tired.

It was only some hours later, during the night, as I was lying alone in my bed with one hand on my stomach, gazing up at the ceiling, that it occurred to me: "disappear" didn't necessarily have to mean "make the final donation." It could just as easily mean "leave," "run away." And if I decided to go, if I decided to run away, I wouldn't be able to keep my promise to Elsa unless I revealed my secret to her, which would mean breaking the promise I had made never to tell anyone about the key card. And I am not the kind of person who breaks promises. I am not the kind of person who betrays a trust. For example, in this story I have not revealed the true circumstances under which I received the key card. Neither of the two nurses who met me when I raced into the surgical department that day has a birthmark. Nor was it either of those two who gave me the key card, and the conversation with the person who did give me the card did not in fact take place in the break room where I sat and waited as I gazed out at the snow-covered park with the pond and the ducks, but in a completely different room in a completely different part of the unit, and at another time. And the code is actually not 98 44 at all.

No, I am not the kind of person who breaks promises. And so now I was faced with a dilemma.

I turned over, facing the side of the bed where Johannes used to lie. I placed one hand on the pillow where his head used to rest. The child in my belly turned over as well. Then we slept.

7

In the newspapers, on the radio and on TV it was early summer.
The national days had been celebrated, first the Norwegian and
then the Swedish, with flag-waving, royalty, and parades with bands
playing. The usual euphoria surrounding those national days was
now gradually evolving into the usual euphoria surrounding midsummer. On the news, on talk shows, and in documentaries,
they had just finished picking over the to-be-or-not-to-be of
the monarchy and the eternal question of why the Norwegians
were so much more energetic in their national celebrations than
the Swedes, and were just starting to fill report after report and
feature after feature with the price of strawberries and new potatoes, and with midsummer poles ready to be danced around,
regional variations on the national costume, wooden horses

from Dalarna, with islands in the archipelago, barn dances and red-painted cottages, with herring and aquavit, drunken parties and drunk driving offenses. Obviously the old traditions were being kept alive out there. But here inside the unit we celebrated neither the one nor the other; we saw no sign of a flag or a midsummer pole. Aquavit and herring were not on the menu. We could get fresh strawberries all year round, they were grown in a greenhouse in the galleria, and I never heard anyone mention new potatoes. Personally, I have always thought that new potatoes taste unpleasantly doughy, somehow.

It was, however, time for the monthly welcome party, and I had decided to go. I had wanted to dress in a feminine way, but none of my dresses fit me any more. So I stuck to pants, shirt and jacket. I had put weight on all over my body, and had even grown the hint of a double chin. For those who didn't know me or didn't know about my condition, and weren't expecting to see a pregnant dispensable person, I expect I just looked fat. That suited me perfectly, because I didn't want to offend any of the new arrivals, didn't want to cause any kind of unpleasantness or consternation. Not tonight. Tonight I was in the mood to have fun. I was in the mood to dance and get to know some new people.

I combed my hair, then stood there looking at my reflection, alternating between the front view and profile. I pushed my hands into my pockets—in the left was the fossil stone, in the right the key card. I stood up straight. I actually looked strong; it was easy to understand why people were happy to believe that I was. I looked indomitable. I looked as if I had authority.

The menu consisted of apple and cauliflower salad with a yogurt dressing, butterfly salmon with teriyaki sauce and stir-fried vegetables, plus, for dessert, chocolate and orange cream with mascarpone and crushed cookies. I was sharing a table with Mats, Vivi and a new arrival, Miranda, who was a sculptor. Like most new arrivals she was very quiet, poking unhappily at her food. I decided to make a point of talking to her during the party, to try to make her feel better. We started chatting, during the meal at first and then later in the bar as we tried out different drinks with umbrellas in them.

The band hadn't started playing yet, and slow, rhythmic music was churning out of the loudspeakers at a relatively low volume. Miranda was telling me about her work. She made small and large sculptures in clay—the biggest the size of a human, the smallest the size of thimbles—depicting humanlike figures in contorted postures. She had, as she put it, "a weakness for contorted bodies," and saw a great deal of beauty in the crooked, the misshapen and the scarred.

"There is," she said, "actually something beautiful in suffering. Even in purely physical pain. Does that sound perverse? Does it sound as if I'm a psychopath?"

"Well . . ." I said. "Maybe it does. But I presume that an artistic eye, an eye that doesn't evaluate and analyze, but primarily observes, ought to be able to perceive beauty in more or less any shape or expression."

"Oh, it's so nice to talk to someone who understands!" said Miranda. "Because that's exactly how it is; it isn't about my evaluation, it isn't that I think it's cool if someone is deformed or suffering or in pain. I just happen to think it's beautiful."

There was something about her that reminded me of Majken. She was like "the dark side of Majken," she was the same but the reverse, you might say. And I told her about Majken's picture of the deformed fetus that was now hanging above the desk in my apartment.

"I'd really like to see that," said Miranda, and I told her where I lived and said she was welcome to drop by any time.

Just as I said that, the rock band came on stage. I only needed to hear the first two or three beats of the intro to recognize the ballad "For My Girl," and out of the corner of my eye I saw a figure approaching from the side with a self-assured walk, straight-backed, lithe, his shirt sleeves rolled up, his forearms muscular, his face weather-beaten and healthy and with a slightly cheeky but somehow shy smile, sparkling eyes, a playful look in those eyes that were—so it seemed to me—seeking mine; and as he came closer I turned slowly to face him, ready to hear him say: "Dorrit, you look lovely tonight," and to bow and kiss my hand.

But it was someone else of course, someone I had never seen before, someone who didn't even stop, but just walked past me with a polite nod.

Miranda said something to me, I didn't hear what it was, the music was loud now. I was just going to ask her to repeat it when there was a movement inside me, a push or a kick. Automatically I pressed my hand against my stomach. Another push now, against my hand, very clear. It was as if we were giving each other a high five, and I wanted to tell someone—no, not *someone*, I wanted to tell Johannes, I wanted to tell Johannes and no one else that I had just done a high five with our baby. I wanted to take his hand and place it on my stomach, feel the warmth of his hand, let him feel the movements of our child. Let him say hello to his baby.

I could see that Miranda was saying something else, closer now, right next to me. She looked troubled, I thought, but I still couldn't hear what she was saying, and suddenly I didn't know how to open my mouth and speak. I must have looked like an idiot, staring at her vacantly and stupidly, as if I suddenly had no idea who she was. But the baby was somehow pressing on my bladder, because all of a sudden I was desperate for a pee, and I came to my senses, smiled apologetically at Miranda, and said:

"Sorry, what did you say?"

"Don't you feel well?" she almost shouted.

"I'm fine, it's just . . . It's just . . . it's this song, it . . . Old memories, you know."

She nodded.

"Do you feel like dancing?" she asked.

"Sure. But I have to go the bathroom first," I replied. "I'm bursting. Back soon, I won't be long!"

I pushed my way through the sea of happy party people, residents and staff mixing together; many well-known faces, roughly the same number vaguely familiar, and a small number completely unknown, I said hi and nodded and waved to the left and the right and soon I had reached the toilets at the far end of the room: a row of doors with people going in and out. Voices rumbling and roaring, laughing and shouting, music pulsating from the main room: "This is for my girl, this is for my woman, for my world. Baby, baby, this is all for you . . ."

The baby must have taken its foot off my bladder—or moved its bottom or head or elbow—because the pressure had gone and suddenly I didn't need to go to the bathroom at all. Perhaps that was why I now noticed three extra doors at the end without the toilet symbol on them. These three were a bit smaller and looked more like some kind of decoration, a kind of fake door rather than real doors. There were no signs on them, no handles, and it was only when I—sauntering up and down in front of the doors in an attempt to look as if I were desperate to pee—got really close that I saw the narrow metal-framed slot in the door frame.

Without thinking—as if I were on autopilot, simply functioning, simply acting, like a robot—I took the key card out of my pocket and swiped it through the slot as if in passing. A small gap in the door frame immediately slid open, revealing a keypad not much bigger than that of a cell phone. In a state that can best be described as a panic-stricken trance, I keyed in 98 44, pushed open the door, stepped over the threshold and onto the other side, and before I gave myself time to see or register where I had ended up, I grabbed the handle on my side of the door and pushed it firmly shut.

It was incredibly bright. I was bathed in a white, harsh neon light and a silence so complete that my own heart sounded like thunderclaps recorded on a loop and played back at a very high speed. It took a little while, I don't know how long, seconds or minutes, before I was able to see in the cold light. And when I finally saw that I was on a landing in a stairwell, exactly as the person I call Birthmark had explained, my feelings caught up with me. Panic grabbed hold and penetrated my body and raced through my veins and arteries, rushing and roaring right through me.

Up or down? I thought feverishly, shrugged my shoulders and started to run upstairs; the party room was on K1, and should therefore be below ground level. It was only when I had gone up a couple of floors that I remembered my experience in the break room in the surgical department, where there had been a window facing onto the outside world despite the fact that it was located on what was called the basement level.

So I turned and ran downstairs instead, two floors, three, then down another half staircase which came to a stop at another door, a substantial door made of metal. This time the slot wasn't hidden in the door frame, but was on the wall next to it, in full view and with a keypad similar to the ones you find in stores for customers to key in their debit pin number.

With my hand shaking—shaking and sweating—I swiped the card, my other hand hovering over the keypad, ready, and—oh no! It was as if the code had been completely wiped out of my memory, the code was—yes, that was it, I remembered, keyed in 94 88. But nothing happened, there was no click. I pushed down the handle anyway, but the door was locked, obviously.

I tried again: 99 48—no.

48 99 then? No.

There was something wrong with those four numbers, they were right but yet they were wrong. My whole body was shaking now, sweat pouring down my back, my mouth was dry and I was on the verge of tears, almost hysterical, my head was spinning— when that trivial refrain suddenly echoed through my brain and stopped the spinning:

This is for my girl, this is for my woman, for my world. Baby, baby, this is all for you ...

All at once I was perfectly calm, perfectly clear, and firmly keyed in the combination 98 44, whereupon the door obediently gave a faint click and I pressed down the handle, pushed open the heavy door, walked out, took two steps, and the metal door closed behind me.

I was out. Outside. There was a breeze, that was the first thing I noticed. I could feel it against my face, I could feel it in my hair, lifting it and messing it up. I could feel it making the legs of my pants flap loosely against my calves. It was almost dark; the sun was drawing its last burning threads from a part of the sky that was already dark and full of stars, toward a still-glowing strip on the opposite side. It wasn't cold, but it was very cool; the night was likely to be quite chilly.

I stood there for a moment just outside the door, watching the wind run its invisible fingers through the leaves on the trees, making the flowers on the lilac bushes nod and bow and the birch trees rustle and whisper. I was in a park. There were lawns and gravel paths; one of the paths led to the left, around the corner of the building. Beyond the corner there was, from my point of view, only darkness. A little way ahead of me, over to the right, I could just see a pond among some low bushes. Tall trees towered up behind the pond, their huge crowns swaying. It was the same pond I had seen from the window of the break room that day in February. My first impulse was to run over there, to get behind the bushes and in among the trees, and to hide myself somewhere. But I realized at once that if there were surveillance cameras out here, which seemed likely, and if anyone saw me running, that would attract attention. It would look suspicious, because why would a staff member run out of the workplace and in among the bushes to hide? No, that would be silly, I reasoned, the only sensible thing I could do was to follow the path around the corner. So that's what I did.

The gravel crunched beneath my feet—deafeningly, it seemed to me—and I expected to hear running footsteps behind me at any moment, to be escorted back into the building by a couple of strong guards, or for a patrol of some kind to be waiting around the bend. But nobody came running and no patrol was waiting. When I got around the corner I saw instead, in the romantic, ghostly atmosphere of the twilight, with its mixture of evening sun and darkness, heightened here by the glow of the streetlamps, that the path led over a patch of grass to a low white wooden fence with an open gate in it. I walked the twenty yards or so to the fence which was ridiculously low, hardly up to my knees; the open gate was completely superfluous, but as the path led to the gate I went out through it anyway, and found myself on a road that was illuminated for fifty yards or so in each direction.

On the other side of the road was a rolling landscape of fields and forest groves and individual farms and houses, their outside lights twinkling like lanterns in a sea of night. Above this sea there was still a glowing, golden pink strip from the sun. So that was the west, I established, or rather northwest, as it was around midsummer. In other words, the road ran north-south—roughly, at any rate. After a moment's hesitation I chose to go north.

When I had gotten beyond the scope of the streetlights, and the golden twilight strip in the northwest had changed to a faint grayish glow, I found myself surrounded by black, cool night. With each step I took it was like climbing further and further into total nothingness. I wasn't afraid, it didn't feel eerie, just uncertain. Since I couldn't see the ground in front of me, I looked up instead, and above my head the sky was so clear that even the most distant stars could be seen—some so distant they have never been named and do not appear on any map of the constellations. The sky was covered with them. Less distant, far below these billions of anonymous stars, was the Little Bear, which Johannes had taught me to find. And there was the Dipper, and there, just to the side and in a straight line from the two stars at the back of the Dipper, glowed the North Star.

PART 4

I did get to see her. Only for a moment, but still. She had black hair. Her face was smooth and delicate, like a doll's. She had Johannes's nose, his upper lip and his mouth. And his chin too, I think. But there was also something of my mother in her face, perhaps something about the forehead, perhaps it was the actual shape of her face. She was a little bundle: arms and legs curled in the fetal position, those incomprehensibly tiny hands clenched, the fingers of one hand curled around the thumb. Eyes tightly closed, her toes alternately bending and flexing in time with her cries.

That was what I saw and heard when the midwife held her up in front of me: that she was real and that she was alive and healthy. Then she was taken away. And I was stitched up as I lay there on the operating table, anesthetized from my rib cage downward.

Petra Runhede had said: "Let me know if there's anything I can do for you, Dorrit."

She had said it that morning after Johannes's final donation, and—amusingly enough—she said it again when I bumped into her in the crowd at the party just a few minutes after I returned from my nocturnal stroll beneath the stars. I had been gone for about an hour and had had time to think about a lot of things, so when she asked me I was perfectly clear about what she could do for me.

"Okay," I replied. "Do you want to know right now?"

"Sure," she said. "Let's go and sit somewhere a bit quieter."

We went out into the lobby. There were low tables, sofas with short backs and round padded stools; it looked like an airport lounge, impersonal and no more comfortable than necessary. I sat down on one of the sofas, with Petra on a stool opposite me. She took a notepad and pen out of the inside pocket of her jacket, then nodded to me in her everlastingly sincere way.

"Three things," I said. "I want to be awake during the C-section. I want to see the child. And I want"—I stretched out my left leg so that I could get my hand in my pocket, took out the fossil stone and held it up in front of Petra in the palm of my hand— "the child to have this, I want the adoptive parents to promise to give it to the child, along with a letter from me, when it begins to ask about its biological parents—or at the latest when it comes of age. The letter will not contain anything that reveals the fact that the parents were dispensable. Can you arrange it?"

Petra scribbled feverishly, then she looked up:

"Yes. I think so. Of course I can't guarantee that the parents will actually keep their promise, but I can certainly get them to sign an agreement."

She promised to come back to me with further information, I thanked her, and we returned to the party, where we went our separate ways; I then went to look for Miranda. When I found her I explained my absence by saying I'd bumped into someone who was upset and needed to talk.

"The way you looked," said Miranda, "I would have thought you were the one who needed someone to talk to."

I laughed, assured her I was absolutely fine, and asked if she was up for that dance now. She was.

It's February again. Eight months have passed since that party. And just about four months since I gave birth. There are two reasons why I've hung on for so long.

For one thing, I wanted to finish writing this—even if it will probably be one of the manuscripts that immediately ends up in some underground passage beneath the Royal Library in Stockholm. That's if it ends up anywhere at all, and isn't simply destroyed.

For another, Vivi was sent for her final donation just after I gave birth, and I wanted to be there for Elsa, because she was there for me after Johannes's final donation.

But now Elsa is gone too, and no one here needs me anymore, not even myself. I only have a few lines left, then that's it. This time tomorrow my heart and lungs will belong to someone else, to be exact a local politician, the mother of two children.

My daughter's parent, by the way, is a single woman, aged forty-two, the director of a small recruitment company within the business and office sector. I've seen a picture of her. She looked nice, but also a bit sad. She's had several miscarriages and has been on the adoption waiting list for a long time. I have also been offered the chance to see pictures of her together with my daughter, but I have declined the offer.

According to Petra Runhede, the adoptive parent was happy to sign an agreement promising to pass on the stone and the letter according to my instructions. Of course I can't be sure that Petra is telling the truth, but I have chosen to assume that she is, just as I have chosen to believe that the adoptive mother will not break the agreement.

In the letter to my daughter I wrote some of the things I would have told her if I had chosen freedom along with her instead of giving her up to someone who can give her security and the chance of a dignified life. I wrote that when she was born she had her father's nose and mouth and chin, and that if I look like my mother, then she had her own mother's forehead and the shape of her face. I wrote that the stone with the cone-shaped fossil had belonged to her father, that he died before she was born, that the stone was the only thing I had left of him, and that I wanted her to have it as a memory of him from me. I wrote that he found it on the beach between Abbekås and Mossbystrand the day we met each other in the November twilight, when he was out collecting stones and I was walking my dog.